PERCEPTION

From Size 0 to 14 Overnight

A Weigh Out Comedy Novel

Cassandra Black

To Anyone Who Struggles
With Their Physical Appearance:

You look fine. Now go make your day!

PERCEPTION

From Size 0 to 14 Overnight

Published by Humor Me Books

A Division of Don't Over Think It Press

Don't Over Think It Qreations, LLC www.dotiq.net

Edited by Peas Coaching, LRB, and Don't Over Think It Press

Cover Design by Rocío Martín Osuna

Photograph by Richard Van Sickle

ISBN 978-0-9742739-4-5

This book is dedicated to my late mother, Lessie Black, who was with me all the way during the creating and writing of this story. Thank you, Mom, for always being there to encourage my love for writing, humor, and creativity.

I Love You Always and You Will Forever

Be in My Heart

A Very Special Thanks To:

Renee Carter

Kris Keiser

Diane Newberry

Elizabeth Panta

A Special Write Out To:

Latisha Butler

Allura Scott

Brenda McGrew

Carla Cain (Diva)

Diane Fulton (Diva)

Liz Panta (Diva)

Rosalyn Campfield

Gloria “Gigi” Campos

Ira Daryn Tucker

Jennifer Williams

My OBS Writers’ Group

Dinner Table of Contents

Chapter One

Slim Fatale

In her high-rise, high-priced, high society, high-profile luxury apartment that overlooks Wilshire Blvd. and the mirror image apartments across the street, in Los Angeles, California, Avery lays on her California King-sized neon pink sheeted bed. She is sweating profusely as it rocks like a sailboat in a winter storm. Her azure almost turquoise eyes roll back as her cotton candy pink colored toenails dig into the mattress, her feet becoming formidable fighting fists as she screams, "YES! YES! COME ON! GET IT! GET IT! WE'RE ALMOST THERE! COME ON! OH YES! YOU CAN DO IT! COME ON! COME ON! ALMOST…OH YES! GO! GO! GO! YES! YES! YES! AAAAAH! FINALLY!"

She pants laboriously and shivers as she reaches over to pick up her cell phone from the pink acrylic nightstand. Her raw and bloody fingers speed-dial her desired contact, leaving crimson smudges on her hot pink bejeweled cover and screen.

A crisp hollow of a man's voice answers, "Dalton."

Avery delights as she yells victoriously into the phone, "Dammit! Dammit! I Did It! Did it! Did it dammit I did it dammit I did!"

Bored already, he asks, "What did you do now?"

"I'm in! I got into Zavier's Zero Zipper Jeans! That's what I did! I'll be ready for the shoot on Tuesday!" she declares proudly.

"I knew you could do it. See what hard work and no food will get you? Another year on your contract. Tuesday."

He's gone.

Physical genealogy states that Avery was supposed to be an overweight child and an obese adult according to the perceived unfortunate shape and projected self-loathing of her five foot two, size eighteen mother who loved to eat to excess followed by an after-dinner complaint. But Avery turned out to be quite tall and willowy despite summers spent at her grandmother's house in Indiana where she loved to visit and bake with her. Together, they would make up wild dessert recipes and present them to family members and neighbors. Avery loved being in the kitchen with her grandmother as it tempered her shyness. In the kitchen she was bold, brash and creative. Avery never wanted to go out and play because her cousins and neighbor kids delighted in ridiculing her because she looked so different from everyone else. Even her grandmother thought she was malnourished. So, she cooked and baked every cheesy, fatty, greasy thing she could to put a pound on her fragile frame. Nothing worked and Avery loved it. She loved to eat and savored every bite. She had no desire to live in a round turbulent body riddled with insecurity and loathing. What they all failed to realize was that Avery's high metabolism was fueled purely by nature.

As she grew taller, slimmer, prettier, and most popular at elementary school, Avery's confidence heightened but so did the taunts at Grandma's house. It wasn't until age nine that Avery started biting back like a shark on a feeding spree as she chomped her chum with the taunts she learned from the other kids at her school. Her verbal swipes even sent the teens away in tears. She enjoyed the power her words had over them and the teasing stopped... on their end.

Avery grew up an only child in an upper middle-class family with her parents, Natalie and Richard. They owned and ran a very successful accounting firm which provided Avery with anything she wanted. They did everything as a family and her parents doted on and showered her with attention. Yes, home and school life were quite terrific... until they met Hollywood.

Avery was discovered at age ten while shopping for candles with her mother in the San Fernando Valley. She was lingering in the food scented aisle concocting dessert ideas to work out at home and send to her grandmother when a woman, who had been observing her, was intrigued by Avery's exotic look.

She approached Avery's mom and introduced herself as Pepper Slausen, talent scout, hired by an advertising agency and invited them to have Avery audition for a national clothing store commercial. Avery nailed the advertising slogan on her first try, which sent the other nineteen kids and their parents in the waiting room, home with no audition. There was something about the way Avery hit the line, "From tops to bottoms you know that Varaline's got 'em!" that shut the audition down. The playful twang in her voice and the joyful expression on her extraordinary face connected with America as she became the official face and voice for "Varaline's."

Avery shot to pop culture stardom and appeared all over the country on television and radio talk shows, award shows, movie premieres, parades, sitcoms, magazine covers as well as becoming the ambassador for several children's charities. Within a year, Avery had become one of the most famous people in America.

As Avery's managers, her parents basked in her rays of stardom. Her mother started changing her own diet to qualify for body transforming surgeries. She also became hyper-restrictive with Avery's caloric intake to avoid any of nature's cruel jokes as she dove into the awkward preteen years. She scrutinized her eating, her skin, her hair, and especially her body. Avery hated all the nitpicking and conversations centered around how she looked, the constant weighing and measuring of herself and food, and the auditing of calories day in and night out. *I wish I would just get fat, and this would all be over.* But she knew she couldn't, not only physically but obligatorily because her parents sold their business and Avery was now the sole household's bread and butter. *I really miss bread and butter.*

Within that year, Avery was offered her own television show called, "Only Avery." It was there that she met and fell in love with the catering on set. Not just the food itself but the preparation of it. She would ask the caterers how they made it and what ingredients it took to do so. The buffet was so beautiful and smelled like paradise. Avery had never seen so much food in one place. Here she was, one of the richest kid stars in America and she was starving. She could have anything in the world she wanted, except for food. That's when the sneak eating began. Thanks to a young observant production assistant, who caught her tucking a turkey croissant sandwich under her shirt, Avery learned how to binge and purge so her body couldn't snitch about the burger or slice of cake she had devoured in a broom closet. After the first season, the show was a mega hit and Avery tailor fitted herself into the wardrobe of on-set diva brat. She was the star and everyone else was atmosphere.

Her parents started believing they were part of the show as well and demanded their own dressing room and specialty food service just for them and refused to eat with the commoners. Because the show was such a hit, Avery and her parents got whatever they wanted whenever they wanted it.

Family time now consisted of memorizing lines, daily weigh-ins, tiny meals, wardrobe choices, marketing, branding, and booking appearances. Avery's likeness and catch phrases were on everything from t-shirts to dolls to games to apps to screen savers to school supplies to clothing lines. Avery and her parents owned it all. Trips to Indiana became more about showing how rich and famous they were than spending time with family. Avery attended festivals, store openings and did local television interviews during their visits. Her grandmother was forbidden from baking while they were in town as Avery ached to be back in the kitchen with her.

The show lasted for six years and Avery, at age seventeen, moved seamlessly into modeling where she traveled the world with her newly rebuilt bionic bombshell mom who was now living the reconstructive life she always wanted. She had gotten so much work done Avery was often afraid her mother would melt if she stood too close to candles. Her father loved his new life wife and even had some work done to keep up with her. Her parents were like two people meeting for the first time every six months as they continued to turn themselves in for regular tune-ups. The three of them looked more like acquaintances than family since all semblance of resemblance had been erased.

Avery soon went from model to super model after firing her parents at age nineteen and hiring Dalton to be her agent. She just couldn't take their self-centered indulgences at her expense and their unprofessional and entitled attitudes. *I'm the one who's doing all the work, not you!* Although they were good at money, they were awful at negotiations. They knew how to demand but not command. Clients could smell their amateur scent and ran with it. The deals became more about what they wanted than what was best for Avery. The turning point came when designer, Pisces Parker, pulled Avery aside and suggested she call super-agent to the stars, Dalton, if she really wanted to go to the next level in modeling.

One day, Avery told her parents she was going to the gym when she was really meeting Dalton. It was money at first sight. Dalton immediately arranged a career caucus with him, Avery, and her parents.

They were extremely upset in the beginning with the idea of severing the umbilical fame cord which consisted of them signing a non-disclosure agreement preventing them from discussing Avery's personal life. Miraculously, when her parents were presented with an enormous check to buy her freedom and Dalton's piece of the pie...they quickly got over it.

They now travel the world and stay in the very best places, mingle with celebrities, and swing with the best-looking couples at the familial mention of her name. Thankfully, with them both being accountants, Avery's money is very well taken care of, to the point where she can live lavishly for the rest of her life without ever working again.

Avery was happy they were happy and happier they were happy away from her. She was finally on her own and could do what she wanted...so she thought. What she wasn't conversant in was that an agent was worse than parents when it comes to expectations. Parents couldn't just drop you and pick up a better kid. An agent could and would, and Dalton was just that agent.

Avery knew she wanted someone who could accelerate her career, but she had no idea it would be this hard. She was used to being catered to by her parents. If they made her do something she did not want to, there was always a wonderful gift at the end for her obedience. Dalton didn't care who she was or how much the world loved her. He didn't have to live with her, and his next sports car didn't depend on her. He always reminded her that she was walking on temporary pavement and that overnight it could turn into quicksand. So, in order to stay on stable ground, she had to comply with whatever he lined up for her as far as jobs, image, appearances (hers as well as events), including who she dated, and who she was supposed to be friends with. It felt more like she was working for him instead of the other way around. But he did deliver. He put together a team that top celebrities would go botox-free for and made her the adult international superstar she is today.

When Dalton told Avery she had to be at least a size two in order to excel in the world of adult modeling, she effortlessly breezed through as she was exactly and naturally a size two at five-feet-eleven. She immediately became the most sought-after silhouette in America. Now he tells her that world renowned worshipped designer, Zavier, (whose ad campaign last year catapulted her career beyond gravity) has changed to only wanting a size zero model for this year's campaign. In order to keep up she had to slim down to continue her reign. Currently, there is no model in higher demand than Avery and there is no higher feeling than being in demand. So, she has to play to stay.

Avery attempts to sit up, but the oppressive jeans she's been battling with for the past six hours are now holding her hostage. The crusade to get up from the bed to her feet begins as she wriggles like a mermaid who has just had her tail dry cleaned and starched. Avery grunts in agony as she rolls onto her stomach and stiffly slides herself down the bed until her feet touch the floor, leaving her sheets looking like the beginning stages of a serious crime. She takes a deep breath as she pushes herself up from the bed like an ironing board with arms. Her torso wobbles back and forth and side to side as she flails her arms to gain control of her stance then face-plants right back on the bed. An hour and fifteen minutes later, Avery is standing.

Forty-three minutes later, she slowly waddles towards her mirror that is across her huge bedroom. She wades and slightly kicks through the pool of various boxes of diuretics, diet pills, cigarettes, and chewing gum wrappers.

Twenty-seven minutes later, she reaches the full-length three-sided mirror. She looks at herself. She is proud, so very proud of what she sees. Her former much envied, now considered obese size two body has been starved, stressed and streamlined down to the new and approved size zero model. Her pink sports bra is plastered to her upper body like a band-aid as she sweats the sweat of twelve marathon runners in the middle of a southern July day. Her naturally tanned skinned is fraught with moisture as her long thick unaltered buttercup petal yellow hair drips like an un-wrung mop.

The constricting waistband of the Zavier Zero Zipper Jeans causes Avery to wince as she runs her hands around her sore mid-section. She is elated to find that her concave abdomen is perfectly intact and that she is free of any back flab and unloved handles. Stand straight, chin up, shoulders back, clavicle out, ribcage prominently displayed. Avery admires herself as she attempts to capture all her angles without losing her balance.

Ahhhh…The glamorous life of a Superior Model.

Chapter Two
Reelationships

Two days later…

Avery poses for famed photographer Knyfe. A waif of a male who moves about the set like a surfer with his wild tangled multi-colored hair in a man loaf high atop his head as it threatens to knock out the hanging lights. He skips around and jumps on everything that is square or has legs including chairs, tables, speakers, and the shoulders of unsuspecting crew all for the divine reasoning of getting that perfectly unique angle. As he clicks and climbs, Knyfe is being photographed by famed self-effacing, green hoodie wearing photographer, Theory, known for making stars out of people who make stars while he is being interviewed by dress pants, torn t-shirt wearing hearsay reporter, Cage, from "Aggrandize Magazine."

Avery sports the same jeans she violated two days ago. Literally, she has not removed them. Upside, the jeans fit like a denim epidermis. She is now able to move around freely and has partially regained circulation in her lower extremities. Downside, she has not had a bite to eat, a sip of water, or used the bathroom in two days.

The music blasts vintage Aerosmith as Knyfe yells at the top of his lungs, "That's right, Avery! Show me what you haven't got!"

Inspired by this command, Avery turns her back and gives a fierce over the shoulder pose as she pouts rudely into the camera, then smiles sweetly, then looks seductive. Wash, rinse and repeat.

Thian Rodgers, Hollywood's biggest action star for the last decade casually strolls in, although there is nothing casual about a thirty-one-year-old six-foot-six man with dark curly hair, hazel eyes, with a face and a body that could have only been designed and constructed by angels. He is so beautiful it almost hurts to look at him. "The mere mention of his name can melt glaciers." (A scholarly quote used to describe him in "Better Looks and Stardom Magazine").

"Okay, now let's change tops and accessories," commands Knyfe as he is assisted down from the stool he was teetering on.

Avery quickly erases the smile from her face and stomps over to famous fashion stylist, Shadoh, a four-foot nine wisp of a woman who dresses like a biker but speaks in tones of pastels and watercolors. Her assistant, Corrinne, known as Cori, better known as nobody, is a true industry outsider. Granted, she would be considered gorgeous, but only in the underground world of "Ordinaries," with her luxurious curly auburn hair that is concealed by the matronly bun and headband that shows off her deep right cheek dimple. She is twenty-six, (elderly in this line of work), had breakfast this morning, and is an unforgiveable size fourteen. She is in an outfit not fit for viewing due to the "no fashion distraction" clause in her contract as assistant to Shadoh. She is not to wear anything that would call attention to herself, away from Shadoh, or cause anyone to acknowledge her presence.

Coming to the shunway today is Corrinne, sporting a bulky gloomy day gray sweater with industrial carpet blue crop pants that hover recklessly just above her black sock encased ankles, finished off by unforgivably comfortable black emergency ward nurse sneakers. You can find this dowdy dress code must-have in a department store near you from the "I've Given Up" section. Even in this lowlier than thou persona and costume, Corrinne's beauty and radioactive personality seeps through like the scent of lavender in a yoga class. If anyone bothered to look.

Without saying a word, Avery holds out her spindly wrists in front of Corrinne and turns her head as if looking at her would cause her to catch a pound. Corrinne removes the bejeweled rings, watch, and bracelets and places them gently on a gold tray. Thian watches as Avery is proposed different tops and accessories and swats them away like a persistent fly. She looks over at Thian and gives him a cutesy wink. He half-waves at her.

Dalton, forty-six, all tailored suit, teeth, hair, and empty soul, struts in with the same cockiness he had as the king of kindergarten. He slides up to Thian and grabs his shoulder.

"There you are, Superstar!" exclaims Dalton loudly in order to ensure everyone around knows that he knows Thian on a casual basis.

Thian rolls his eyes.

"That never gets old to you, does it?"

Dalton guffaws, "No, it doesn't, and you better hope you don't either."

Thian shakes his head.

Dalton looks over at Avery. "She looks amazing! I sure know how to match 'em. You know everyone's calling you two 'Thievery' because you've stolen the world's heart."

"Whatever," says an unamused Thian. "Who's that assisting Avery?"

"Who?" asks Dalton incredulously.

"The girl in the blue pants."

"Thian, I see no one else in this room unless they're

making me money."

Thian looks disgusted and says, "That's a bit crass."

"That's about cash." retorts Dalton. "Listen, you and Avery are stars. Anyone else is just black sky."

"Is that all you think about?"

Dalton looks hurt and makes eye contact with Thian (something he rarely does) and says, "I can't believe after all these years you still think I may be better than that." Dalton laughs.

Thian looks away and responds, "Glad I don't think that way."

Dalton puts both hands on Thian's shoulders in a father giving his son a pep-talk before the big game kind of way and says, "You don't have to. That's the twenty percent of your brain I get paid to use. Now go on over for that spontaneous photo op. Kiwi Meyers from 'Wish You Were Her' magazine just walked in."

Thian slumps in dread.

"Why? Why do I have to keep doing these phony photo ops?"

Ignoring Thian's juvenile whine, Dalton proudly states, "And I have an intern putting an anonymous tip to 'Who's Doing Who T.V.' where you two will be having an intimate late-night dinner tonight. Remember to act slightly annoyed that they found you."

"I definitely won't be acting," says Thian under his breath. "Listen, can't we just order in?"

Dalton gives Thian the, 'You old dog you,' look and says, "Oh, a little quiet one on one time together! I knew you'd come around."

"Actually, the delivery guy can come to my place and then hers," says Thian.

Dalton laughs heartily then quickly turns it off. He turns and whispers sternly to Thian, "Expect an announcement on your and Avery's engagement in the near future."

Thian jumps in astonishment. "Engagement? We're not getting married. I would never buy her a ring!"

Dalton pats his right pec, "Don't have to. I've got it right here in my breast pocket, just waiting for the right moment. Right next to my heart."

"Your heart's on your left side," Thian corrects him dryly.

"Left, right, whatever. I'm thinking you propose at the Academy Awards."

Before Thian can formulate his thoughts and rewire a sentence to make sense, Dalton's phone rings. He answers it.

"Speak." And with that, Dalton walks away.

Dalton has been Thian's agent for the past ten years. He discovered Thian when he was having an indoor grotto built onto his mansion. Thian had been working construction with his brother, Dominic, in their father's real estate contracting business for two and a half years before he transitioned from construction worker to action hero. Thian landed the part as Rogan after Dalton's other client, Briken Conrad, decided he wanted to do more meaningful roles. Dalton had to quickly find someone to show up for a read at the studio in three days. Thian did it as a goof and a dare from his brother and the rest is action hero history. Today, Briken Conrad sells pet bird insurance.

Dalton's proudest packaging deal to date for Thian and Avery has been their pairing. The world went wild when they saw the staged pictures of them leaving hand in hand from the famed comedy spot, "Mother Chuckles" (an establishment Dalton happens to be a partner in). Thian and Avery have been fake dating for about nine months and rumors set ablaze by Dalton that an engagement announcement is imminent has the world sitting on the edge of their prickly seats waiting for the day.

Thian first met Avery as she was coming out of the pool, slow motion style, at the hotel she was staying in Milan.

He was reluctant to go through with this charade because he had heard how difficult and demanding she was. Thian lived a chilled lifestyle and had no desire for drama unless it was made for the big screen. She approached him slowly, allowing him to catch his breath before she reached speaking distance. *Why is she walking so slow?* Avery was dripping wet and gave him her famous sultry pout as she got closer. *Why does she look so angry?* He put his hand out to shake hers but instead of shaking his hand, she gave him a hug that left a fully soaked outline of her body on his white shirt and white jeans. Leaving him with a bad impression.

Avery thought that Thian was out-of-this-world-but-in-her-league handsome and was ready for him to fall in love with her. *How could he not? I am* the *hottest human in the world. The fantasy everyone wants and wants to be.* This union was going to be easy. They were both on the same level looks and career-wise. *We will have such beautiful children.* Avery's ovaries were fully invested. She only knew what she had read about him in the trades. He seemed rather boring, a non-Hollywood type, a homebody nice guy. *He's just saying that to keep the dowdy college girls and broke down housewives interested with the thought that he seems so accessible and they would have so much to talk about if they ever met. Who needs to talk when you look like we do?*

Thian thought Avery was beautiful but empty and mean. He wasn't like some of the men in Hollywood who would take advantage of this situation and Avery. She was more than willing to play along on and off the court of the public eye. He could tell she hoped this could turn into something real.

Their "dates" consisted of Avery being aware of who and what angle people were looking at her, constantly checking her makeup, taking calls, and answering texts. When she noticed someone was looking, out of nowhere, she would grab Thian's hand and gaze up at him or laugh as if they had shared an inside joke. It made his stomach turn. It wasn't until he placed himself in the mindset of being in one of his movies and that this was all make believe, was he able to choke down a meal, applaud her strut down the runway, and put his arms around her waist for photo ops.

The world ate it up. They were even voted "World's Most Couple To Be." Everyone just loved the scripted quotes of undying love they said to and about each other. The phony smiles and forced kisses for the camera to sell the product of lies. Avery rather liked the idea of their relationship and had at one time hoped there could be more but Thian basically ignored her and did not want to touch her. She rationalized that he was intimidated by her because his career was in a slump and he needed her as a boost. This delusion of a conclusion helped her ego tremendously. Believing she was the one saving his career and the one with the power, Avery became much more demanding. He had to do what she wanted in order to stay on top. She was the hero in this film.

Avery skips up to Thian like a five-year old approaching an ice cream truck and jumps into his arms. He does not embrace her until he sees the pictures being taken. Avery and Thian playfully smooch and laugh as they talk softly.

"At least pretend you like me."

"I'm an action star not a thespian."

"Just remember, I'm the reason anyone knows your name."

"What are you talking about? I was making Rogan's Rage when you were in middle school."

"That's right Old Man, now you're finally relevant."

Kiwi Meyers gives them a thumb's up and turns away. Avery and Thian break away in disgust and go their separate ways. Avery happily returns to the photo shoot and Thian walks over to Corrinne. She is frantically searching the rack of tiny clothing in preparation for Avery's next change while Shadoh sits in a corner fighting the temptation to eat a baby carrot.

"Need some help?" Thian asks Corrinne.

Corrinne doesn't look up, "Nope."

"Want my advice?"

"Nope."

"Want my autograph?"

"Absolutely nope!"

Irritated, Corrinne looks over at Thian and immediately shrinks back in surprise. She quickly turns away as to not make any further eye contact, "Oh! Oh! I didn't know it was you, Mr. Rodgers!"

Thian chuckles, "Did you call me Mr. Rodgers? I think my parents used to watch him when they were kids."

Corrinne catches her giggle and explains as coherently as she can, "I…um...thought it…you were Andy from lighting."

"Andy from lighting huh? So that's my competition?"

Corrinne fights a smile as she diligently looks through the clothes, trying to ignore him. *Is he serious? I'm just trying to work.*

Thian continues to stare at Corrinne. *Gosh she's beautiful!*

Corrinne catches a glimpse of him looking at her. *Gosh he's beautiful! I wish he'd go away!*

There is an uneasy moment of silence as Thian racks his brain to think of something clever to say.

"Do you need me to pull an outfit for you?" asks Corrinne in a professional tone, knowing she's opening the forbidden door to banter.

Thian grabs a tiny pair of rhinestone studded jeans and holds them up.

"I think these would look rockin' on me."

Corrinne looks over and bites her bottom lip to stifle a laugh then quickly turns back to the rack. Never one to turn down an opportunity for a quick response, even if it could get her fired, she quips, "Perfect. The dressing room is to your left. If you need help, just holler."

Thian laughs out loud. Corrinne's face quivers with the asphyxiation of her own outburst. She almost releases a squelched smile when Avery suddenly appears. Her presence dissipates all levity. She takes the tiny jeans from Thian and tosses them dismissively at Corrinne.

"Thian, Baby, stop distracting the wardrobe girl. You know talent and help don't mingle." Avery looks over at Corrinne and sneers. "Let's not get Blue Pants fired."

Avery kisses him possessively on the lips and leads him away.

Corrinne removes the tossed jeans from her shoulder as some of the rhinestones are caught in her hair. She struggles to remove them while sacrificing several strands. As she pulls it free, her cell phone vibrates. She looks around to make sure she's not being watched then slides it out of her pocket to read the text from her best friend, Malinda, that states, "Still meeting at Coffee Being at 3:30?"

Corrinne types quickly back, "Yup! So much 2 talk about."

Like the doorbell from hell, Avery's shrill and demanding voice rings Corrinne to duty, "Blue Pants! Where are my accessories?"

Corrinne jumps and slips her phone into her back pocket but misses and it falls into a basket of scarves. Corrinne grabs the tray with the rings, bracelets, and earrings she selected earlier and runs to the set. She presents Avery the ornate vanity tray and looks away as Avery picks through them like a box of nuts and chews from See's Candies.

"Good enough. Do this," Avery finally states and holds out her hands to be adorned.

Meanwhile, Thian has made his way back to the clothes rack where he and Corrinne were talking. He notices her cell phone atop the colorful scarves in the basket. He picks it up and it suddenly vibrates. Startled to the point of almost dropping it, Thian fumbles with the phone like a hot potato. He finally gains control of the rogue phone and reads the text that is the cause of this mayhem.

"Hey Corrinne make it 4 at Coffee Being running a little late c ya!"

Thian smiles.

A young, nervous cat of a girl, Rella, walks by Thian trying not to make eye contact. Thian notices her and says, "Excuse me…"

The girl jumps as if she had been greeted by a taser gun. She looks down at her feet and responds with the confidence of a lamb surrounded by wolves, "No, no! Excuse me. I'm sorry I shouldn't have been breathing in your space. I…I shouldn't be breathing at all. I'll stop." She takes a deep breath and holds it.

Thian looks puzzled and says, "Okay…Um, can you please make sure the young lady in the blue pants gets this back?"

He reaches out to hand her the phone. She looks at it and takes it as if Jesus had turned water to Red Bull right before her eyes. Thian gives her a strange look then walks away. The nervous cat stares at the phone in awe then licks it.

Chapter Three
Caffeine Crush

Malinda Monroe, age twenty-six, size fourteen, and fashionably fierce in a pink pencil skirt and crisp yellow blouse, sits at the octagon shaped table with the words "See Every Angle Before Judging," carved into it at Coffee Being. Her pin straight black hair (that takes her thirty minutes to straighten every morning) lays obediently down her back while her surgically precise sliced bangs sweep across her forehead and left brow like a crescent moon.

Corrinne enters the experience that is Coffee Being, with its chartreuse walls littered with multi-colors of post-it notes on what being a Coffee Being means to the patrons who believe in their philosophy of "Drink In Life." The atmosphere is alive with up and coming creatives who are about their art more than becoming a star.

Corrinne approaches the yellow lacquered counter and is greeted by a familiar "host," Jason, a tall, great-to-look-at guy in his early twenties. He is a cross between a day trader and boyband member with his perfectly gelled hair and the tattoos on each wrist that read, "Left" on his right wrist and "Right" on his left wrist. He is dressed in the company uniform of a chartreuse t-shirt with thick brown lettering that reads, "Coffee Being; Pressed and Highly

Savored."

He greets her with a big smile, "Hey Corrinne, what can I get for you?"

Corrinne peruses the menu overhead.

"I'm going have your Live Today with a shot of Tolerance." Which translates to coffee with cream, sweetened with vanilla bean, and a shot of lavender.

Jason chuckles, "Oh, it's been one of *those* days!"

"It's been *three* of those days!"

"Will that be a decent, divine, or decadent?"

"I'll take a divine."

"Anything else?" he asks with the hopeful smile of possible flirtation.

"No, I'm good for now. Thanks."

She innocently flashes him her electric smile that overtakes his heart.

"That'll be five dollars and seventy-five cents."

Corrinne swipes her Coffee Being card.

"Thanks," she says as she replaces her card into her wallet.

"I'll bring it to you."

"Thanks again."

Corrinne looks around, sees the back of Malinda and walks towards her. She sneaks up and grabs her shoulders just as Malinda is about to pick up her large green cup with the yellow cardboard band around it that reads, "Being."

"Gotcha!" says Corrinne suddenly.

Malinda jumps and looks around, annoyed.

"What the heck was that for?"

Corrinne laughs and sits across from her.

"That was for...."

Malinda holds up her hands, shakes her head in disbelief and says, "Whoa whoa whoa! Wait a minute. What are you wearing and why haven't you been arrested?"

"Sorry, I came straight from work and didn't have time to change."

Malinda looks surprised and says, "Work? Where are you working? On a farm?"

"A farm would be much more civilized."

Malinda looks around with deep concern and whispers, "Did anyone see you come over here?"

"Yes, they did. In fact, I went to each table and told them I was coming here to meet you...and that you lent me this outfit straight from your closet," Corrinne answers sarcastically.

Malinda laughs, "That really isn't funny. I'm only laughing to keep from shedding tears that would mess up my flawless mascara work. Seriously though, you should not be in public looking like this." She takes a deep sigh and looks at Corrinne. "Oh, I miss your corporate fashion days. We were always the best dressed girls in the office."

"I know, me too."

"But the crazy thing is, now that you work in the fashion world, you've lost all your fashion cache."

"Well not all of it," says Corrinne as she plucks the plain nails that are covering her perfectly manicured tropical ocean blue nails. "Just during the day."

"But that's when it counts, when everyone's awake and can see you," Malinda chuckles and picks up her drink. "Is it safe for me to take a sip now?"

Jason comes to the table with Corrinne's drink. "Here ya go, Corrinne," he says as he places her cup gently in front of her.

Corrinne looks up at him, "Thanks, Jason."

"You're welcome. Let me know if you need anything else."

Corrinne smiles politely, remembering how inviting her smile can be.

"That I will definitely do."

Malinda looks offended and chimes in, "Hey, what if I need something else?"

"Then you'll have to go through me," declares Corrinne playfully. She laughs and looks up at Jason who looks down at her with the smitten expression of a first crush. Oops! She did it again. Sometimes her humor is misconstrued as flirting.

"You got that right," says Jason as he winks at Corrinne in conspiracy. Their bond sealed. He walks away cheerfully, planning their first date and tenth anniversary.

Malinda follows him from the corner of her eye then looks back at Corrinne and says, "Somebody's got a big ol' crush on you."

"Think I should go out with him?"

Malinda takes a sip of her "Fly With Me," (better known as black coffee with sugar and five shots of cocoa) and responds, "Over my dead Prada."

Corrinne laughs then stops short, suddenly anointed with annoyance and asks, "By the way, what were you thinking setting me up with that weirdo last night?"

Malinda looks genuinely confused, "What? I thought you two would hit it off."

"Really? You told him I was a casting director."

Malinda answers sheepishly, "I know! But he was so cute, and I figured he would let his pompous guard down and try to impress you. He seemed really nice at the dry cleaners."

Corrinne looks unconvinced and says nothing.

"I thought you two would have the cutest babies!"

"He rapped Shakespeare while river dancing. Is that what you want for my children?"

Malinda laughs, "Oh no! I wish I could have seen that."

"Oh, you will. I filmed him on my phone and promised him he'd be getting a call from Spielberg next week. I can't stand those Hollywood types."

Malinda throws up her hands in wonder.

"Then why in holly would you work with them?"

"Love the business. Hate the people."

"Like that cardboard cutout, Avery?"

Corrinne curls her lips and crosses her eyes like a baby tasting lemon for the first time.

"I haaaaaate hate hate hate working for her! Today was the fourth time I've worked with her and she still calls me by whatever I'm wearing."

Malinda gasps and says, "Oh no! She calls you ugly?!"

Corrinne gives her a phony "Ha ha."

Malinda leans in close and asks breathlessly, "So…have you seen Thian Rodgers?"

"Actually, he came by today."

Malinda grips the sides of the table as if steadying herself in stilettos caught in cobblestone.

"What? Oh my Gucci! Are you serious? Is he really that tall and good looking?"

Hating to have to admit it, Corrinne nods her head and responds reluctantly, "Even better. I accidentally looked him in the eye, and he is absolutely drop jaw magic."

Malinda throws her head back in ecstasy.

"I knew it. I knew it!"

"But he's a jerk."

Malinda snaps out of her fleeting fantasy and sits up.

"Why? What did he do?"

"He came over and talked to me."

Malinda looks and responds with horror, "He did what? How dare he! What kind of animals are you working with?!"

"I think he was trying to get me fired. He knows we minions are not to be acknowledged outside of orders."

"You're exaggerating."

"No, really, it's in my contract. I think he was showing off for Avery."

Malinda gives her a devilish look and says, "Or…maybe he likes you."

"HA!" The sound erupts from Corrinne's diaphragm with the force of a dislodged chicken bone and startles everybody in the dwelling. She looks around apologetically.

"Okay, now we have to go. Everyone has officially seen you with me."

Malinda gets up and grabs her oversized lavender purse from the chair next to her and gracefully slides it onto her shoulder. Corrinne gets up and searches for her keys in the blue fanny pack hidden beneath her bulky sweater. Malinda looks as if she's seeing a giant goblin.

"Do I have time to change before we go to the movies?" asks Corrine as she rummages through the offending pouch.

"Let's be clear, there will never be a time when there's not enough time for you to change out of that," retorts Malinda as she picks up her cup and turns to walk towards the door.

Corrinne finds her keys, picks up her cup and says loudly as she follows Melinda, "Of course I'll get these pants and sweater cleaned before returning them to you!"

Malinda suddenly stops, throws her head back and bursts into laughter. Corrinne laughs too as she catches up to her. Malinda puts her arm around Corrinne's shoulder as they continue their merriment out the door.

A female host delivers a mountain of a blueberry crumble muffin to a man sitting at the table next to where Corrinne and Malinda were as he finishes up his decadent sized "True Is You" coffee.

"Here you go, Sir. Enjoy."

He looks up at her and responds graciously, "Thank you."

The host double takes and opens her mouth to squeal when Thian puts his finger to his lips.

Chapter Four
Realationships

Malinda happily sifts through the colorful dresses and skirts in the lavender and mint room that is lined with racks of clothing neatly hung and compartmentalized by style with signs that differentiate each section. She is in the "Get Dressed" section. On the wall next to her is "Jean on Me" where racks of jeans in all colors and designs reside. On the next wall there is a long rack of tank tops and t-shirts labeled, "Top of the Line" and on the fourth wall, coats and jackets under "Jacked." Each wardrobe area houses a lavender and mint glam decorated full-length four-sided mirror. In the middle of the mahogany wood floored room, a four-sided mint tufted chaise lounge poses elegantly as it summons the fabulous to gather. Malinda pulls out a red and black damask patterned sheath dress and walks to the mirror. It lights up automatically as her reflection to be steps up to it. She admires herself in the photo shoot type lighting as she holds the knee length dress up and poses.

"I'm going to wear the black and red sheath tomorrow," Malinda calls out.

"Go for it," responds Corrinne as she sits in her spacious powder blue powder room at her lit sky-blue granite-top vanity table. She applies the last coating of coal black mascara to her immaculately eye-lined lashes that extend protectively above her caramel colored eyes. She smiles as she sees her usual glamorous image winking facetiously back at her.

"Remember to take a picture of yourself in it and send it to me for my look book."

"Have I never?" Malinda calls back.

"Never have you never," laughs Corrinne.

The doorbell rings.

"I'll get it!" yells Malinda as she gives herself three last looks in the mirror from all angles. She lays the dress gently on the chaise and walks out of the room. "I bet I know who that is."

"I bet you're right," answers Corrinne with a giggle as she continues to apply her makeup.

Malinda strolls through Corrinne's spacious and colorful five-bedroom, four-bath house. It is very unassuming from the exterior with its ranch-style wood paneled white frame and neatly manicured lawn and vibrant garden. Passing by this home one would never suspect the opulence that is swirling about inside. Each room is decorated tastefully with high-end furnishings and accessories designed for her. Corrinne refers to it as "A place where creativity and peace come to live."

Four of the bedrooms are used for designing, making, and housing Corrinne's original clothing designs. There is the materials and fabrics room, the design and sewing room and last but fashionably not least is the dressing room where all her finished products are hung and displayed like her own section in a department store. It was expanded into an even larger space by knocking down the wall of room four. But the piéce de résistance is the custom-made-to-her-style master suite that is Corrinne's quiet sanctuary, painted and bedecked in all things aqua, even the marble flooring is a Caribbean blue shade; which makes it less of a room and more of an oceanic gateway.

Having grown up with unlimited wealth her whole life, Corrinne and her twin, Lorrinne, never wanted for anything material-wise. For their twenty-first birthday, they were gifted their own choice of homes from their father. They both knew by age four that their living together should be a temporary situation. Although they are identical twins, there is nothing the same about them, especially looks-wise. Lorrinne is slim and delicate while Corrinne is curvaceous and sturdy. Lorrinne took pride in referring to Corrinne as her not-so-thin-twin. Even to this day. Corrinne takes it in stride and is still in awe that Lorrinne even knows how to rhyme.

When probation was granted at eighteen, Corrinne did

not hesitate to flee for college dorm life. That same year, her parents' marital sentence was up with time served, inspite-of bad behavior on both ends. He had married for beauty and she had married for money. Perfect foundations for a successfully disastrous marriage.

Corrinne studied and excelled in clothing design. Lorrinne, on the other hand, was and still is co-dependent on their mother, Priscilla. She elected to stay home with her and remain responsible and independent free in the Bel-Air estate they were raised in. The same staff they grew up with continues to manage their beauty busy lives as they are constantly in training and preparation for pageant seasons.

Corrinne has been designing and making her own clothes since age seven when her mother refused to purchase anymore clothes for her until she lost weight. Thank goodness for her aunt on her father's side, Tally. She stepped in and made Corrinne some of the most exquisite outfits. Even the jeans and t-shirts, were fashionably detailed with stitching, hidden pockets and fun designs. Corrinne and Tally spent countless weekends and days after school designing and making Corrinne's wardrobe from everyday wear to special occasion to bathing suits to coats and jackets to book bags and purses. Corrinne had gotten so good at designing and sewing, she even offered to make her mom a dress.

"Darling, that's something you do when you don't have money to buy clothes. We're not livin' out on some prairie, driving horses with carriages. And I don't have your problems of finding clothes to fit me."

"Me neither!" Lorrinne chimed in proudly.

"I wasn't going to make you one anyway!" Corrinne bit back.

"Don't yell at your sister! It's not her fault you're too fat to shop with us."

Corrinne never offered again.

To Priscilla, work was only for men and for women who couldn't attract rich men. For this reason, she encouraged Corrinne to hone her skills as a seamstress. Even though Corrinne was the much prettier twin, Priscilla was convinced that a thin figure beats a pretty face any day.

Priscilla would tell Lorrinne, "You will never have any real friends because they will always be jealous of your perfectly proportioned model thin body you inherited from me. But you will never ever be without male suitors. You will marry very well." Her profound advice to Corrinne was short and bitter, "You, on the other hand, will have plenty of friends. Be grateful to any man who looks your way because your choices are slim, and you are not."

Corrinne took on her father's independence and work

ethic. She made it a point to learn their family business from top to bottom. She was always curious about how and why things were designed. It wasn't enough that toys were pretty or made funny noises, she studied the way they looked, felt and fit together. Corrinne's mother thought it was peculiar while her father thought it was genius.

So, every chance he got, her father either took Corrinne to work with him or had the au pair drop her off when Priscilla wasn't taking the girls out for exhibition. She was so proud to have twins because it made her more special than the other plain and ordinary mothers who could only produce one at a time. She only took them when she knew the moms and not the "domestics," as she calls them, would be around. When their size difference became obvious and they no longer looked like twins, Priscilla stopped taking them both out. Just Lorrinne, who loved and lived for the extra attention. Corrinne was relieved.

It wasn't until fourth grade when Corrinne met her true sister for life, Malinda. It was fashion at first sight as they looked and acted more like sisters than classmates. They were both the most stylish and style-conscious of the batch.

Malinda is the only child of famed day-time soap opera stars, Perry Monroe and Valaria Pine, who have starred on the multi-award-winning, top-rated soap opera, "Magenta Falls," for forty years as young star-crossed lovers who eventually marry, have affairs, murder their rivals, embezzle from companies, become fugitives, get kidnapped and rescued all while professing their undying love for each other.

Away from the cameras they were a happy family. Malinda was raised by her loving parents with a little help from family members when they were filming. Her parents dropped her off and picked her up from school, they traveled together, had meals together and lived a rich and happy life as rich and happy people.

Having grown up on the set of her parents' show, Malinda spent a lot of time in the hairdressing trailer. It was there that she grew to love and respect the art. She learned all the terms and techniques at a young age and was even allowed to experiment with her mom's hair. By age twelve, some of the styles she came up with were worn on the show. Her parents loved her ambition and encouraged it with her own beauty salon in their home when she turned thirteen. It was there that she would wash and style her friends and family's hair and eventually makeup. Corrinne would make and design clothes for her, and Malinda would do her hair and makeup. By high school, they were the most fashionable girls walking the halls. Aside from catty weight notifications from some of the girls, Corrinne and Malinda were quite popular.

While Corrinne went to design school, Malinda went to beauty and barber schools all over the county to learn how to do all types of hair. She did not believe in being limited. She can do anything from blowouts to barber, to braids, to weaves, to press and curl to perms to color to finger waves and more. She interned at salons from Beverly Hills to Baldwin Hills from Calabasas to Korea Town to Sunset Blvd. to Crenshaw Blvd. from Boyle Heights to Ladera Heights and from Hollywood to Inglewood. She worked hard, made lots of friends, and earned much respect. And no one knew who she was.

After graduating college, Corrinne and Malinda interned together at a marketing firm for clothing and beauty products to learn and understand that field for their future business ventures. They fetched coffee, took notes, ordered lunches, cleaned conference rooms, offices, and kitchens, answered phones, made reservations, ran personal errands, and walked and cleaned up after dogs all while looking fabulous.

After a year and a half, Corrinne decided to go deep undercover and work for designers and stylists in order to truly understand the business from behind the scenes. She got the assistant gig working for Shadoh and various stylists as a favor from one of the executives at the firm who really appreciated her work ethic and ambition. While working for the stylists, she always went by the name Cori and dressed down to remain unassuming. She knew that if anyone knew who she really was, they would treat her with faux mink gloves and not let her do and learn what she needed from the ground up.

The doorbell rings persistently.

"I'm coming! I'm coming! Keep your brows on! This isn't an emergency room!" Malinda yells as she briskly walks towards the door.

Corrinne laughs as she slips on a dress in her turquoise walk-in, dance-in, dream of a closet.

Malinda looks through the heart-shaped peephole, rolls her eyes and smiles. She opens the door.

"We've been expecting you."

As Corrinne continues to dress, she giggles at the distant playful banter and laughter between her guest and best friend.

Corrinne's confident stride, solidified in a pair of plum four-inch stilettos that elevate her five-foot-nine stature to six one, can be heard as she makes her way to the living room wearing a pistachio green trench coat dress with cuffed long sleeves that show off the bright purple lining. Her popped collar with matching purple lining would rival any vampire's cape. Her waist is cinched immaculately with a thick purple looped belt that fastens to the side with an interlocking CM, (Corrinne's initials and insignia). Her hair has been released from the confines of the day's bun and the coiled strips of chocolate ribbons cascade down her back and dance joyfully about her shoulders as she enters the living room.

Malinda smiles at Corrinne in relief and gratitude for her wardrobe upgrade.

"Welcome back! Oh, how I've missed you!"

Corrinne laughs then playfully scowls and puts her hands on her hips. She gives her guest a chastising look.

"A jerk? You really thought I was being a jerk?" asks Thian laughingly as he removes his baseball cap.

Corrinne bats her eyes and puts her hands to her chest and answers coyly, "Why, whatever are you talking about Mr. Rodgers?"

"Okay, this is about to get weird. I'm just going to go finish shopping."

Malinda leaves the room shaking her head.

They laugh. Thian rushes Corrinne and envelops her in his muscular man arms that only millions of women around the world could dream of experiencing. They kiss passionately.

"Mmmmmm...you look so good," says Corrinne.

"Not as good as you," counters Thian.

"Yeah, well, that would be pretty impossible," she giggles.

"You're right about that. So, how long did you know I was in the coffee shop?" he asks.

"The moment I walked towards the table. I know the back of you like I know the back of myself."

"And I am very pleased to know the back of you as well," says Thian with a raised brow.

Corrinne laughs as she caresses his face and kisses him gently, "You're also wearing the cologne I had made for you for your birthday."

"Oh, that's right! I can never fool you. It's the only cologne I've worn since and the only one I'll ever wear."

Corrinne pauses and looks into his eyes. He always says the best things that make her fall in love with him more without even knowing it. Never cheesy or stated as an ulterior motive. Just kind. Just sweet. Just him.

Corrinne and Thian met a little over a year ago, according to Corrinne. According to Thian it would be exactly thirteen months and nine days ago. When something momentous in his life takes place, he remembers how and when to a tee.

They met at Corrinne's family business, "Mayars Majestic Materials," the ultimate fabric and materials mall. It has been in the family on her father's side for over a hundred years. Her father, Lloyd, took it over from his father ten years ago after he retired. Mayars, whose philosophy and tagline has always been, "Where every budget comes to shop," is a seven-story brick building in the heart of downtown Los Angeles with plenty of free parking and no pretentious valet for the famous and fabulous. Each floor is compartmentalized according to types of materials needed from clothing to furniture to flooring to automobile interiors and beyond. It is extraordinary with its wall to wall, floor to ceiling materials imported from all over the world. "If it isn't at Mayars then it doesn't exist." It has been a landmark tourist attraction for the past sixty years. Everyone from the hobby knitters to the most famous top designers shop side by side in this Disneyland of materials. Grandpa Mayars was always big on customer service. Every single person who walked through those sliding glass doors, whether they were coming to purchase one button or a truckload of fabric for the season's fashion line, received the same V.I.P. treatment. Corrinne loved working there and being part of the family style atmosphere.

One day, Corrinne was helping an older woman pick

out material to have a dress made for a special occasion. What should have been a few minutes of helpful advice turned into forty-five minutes of fashion advice, laughter, and shared stories of fashion disasters. Thian watched the whole scene from the next aisle as Corrinne and his mother enjoyed their time together. By the end of their conversation, Thian's mom, Britta, wanted Corrinne to design and make her dress. There was just something about Corrinne she really liked. Thian could see it too. It was something intangible, an ease and sincerity in which she moved and spoke to people that was as attractive as her physical beauty. He had no idea Corrinne was the owner's daughter and just thought she was an incredible employee. He was attracted to her immediately and knew that him being who he was would be impressive enough to at least gain him a cup of coffee with her.

When Thian walked up to his mom and Corrinne, they were caressing and discussing a coral silk fabric. Corrinne was telling Britta how good she would look in petal sleeves with layers of petals on them. He noticed Corrinne's dimple right away as it communicated years of smiles and laughter as she spoke.

"There you are!" said Britta as Thian walked up. Corrinne looked at him and he suddenly became nervous.

Come on! You're Thian Rodgers! The Bravest Man in the World! You have saved hundreds of thousands of lives from aliens, terrorists, pirates, corrupt systems, car chases, rabid chickens, dinosaurs, and even poisonous butterflies. Surely you can carry on a brief conversation with the salesgirl in a fabric store. Corrinne smiled at Thian as she held a fabric swatch against his mother's face and complimented her coloring. *Why is my throat so dry? Come on saliva, do your job.*

"Greggery, this very nice young lady, Cori, has helped me pick out the fabric I want for my dress."

Thian's un-Hollywood name is Greggery Rodger Thianopolous. Dalton felt that Greggery Thianopolous was too small of a name for such a big guy and renamed him Thian Rodgers, and from that name on his career was as built as he is. He was born and lived in Greece for the first five years of his life with his mother, father, and older brother, Dominic. They moved to Los Angeles where his father opened his own construction business that built thousands of establishments throughout California. He lived a comfortable, upper-class life with his tight-knit family and eventually joined the family business, for a limited time only.

"Isn't it beautiful?" his mother asks.

"She sure is." *Did I just say that?* "I mean, it sure is."

He slightly lifted the bib of his cap so Corrinne could see who he really was, and hopefully be half as impressed with him as he was with her. Their eyes made contact and he felt his heart stop as everything went silent for just that moment. He felt the inexplicable feeling of a switch happening in his life. Suddenly nothing else mattered but trying to get to know this salesgirl.

Corrinne could feel her face getting hot as a blush started to crowd her face. She smiled politely and said to him, "You have a good eye for color," and went back to tending to his mother, business as usual. She wanted to say, "You have incredible eyes, please never stop looking at me." She knew right away who he was, but it didn't matter. She grew up around celebrities and beautiful people. She had even seen his movies. Hearing the thunder of his fashion work boots that made her turn and look his way caught her quite off guard. All she could see was a tall strapping lumber jack whom she was sure was in the wrong section. When they were introduced, a gust of electricity swept through her as his hazel eyes gripped her attention for seconds too long. *Get yourself, Corrinne! He's not real. Just a manbot built by writers and trainers! He's not human.* His presence was unlike anything she had ever felt, and she couldn't understand why. But Corrinne carried on as if he were just another customer.

Wait! What is happening here? Surely, she recognized me. I'm Thian Rodgers, action hero, Rogan's Rage, not just Greggery. Why isn't she impressed or at least giving me a lingering look? Thian removed his cap as if it were getting hot and fixed his curly hair to give Corrinne the unmistakable opportunity of knowing who was truly in her presence. She glanced over quickly to see what all the physical fuss was as she started to pull the long roll of fabric out to be cut for his mother.

"Here, let me get that," he said in his best Thian Rodgers voice as if he were rescuing her from bullet shooting fabric rolls.

Corrinne looked at Thian then allowed her eyes to surf the waves of his hair as she continued to pull out the roll.

"Thanks. I got it. There's a certain way you have to extract it in order to keep the fabric's full luxurious integrity." She smiled at him with a slight devilish wink, "It's a company secret, but you can carry it when I'm finished."

Thian was elated that she had acknowledged him and that he was able to do something for her. *I absolutely can carry a roll of fabric, heck, I've carried cars, towed planes with my bare hands and fought off ninjas while carrying an injured tiger, of course I can carry this for you.*

She looked and spoke to him like…like…like he was an actual person, a customer, a human making human contact. *This feels good. This feels great.* He felt so happy in that moment and never wanted to leave that store unless she was coming with him.

"You got it," he responded, hoping to sound casual yet willing but not too casual or too willing, just cool but not too cool as not to come off aloof and Hollywood. *What are you doing? What is wrong with you? Pull it together, Man. What's with all the mind crowding? Just be you. Be Greggery,* Thian thought to himself as the long roll of silk material made its way out of its coveted slot and into Corrinne's yellow bell-sleeved arms.

Thian took the coral material from her arms like it was their first newborn and put it over his shoulder. Corrinne looked up at him and smiled broadly.

"My hero."

"That was a close call today on set. What were you thinking?" asks Corrinne.

"I was thinking there's the love of my life over there being socially abused by the woman I'm supposedly dating. All I wanted to do was go over there and give you a hug," Thian answers pensively.

"Don't ever worry about me. I can hold my own."

"I know, it's just that I've never been on set with you or even that close in public with you. It took everything I had in me not to run over to you and say, 'Hey Cori, why don't you come over here and give me a smooch," says Thian in his exaggerated Rogan's Rage theatrical voice.

"Is that really what you would've said?"

"No, actually I really wanted to say, 'Hey everybody, listen up, listen up, yeah, you over there with the camera and hair tower, listen up. See that woman over there in the flooding blue pants and gray sweater masking her incredible beauty, talent, and intelligence? Yeah, her right there, the one that this model you all worship, like the founder of silicone, is ordering around like a servant. Well, she's my **real** girlfriend and the **real** woman I love.' Then I would have dramatically slow walked over and kissed you."

Corrinne smiles at his sweet goofiness, although she knows that is exactly what he wanted to do. Thian has been itching like a dog full of fleas for them to come out and let the world know about their relationship.

Sensing her discomfort at his bringing it up, Thian quickly changes the subject.

"And by the way, you said my River Dance was good last night. You know I've been practicing that forever for tonight's big Rogan's Rage escape scene."

Thian river dances as he pretends to dodge bullets and fight off attackers.

"Then he sweeps in and rescues the damsel in this dress."

He effortlessly scoops Corrinne up in his arms as she gives a slight scream of surprise and delight and gently sits down on the couch with her in his lap. They laugh giddily like two kids on swings at their highest speed.

Yet another thing she loves about him, his playfulness. He did not take his success as the world's biggest, highest paid, most-want-to-be-slept-with superstar seriously. He was always present, attentive, loving Gregge.

"You should come by the set after the movie," suggests Thian as he plays with her luxurious curls.

Corrinne chuckles, "Sure, I'll come by as your assistant or bring your coffee."

Thian sobers, "I'm serious. I want us to step out of this love armoire."

"Armoire, huh? I love when you talk furniture to me," she counters as she playfully squeezes his chin.

"Don't change the subject."

Corrinne sighs and rolls her eyes as she tries to get up. Thian holds her tighter.

"I'm serious."

"I know you are."

"You're the one I want by my side, holding my hand, taking pictures, and being a solid part of these momentous occasions with me. Without you there, they are just empty moments to get through until I can see you. Even more than that I want us to sit in coffee shops, restaurants, stroll down the street, take trips and be the real couple outside."

"We go out," says Corrinne in a small voice as she feels the weight of Thian's sincerity and his sacrifice for her request to remain incognito.

"Yeah, with me in disguise as Gregge, your construction worker boyfriend. I'm tired of putting on all those prosthetics and the twenty-five-pound gut so we won't be discovered. Now, don't get me wrong, I will continue to do it if it means being with you."

Corrinne looks deep into his eyes, "I am so sorry. I had no idea you felt that way. I thought you were having fun."

"I'm always having fun when I'm with you, but I want to be with you as *me* all the time. I want people to know that *you* are with me."

"What about the paparazzi?"

"They only come around when they're alerted by Dalton. He's the one who arranges those dinners and spontaneous pictures with Avery. No one followed me here, and I bet we can walk around the block, go into grocery stores, farmer's markets, and movie theaters with no problem."

"Speaking of Avery, was it necessary for her to kiss you on the mouth like that?" Corrinne asks reviving that twinge of jealousy she had earlier in the day when it happened. She had an overwhelming urge to snatch a patch of that batch of attached hair from Avery's head.

"It absolutely wasn't, and it caught me way off guard. I think she was feeling protective."

"Of you?"

"Of her image. She loves being the love interest of the current world's hottest star while she's the world's biggest model, even though she can't stand me, and I barely tolerate her."

Thian was dating Corrinne around four months before Dalton proposed the idea of him and Avery becoming America's Sweethearts. Thian begged Corrinne to let him confess and profess his love for her publicly in order to shut this stupid idea down. Corrinne refused the offer because she wasn't sure their relationship was going to last past six months, (even though it had become very strong in such a short period of time). They had been to each other's parents' homes for dinners, events, and celebrations and everything remained undercover quiet. Why ruin such a good thing?

After much convincing and much refusal, Thian acquiesced and the relationship deception began with Corrinne aware of every move along the way. Thian showed her all the texts from Dalton, put him on speaker phone whenever he called with the next date meetup, and told her all the gruesome details of his agonizing time spent with Avery. Corrinne wasn't afraid he'd fall in love with Avery. She wasn't his type. Thian was a diver and Avery, shallow water. In fact, this arrangement worked very well for Corrinne. It bought her more anonymity time. She wasn't ready to be so exposed.

"See? This is what I mean. I just don't want the hassle and all that comes with it."

"Oh, so now I'm an it?"

Corrinne playfully slaps Thian on the shoulder, "Of course you're not an it. The **it** is the Hollywood machine, the gossip, the noise, the who's better than who, the shaming, the…

"Hold up. Shaming? What shaming? Who's shaming?" asks Thian incredulously.

Corrinne gets up. Dammit, she didn't mean to go there. She's always been so confident, never letting anyone see her sweat because she hasn't...until now. This was just supposed to be fun, dating a huge celebrity in a cocooned existence. Now she was in deep. He in deeper. No life raft or Coast Guard on the way. Just open love water and now is the time sink or swim. Love or let go. Step out or stay in.

Thian continued to stop by to see Corrinne as often as he could for any reason just to be in her presence. He went to every one of his mom's dress fittings and alterations. He made suggestions and jokes that genuinely made Corrinne and his mom laugh. He brought Corrinne her favorite coffee once he found out what it was through a casual, pre-planned, well-rehearsed conversation he initiated on different coffee shops and types of coffees they serve and what he likes. Corrinne took the bait, knowing exactly what he was doing. His mild nervousness yet confidence to keep coming back and try again was endearing. She found herself excited to see him when he would round the entryway behind his mother even though she was more than capable of coming in on her own.

One day he came in on his own and asked her out to lunch. She refused because it was against store policy to date customers. He told her that it wasn't really a date but that he needed to discuss another dress he wanted to have made for his mom during a time when he needed to eat. He would do anything just to spend more time with her, even if it meant designing a dress, something he knew nothing about. Corrinne shared her lunch she bought in the café that morning with Thian after it looked like he was staying through her lunch time. He was intrigued and comforted by her freedom around him. She never tried to impress him. Instead she moved confidently about him which made him forget he was famous.

He eventually coughed up the nerve to ask her out on a real date once his mom's dress was finished. Not just any date, but the date of a lifetime. Thian was the special guest presenter at a gala that was honoring Corrinne's father for his philanthropic deeds all over the world. Thian thought that the invitation would impress and wow her to the point of a kiss. He came prepared, double minted breath and all.

Corrinne was taken off guard but didn't show it. She had also forgotten who she was and that Thian didn't know. To him she was the floor manager and seamstress in the materials store. She knew it was coming eventually and fantasized about it constantly. What she didn't expect was for him to ask her out to her own family's gala! Corrinne wanted to go out with Gregge, the regular guy who came to visit her without the fanfare, photographers, and fans. She knew once she said yes, this magical world of anonymity on both their parts would be over.

"Oh, um, actually I'm going to be working the gala, so I guess I'll see you there."

Her mind raced. *Why did I say that? Now I'm going to come off more as a liar than a truth concealer. Anyway, he never asked, so I never told who my father is. Perfectly on the up and up.* Things were now getting too close. It was time to come clean. She knew he liked working class Cori, but would he feel the same about heiress to a billion-dollar empire? He was so unpretentious, human and kind. *Wait a minute! Does he think he's doing me a favor? Superstar slums it with ordinary working-class girl only to bring her up in society because she is with him. Well, who does he think he is? I was stratospheric society way before he was even famous! How dare he! Why are you angry with him? I'm not. I'm scared. Now I'm a liar. Fix it, Corrinne!*

He looked so disappointed. Like a hungry man who finally gets to order, only to find out they've run out of food. Not even a breadstick.

"Oh, okay, well…I guess I'll see you there."

He was so dumbstruck and disappointed that she turned him down he didn't even realize he had repeated exactly what she said.

Thian stood there, waiting for her to change her mind, like they do in his movies when he convinces an unwilling law maker to become a law breaker. That's what he wanted her to do. Break the law of company policies and run off with him to fight crimes of love and happiness! *Did*

I just think that? Wow! She's really got me! Thian knew in that moment there was not one thing he wouldn't do to have Corrinne in his life.

"Corrinne? Talk to me. What's really going on?" Thian probes as he puts his hands on her shoulders.

Corrinne takes the deep quivering breath of a swimmer going to the bottom of the ocean because this was where she was going, to the depths of her hidden insecurity. She never had to go there because the opportunity never presented itself. But here it is, in her face with nowhere to hide. All the excuses, all the hoops Thian had to and continues to jump through just to make and keep her happy and in his life. He never flinched, complained, gave ultimatums, or even asked why. He just did it. And she has been so selfish this whole time because she was so earth shattering afraid of losing Thian once the public got a glimpse of her and the opinions they would have about her size. He would see her in a different light, her confidence would wilt, and she would never want to leave the house again. She just couldn't take the scrutiny, the teasing, the shaming, the questioning of Thian's taste in women. Was she a fetish? A pity-date?

She had opened up to Thian about many things in her life but never her weight. She was so confident and that is what he loved. Would he look at her differently if she told him the truth? Would he suddenly see her and think she was too fat for him? *Did I really just address myself as fat?* She had never done that before. Corrinne is spiraling in a corner she can't run away from. She spent so much time being her best self and now it could crumble because of this man. Is it even worth it? Is he worth it?

It felt like hours before Corrinne turned around to face Thian.

"I'm scared," she says bluntly.

"You don't have to be. I'm here to absorb all of that for you," Thian says sincerely. He means it. He would take any type of attack for her.

Corrinne shakes her head as she looks up at him and says tearfully, "You can't take this one for me."

"What is it? How can I help? What can I do?"

"Nothing."

"They want me to propose to Avery at the Academy Awards."

Corrinne stops cold and feels a bit woozy from the verbal blow she was just served.

"Dalton already has the ring."

Corrinne is unable to catch her breath.

"But I got one first," Thian states softly.

Corrinne is crushed. This is it. She played the game too well, too long, too selfishly. She musters up enough air to say in a cracked voice, "Well, I guess you gotta do what you gotta do."

She turns away from him. She doesn't want him to see her cry.

"I sure do," he states matter-of-factly.

She expected a bit of a fight or other alternatives from him. He always had one. *What's changed now? Maybe he's finally started to fall for Avery. Have I waited too long and now his affections have waned?*

Fear has a vice hold on Corrinne that she's never felt before. She can't let him go. She won't let him go. Corrinne turns to face Thian, who is on one knee with an open small aqua-marine silk box that houses the most beautiful diamond ring that shimmers and creates a prism on her walls.

Thian smiles with tears in his eyes, "Let's fight this together."

Chapter Five
Disorderly Conduct

A giant image of Avery, wearing the hostile jeans she fought so hard to conquer and a pink tank top with the words, "Thin and Now," sits high atop and stretched down and across twenty-two stories of a high-rise building on Sunset Blvd. in the heart of Hollywood's elite shopping, eating and clubbing circuit, that reads:

"You Only Count If You're a Zero

ZAVIER ZERO ZIPPER JEANS

WHEN NOTHING IS EVERYTHING"

Parked right underneath it is a midnight black over-sized SUV with illegally dark tinted windows. The unequivocal sounds of overheated and much needed passion are made as Avery cries out in breathless grunts and squeals, "Oh yes! Oh yes! I have been waiting so long for this! You have no idea how good you feel right now!"

Her eyes are closed in ecstasy as she sits on the backseat floor in gray sweatpants and an oversized t-shirt stuffing her face with pepperoni and sausage pizza, french-fries, peanut butter cups, spaghetti, orange chicken, waffles, and cookies. Her cell phone rudely rings, interrupting this torrid fast food love affair. Never one to miss a call, no matter what, because it could be the difference between a career changing campaign and being mercilessly tossed back into the world of a mere civilian. She is hard pressed to find her link to relevancy amongst her chaotic backseat buffet. Between nibbles and finger licks, Avery searches under sectioned containers, cartons, soda bottles, soiled napkins, plastic utensils, and bags as she follows the ring like a cat to a laser light. She finally finds it in the pizza box covered with strands of congealed melted cheese. After a couple of greasy fingered attempts, Avery manages to slide the answer call button on her screen. She swallows hard as she tries to sound dainty.

"Hello?'

"Hey Doll! I just drove by and saw your ad on Sunset! Have you seen it?"

Avery caresses a peanut butter cup lovingly, mesmerized by its ridges and smooth middle.

"Yeah, it's great," she responds breathlessly, talking about the delicious ribbed item approaching her awaiting mouth.

"Great?! Baby it's monumental! It's revolutionary! Do you know how many millions of eating disorders you've started just from that image alone? It's genius!"

Avery pops the peanut butter cup in her mouth and chases it down with a swig from a liter of cola.

"Mmmhmmm!"

"Are you eating?" asks an annoyed Dalton.

Avery snaps out of her feasting fantasy.

"Eating? What does that even mean?"

"Well if it isn't teeth, tongue or Thian, get rid of it! You have two more photo shoots and twelve interviews this week."

He's gone.

"Gotta make room for round two."

Avery sticks her two pink salon perfect talons down her throat and projectile vomits into a trash bag.

Chapter Six
Our Lord and Zavier

Brandyn Greer, early twenties, (on her resume), extremely thin, all cheekbones and lashes, is as perky as caffeine on caffeine as she perches herself like a proud trophy onto the green plexiglass low back scoop stool, designed to make her sit up straight and not want to be there for long. She is getting last minute makeup touchups to ensure no one will ever know that she has freckles, an elongated chin, and a weak jawline. All the attributes she was born with and never had an issue with until she became an entertainment correspondent five years ago. She has now hit the pinnacle of her career as the host of the leading nightly entertainment "news" show.

An authoritative male voice booms over the stark set of the two chairs set against a green screen to make it look to the viewing audience like they are levitating atop the Hollywood sign surrounded by the untouchable and dazzling lights of Los Angeles. "Quiet on the set! Zavier has entered the building and is being escorted to the set! Quiet please and all eyes averted as he passes!"

Not just a hush but an audible blackout befalls the whole studio. Heads drop simultaneously as if in communal prayer as the distant echo of two sets of footsteps, (one discount and sensible the other expensive and unreasonable), break the barrier of silence built on the backs of the obedient crew and interns.

Brandyn, shaking in anticipation and hunger, can barely contain herself as the sound of the divine designer nears her hemisphere.

The director holds up two fingers and announces, "And Brandyn, you're on!"

The cherry light of the camera pops on alarmingly bright signaling, it's time to talk and roll.

Ever the pro, Brandyn composes herself, looks into the camera like a best friend at brunch, and recites with over enthusiasm, "Welcome back to Excessive Hollywood where we make something out of nothing then run it into the ground and resurrect it again! I'm Brandyn Greer and I have the ultimate privilege of being in the presence of the Apostle of Apparel, Trend Creator, and The Last Word in Fashion for Women Who Can't Speak for Themselves, The Legendary, Hero of Hemlines, is right here with me on this sign! Zavier!"

The camera moves dramatically from Brandyn to reveal the demigod of dress who became famous for his uncanny talent for designing dresses that fit perfectly just from a single photograph. Here sits Zavier, sixty-three, an average sized man of six feet with a head full of startling silver hair and piercing gray eyes that reflect confidence and judgment. His impeccable made to pleasure black suit and cornflower collarless shirt is purposely buttoned two holes down to subtly reveal the thin gold chain linked by z's as it languishes boastfully on his hairless chest. His famous perfectly etched jawline still houses the undeniably sublime symmetrical face that launched his modeling career over forty years ago.

"Oh, Zavier it is such an absolute honor to have you here tonight!" grovels Brandyn.

"Goes without saying," he answers in his too cool for this planet tone.

"How are you?" asks Brandyn feeling like a peasant begging for crumbs.

"As good as I look."

"Well then you're doing quite fantastic!" She flirt winks hoping for an after show ride back to his place where she'll captivate him to the point of moving her into his mansion by end's week and never having to work again because she would be pregnant by the end of the year.

Brandyn stands up and poses proudly. She has been waiting for this moment her whole life.

"As you can see, I'm wearing one of your dresses from the Zavier All is Nothing line and it fits like a hug!"

Zavier looks her up and down. She got him. He can't take his eyes off her. *This must be the day he's been waiting for as well. Finally, a chance to meet me.* Brandyn is so confident as she twirls and poses, exposing their undeniable connection.

"Yes, it does. After they put in several more inches."

Brandyn is dispirited and sits back down. She quickly pulls herself together and laughs it off. *Obviously, he can't let people know he likes me. Play it cool, we'll laugh about this later in bed.*

"Oh Zavier, you're such a kidder!"

"Sweetie, I'm not kidding. I'm offended. It looks like an extra yard has been added to this dress."

This exchange between Brandyn and Zavier is seen all over the world and lands as the "Hot Entree" on the popular dining room table talk show, "Chews 'n' Views." An all women, all eat all show that serves entertainment news each weekday morning. Five women of all ethnicities from age twenty-one to sixty and from size three to sixteen sit at a restaurant style counter eating meals and snacks throughout the show as they comment on the menu items for the day's topics in front of a live audience. They are accomplished, outspoken, attractive women with husbands and kids who are over the "Look at me, please like me" stages of their lives. Except for Bloom, the token immature outsider of the pack who is fresh on the hunt to capture that inexplicable “It” factor all the magazines and commercials tell her she needs right now, only to change next week. She refers to her co-hosts as Frump, Frumpy, Frumpier, and Frumpiest (not to their face of course). She is convinced they are all having a mid-waist crisis because they refused to host the show in bikinis for their summer season. Her idea of course. The thought of pushing out a kid then a stroller makes the enamel of her three original teeth melt.

Sharla, age sixty, the show’s captain munches on pop-corn as she welcomes viewers, “Good morning Diners and thank you for joining us at “Chews ‘n’ Views where we feast on the latest news feed.”

DeeAnne, age, fifty-one, eats an omelet, “Today we are absolutely consumed with designer, Zavier.”

Liza, age forty-two, eating a croissant states, “I can’t wait to get to this. I am literally chomping at the bit!”

Bloom, age twenty-one and size three, scoops out an ice chip, “He took my appetite.”

“Can you even believe that interview? What an indul-gent misogynist!” says Sandy, age thirty-six, as she eats a break-fast burrito.

“His words were so biting! I mean he just devoured poor

Brandyn," declares DeeAnne

"I'll take a Zavier with a side of hubris and narcissism, please," states Sharla between chews.

"Who would even listen to this glutton for fame?" asks Sandy.

"I binge watch everything he's on," states Bloom proudly.

She looks in her cup to scoop another ice chip and looks horrified.

"Oh, my gorge! They're gone already! I've eaten too much!"

Liza looks over at her cup.

"Your ice chips just melted, Honey."

Bloom looks relieved and smiles.

"Ooooooh."

The next day…

A long line of over two hundred extremely thin women of all ages is wrapped around the blocks of Beverly Hills waiting for Zavier's couture boutique, "THINVIOUS," to open. This event only happens once a month and the women line up like it's the last concert tour of their favorite singer. The hope is to catch a glimpse of Zavier and to fit into one of his latest designs. It is an onyx mirrored building so that everyone who walks by can be self-consciously aware of their image for half a block. Some days Zavier and his minions spend the entire day standing at the windows inside observing, scrutinizing, and rating everyone who walks by. The fourteen-inch door is only welcomed to those who can fit through it comfortably without touching either side. Approximately one out of every thirty-eight makes it through.

The ingress to insecurity is finally granted and a wave of screams filter throughout the blocks with the hopes of making the cut. There is a nervous energy as the first five women attempt to pass the doorway initiation attended by twenty-year-old, Sea, donning the Zavier trademark of low tolerance and high judgment for imperfection. All his staff are super thin females from eighteen to twenty-one with dyed polar bear white hair in skin-tight black leather jumpsuits with a small gold Z just under the left shoulder teetering on five inch black and red strappy stilettos.

Inside, the walls are a cherry red from floor to ceiling with black marble floors, (basically what a store would look like in the fashion section of hell). The walls boast huge black framed pictures of the most famous models and celebrities wearing Zavier's iconic dresses. Avery's latest gold framed poster is front and center. The large room is empty but for one tiny floor length red gown entombed in all its glory in a lit glass box that levitates eight feet from the floor. It is secured to the ceiling by a glimmering gold rope. The embellished sign on it reads: "Break in Case of Perfection." It is the Holy Grail of Gowns. Actually, it is more like the carnival game you can never win.

Zavier's store has been doing this monthly challenge for the past five years and no one has ever been able to break the glass. Along with being able to fit into the dress size-wise, the woman must be able to compliment the dress with her facial beauty and character as well. In order to do so they must make it through all four of Zavier's "Appraisers" better known as his devoted soulless, esteem decimating assistants.

After two hours, six women are allowed in. They stare at the dress in speechless, tearful awe, for only a few have made it this far into the vault of fashion. This is the day they've dreamed about and worked so hard for. To be The One to fit into this impossibly sized dress to let the world know, "Hey! I'm better than you! Know why? Zavier said so!"

The undernourished appraisers guide the grateful women to different stations to see if they will qualify. First station is with Vo, a non-charismatic entity of a nineteen-year-old dressed in the uniform of thin, bored, and cool.

Here, the women are weighed-in wearing paper towel bikinis on a pre-calibrated gold scale that announces their weight in "Yes," "No," and "Not even Close."

On the rare occasion that someone passes the first judgment, she moves on to Sparrow, who has the personality of a mushroom, and is quizzed in the monotone voice of a peaceful snore.

"Favorite food?"

"Cucumber chips."

"Last time you ate?'

"Two days ago."

"Why are you here?"

"To prove that I'm better than other people."

"Move to station three."

Station three houses twenty-year-old, Fig. No words as she walks around the candidate assessing by sight and tape measure.

"Sorry, according to my exhausted tape measure you are a size one and you need to be less than a size half to break this glass," she informs with the care and concern of a napping cat.

The woman is hysterical.

"Nooooo! This can't be! Do you know what I've done to try and fit into that dress? Nothing! I've eaten nothing, I drank nothing, I smelled nothing!"

Zavier enters the store from a much wider side door that opens part of the red wall amidst a chorus of gasps and whimpers from the blessed women who are now in his presence. They stare in adulation as the outside light gives him an angelic glow. The wall closes behind him.

In a glance, Zavier surveys the rest of the women in line waiting to be called to the first station and taps some of them on the shoulder and says, "No, no, no, never."

One by one the dejected women step out of line with a heart empty of hope but the holy acknowledgement of Zavier. He approaches the dejected puddle of a woman on the floor in the measuring station and looks down at her, literally. Feeling his presence, she looks up and sees him.

"Stand up," he commands.

The woman stands up immediately.

"What is your name?"

"Breaze."

"Less lettuce more gum. You're almost there."

The woman cries in gratitude as the others look on in envy. She is suddenly empowered as if anointed with a special gift from the gods. She stands tall, her head held high, and announces in a strong voice, "Yes Zavier, I will. You'll see. I'll be nothing in no time!"

To be rejected then given such sage and caring advice from Zavier was as good as getting into that dress. Well, almost.

Zavier turns and heads to his office upstairs. His main appraiser, Teal, twenty-three, approaches him at the bottom of the stairs. She has been with Zavier for over five years and is his eyes, ears, protector, and devoted groupie who would be up for retirement if she weren't so good at what she does; which is any and everything Zavier tells her to tell others to do.

"Uh, Sir, Thian Rodgers is waiting for you in your office. He's been here since noon," she informs him.

"Hmmmph, I'm early. It's only one-thirty," Zavier responds casually as he makes his way up the stairs.

Zavier's office is quite the contrast to his store with its lush, lavish, ornate modern furniture, mirrors, various sculptures, and designer paintings of him. There are four chandeliers hung purposefully to have him in the best lighting no matter where he is in the room. Behind his gold and glass top desk sits a plush comfortable and cushy office chair. On the other side of his desk sits two eight-inch clear lucite chairs for visitors and meetings which are the only seating available for anyone else.

Thian tried to sit on one of the chairs and almost fell over. So, he opted to stand and pace the floor for an hour and a half. If this weren't such a big deal to him, Thian would have walked out an hour and twenty-nine minutes ago. One thing he really hates is being kept waiting. But one thing he loves more is surprising Corrinne.

Zavier swoops in with the air of royalty. Thian takes in the scene with morbid curiosity. Two young model-type women appear out of nowhere on each side of him and remove his overcoat in unison. Why he had on a coat over his suit in eighty-five-degree weather is lost on Thian.

"Dismissed," Zavier orders and the women silently leave. Zavier observes Thian as he approaches him. *Hmmm... He's a lot bigger than I expected.*

Thian smiles as Zavier strolls towards him. *Hmmm... He's a lot smaller than I expected.*

They had passed each other on red carpets and events amidst flashing cameras and people calling for their attention but had never actually met. Thian had no interest in fashion, unless it was Corrinne's and Zavier had no interest in anyone he couldn't dominate or manipulate.

"Thian Rodgers of "Rogan's Rage. World-famous action hero. Welcome," Zavier greets him magnanimously as he shakes Thian's hand.

Thian is surprised by how reasonable his handshake is. Most men who meet him try to shake him down by proving they are as strong as he is.

"It is such a pleasure to meet you," responds Thian while thinking, *It would have been more of a pleasure an hour and a half ago.*

"Of course it is. Please, have a seat. Have two," Zavier laughs in superiority as he struts to his cozy seat while Thian pieces together some form of a seating arrangement between the two devil chairs.

Zavier sits behind his desk in comfort as Thian teeters like a teacup in an earthquake.

"Now, what can I do for you?" asks Zavier, secretly thrilled to have such a big star coming to him. It never got old, but he had to act like it did.

"Well, this is a big secret only you and I can know about," says Thian, sounding like he's getting ready to pledge blood brotherhood to his best friend.

"I invented secrets. Remember my clothing line, 'Zecrets?' Zavier puts his finger to his lips, "Shhhh…No one has to know. It was brilliant!"

"It sure was!" Thian agrees, having no idea what Zavier is talking about. "Anyway, you know the Academy Awards are coming up and…"

“And you’re nominated for Best Actor. How exciting. Congratulations,” says Zavier trying not to sound as impressed as he is.

“Thank you. Now, what I need from you is a specially designed, one-of-a-kind dress for the love of my life. The catch is, she can’t know it’s being made for her. It’s a surprise!” Thian blurts enthusiastically.

“Oh, that won’t be a problem. Avery is already my spokes-model and I’ve already finished her dress. But tell you what, I’ll say you had a hand in the design,” replies Zavier in modest grandiosity. “This is something I never ever do.”

Thian looks uncomfortable. He had gotten so wrapped up in Corrinne saying yes to his proposal and finally agreeing to go public, that he had forgotten all about Avery. In fact, he hadn’t shown up for their last two “dates” and Dalton is furious. He spent a lot of money on the spontaneous paparazzi to capture their every move at a local bowling alley.

“Oh…Avery and I haven’t dated in a long time. It was just publicity to propel our careers. Actually, we can’t stand each other.”

Thian laughs.

Zavier doesn’t.

"Then who am I designing for? Is she famous?" asks Zavier barely containing his annoyance at his assumption being wrong.

"No, but she's the star of my heart," replies Thian, surprised at how publicly corny he has become. That's what happiness will do to you.

Zavier chuckles at Thian's pedestrian silliness, "Oh, you've got it bad.

"No, I've got it good!"

"I think I'm going to be sick."

"Love-sick I hope." Why can't he stop? Because he doesn't want to.

"My goodness. She must be out of this world gorgeous if you're willing to toss aside Avery," says an intrigued Zavier. *And possibly your career.*

Zavier stares Thian down as he fake-contemplates his answer. His mind races, *Of course I'm going to do it! To design the dress for the biggest Hollywood relationship upset? Any designer would be a fool to turn this down. Whoever this model takeover babe is, she's going to be the biggest most sought-after fashion queen! And I, Zavier, will be in the center of it all. I may even call it "The Model Take Down Gown." I love it! I love it! Love it! Such genius! The line will consist of dresses to steal any man away from the relationship he's in. I'll call it 'EmbeZZle.' Oh! Sometimes I can't stand myself! I really can't! The Academy Awards will be my night as well!!*

"Well, since it's you and I am a big fan…just so you know, I never do this, especially on such short notice. I am booked seasons ahead of time as well as busy with future creations. However, I will make an exceptional exception for you and the woman who has purloined your heart and all sensibilities."

Thian jumps up from the supposed chairs, knocking them over, and cheers, "Yes! That is awesome! She's going to be so excited when she unwraps it just before we get ready for the show. She's such a big fan of yours. A Zavier original! Made just for her! I can't wait to see her face!"

His enthusiasm spills a bit onto Zavier as he happily stands up and smiles broadly from the thought of his takeaway from this whole love triangle.

"Now, let me see a picture of your girlfriend. You know my genius is that I can design a perfectly fit dress just from a photograph."

"Even better! I was wondering how I was going to get her measurements without casting suspicion," Thian says happily as he swipes through his phone of over a hundred pictures of Corrinne and himself to find the best full-bodied one of her.

"Oh, here we go."

"Great, send it to my printer, ZAVBEST1."

Thian types in the conceited code on his phone.

The custom-made red printer hums as Corrinne's color photo of her wearing the pink ballgown she wore at her father's gala where he invited her to be his date. This is his favorite picture because that was the night they shared their first kiss in one of the ballroom's dressing rooms. He remembers it vividly as the room spun and he could swear he saw doves flying about her head. He told her that he would do anything it took to make her happy if she would just agree to always be in his life.

Corrinne had taken Thian by the hand when she turned him down to be his date and revealed who she really was. Thian was dumbstruck that she could keep a secret like that but most of all that she was so grounded with all the privilege and money she comes from. He had finally found his match. A woman who wasn't after him for the Hollywood scene or a career come up. She was solid, she was talented, she was beautiful, she was humble, she was Corrinne. She never wanted the spotlight and was afraid of the same thing he was…disingenuous people.

"Let's think about this, let it soak in for a few days. If

this is something we want to continue, then let's meet at 11:03 p.m. at the gala in the Petals dressing room," she told him.

"I don't need to think, and I don't want to wait." he wanted to tell her because he knew right then, right there that this was not only something he wanted to continue, this was something he had to continue.

The three days away from Corrinne were the worst days of his life. They felt empty even though he was on set running into burning buildings, fighting creatures from other planets, and saving penguins from mutation. He missed her and vowed that there would never be a day he would not have contact with her face or voice.

Corrinne's picture completes printing and Zavier takes it. He can tell by her face that this was not going to be good. He studies it, walks back to his desk, and looks at an excited Thian.

"You really expect me to believe that you're dating ***her****?* And you expect me to make a dress…for ***her***?"

Zavier callously tosses Corrinne's glamorous smiling face to the desk where it slides and almost falls off the edge.

Thian looks confused.

Zavier reaches over and picks up the picture again and studies it. Then he laughs.

"Oh! I get it now! This must be that practical joke show, Fooled!" Zavier looks around. He yells out as if there is a hidden crew. "Where's the cameras? Did my staff put you up to this?" He laughs, "They must be getting me back for that water and orange peel diet I put them on last month. Wasn't my fault they started looking like they ate a meal a day! All right! Come on out! I can't be fooled!"

Thian watches him in anger and disbelief.

Zavier is oblivious to Thian as he revels in the belief that he is being filmed, and happy that he's going to appear on America's favorite practical joke show looking as good as he does today.

"It's not a joke, Zavier."

Zavier tapers his maniacal laugh then sobers as he looks at a thoroughly annoyed Thian. The two men stare at each other. Thian wants to reach over and grab Zavier by the throat and make him sit in one of those ridiculous chairs and apologize a thousand times.

Zavier wags his finger at Thian playfully, "You're good, Thian Rodgers. That's why you're nominated for an Oscar!" He starts to laugh again.

Thian just stands there. He now understands Corrinne's fear.

Chapter Seven
Faking Up Is Hard To Do

Avery is enjoying an all-eyes-on-her day on the rooftop of an exclusive hotel in Beverly Hills for a Zavier photo shoot. Her phone rings off set. Her assistant, Rella, (whom Avery says is short for irrelevant) looks at the screen. It's Dalton. She answers it.

"Hello Mr. Dalton, it's Rella. Avery is being immortalized." This is what she is to tell anyone who calls while Avery is being photographed. An instruction given by Avery.

"Put her on the phone. It's an emergency."

"Oh, okay, okay, okay…hold on," Rella responds nervously as she walks towards the exclusionary spotlight not meant for her. She timidly walks up just out of camera range as if it were a gun and signals Avery.

Avery whips her head around. "What!?" she says sharply, verbally stabbing Rella to the point of her slightly stumbling.

"It's Mr. Dalton, he says it's an emergency."

Avery leaps out of her perfected posture and beckons Rella to give her the phone.

"Dalton?"

“Hey Doll, I got some bad news to tell you and I thought I should tell you in person, but I changed my mind. Listen, Thian has fallen in love with some girl and is taking her to the Oscars.”

“Wait! What?! He’s been cheating on me?” screeches Avery incredulously.

All at once, everyone clears the set and entire area, so as not to be hit by any shrapnel.

“Okay level off. He’s not really your boyfriend remember?”

“Yeah, I know. But it still isn’t right. I have been nothing but gorgeous to him!” she spits out indignantly.

“Well, Doll, not everyone is as depthless as we are. It’s a gift.”

“Who is it? Don’t tell me it’s that pretentious, flower dress wearing, singer, Thistle.”

“To tell you the truth, for once, I have no idea who she is, and I really don’t care. Thian is my Oscar Baby right now and he can do whatever he wants.”

Avery sighs in frustration.

“Is that all you care about?”

“Why do people keep asking me that? Yes! Yes! The answer’s always yes!”

"You better make sure they all know the breakup was my idea."

"Already wrote a press release to come out the day before the Oscars. This will make them really want to watch, just in case there's a catfight on the red carpet. I can see the headline now…'Red Carpet turns into Bled Carpet.' I love it! Hey, how good are you at kickboxing?"

"You are one evil man, Dalton."

"Stop, you're making me blush," he giggles.

"So, who am I supposed to go with? I can't go by myself."

"Don't worry your unfed head. I've already arranged your escort."

"Well, who is it? Is he as famous or more than Thian? He better not be one of your new discovery, up and coming, boy band acting losers."

"No, it's not, because all of them have dates."

"Just tell me! Who is it?"

"You'll see on Oscar night. Just be breakup beautiful and on time for the car.

"Why can't I be your date?"

"Because you're not going to sleep with me. My date

will."

"I'm open to negotiation."

"There is none. I don't sleep with my clients."

"Really? I always thought you had no scruples."

"I don't. This is just my professional rule. Funds over buns, checks over sex, pay over play, banks before spanks, money over honey, bread over bed, coins over loins, dollars over hollars…"

"Okay, I get your point."

"Thanks for the visual though."

"That's not what I meant. I…"

"Gotta go, I'm bored."

He's gone.

Avery angrily throws her phone in the pool. Splash! In goes Rella to rescue the waterproof vessel of communication.

Even though she and Thian were in a relationsham, she liked the idea of people thinking he was her boyfriend. It made her feel special that others thought the sexiest man in the world loved her. Now it's over, and the public will probably hate her for breaking up with such a great guy, even though he was cheating on her. But his cheating will probably be justified by the fans because of something she did in the relationship. Maybe she wasn't nice enough, catering enough, gone too much, not pretty enough, not thin enough. She had kind of hoped things would really work out for them as a couple. *I mean, what's not to like? I'm a superior model, famous child star, and envied by everyone.*

When she met Thian for the first time at the pool, Avery already had a huge crush on him and was thrilled that they were being hooked up. Dalton was her own personal dating site and he got it right. She thought she would impress Thian by doing her famous exit from the pool like she did for the perfume commercial "Caution." It was freezing that day and she would have rather been inside wearing a sweater and wrapped in a blanket. But no, Dalton said to make a big impression. And so, she did. He barely reacted and seemed annoyed that she had gotten him wet. Rejection is bad but rejection in an ass floss bikini after doing a slow seductive walk out of a pool is worse.

After their first dinner date, it was clear to Avery that Hollywood shop talk was of no interest to him and neither was her model look-book nor was her list of all the people she knew she was better than. She realized they had nothing in common and resented him for not being so entranced by her beauty and fame. *Who does he think I am? How dare he not worship me!* Then she rationalized that he must be intimidated by her career and empowerment. *He wants a woman who will stay home and cook for him. I could do that. If he would just ask.*

For once, she wished something could be real in her life.

Chapter Eight
Clothes Minded

Two months later…

Zavier's broody brood enters his office ready for the day's command of idiocy. They stand before him in their uniforms and wait silently while he sips his tea and reads the latest entertainment and fashion news quietly. Fifteen minutes pass when he finally speaks without looking up.

"I need you to take that to the car."

Zavier dismissively points to a red garment bag with a 24-karat gold hanger protruding from the top.

They turn and look at it in complete awe. To be this close to a Zavier original is a privilege, a moment that can never be taken in again, a moment to be wholly inhaled and marinated. Teal, Vo, Sea, and Fig briskly walk over to the garment bag and try to pick it up, but it's too heavy. They all struggle as if they were lifting a car. After a few attempts they manage to get it off the couch only to struggle and sweat their way towards the door.

"This is so heavy, Sir, there must be a thousand pounds of crystals sewn into it," says Teal, exhausted.

"Close, it's a size fourteen," says Zavier.

"What?!" They all yell as they drop the garment bag and stomp on it in fear and terror as if it were a pile of deadly spiders.

"How did this get in here?" shrieks Vo.

"This is horrifying!" cries Fig.

Zavier jumps up and stops his protective squad from stomping on the garment bag.

"No, no! Stop it! Stop it! It's all right!"

"Where…where did it come from?"

"Should we call the police? Are we in danger?"

They're all trembling.

"Okay, okay, everybody, calm down. Calm down!"

Zavier takes a deep breath, looks up at the ceiling for guidance from above (his portrait), then hangs his head low and shakes it in shame.

"What's happening?" asks Vo.

Zavier musters enough courage to face them and says in a small, cracked voice, "I made it."

It's thin world Armageddon as Teal hysterically screams, "Noooooooo!" and runs out of the room.

Vo holds her stomach and dry heaves her breakfast of oxygen as Sea drops to her knees and weeps next to a passed-out Fig.

They took it much better than Zavier thought they would.

Chapter Nine
The Size The Limit

Thian rushes to the door of his eight-bedroom mansion in Sherman Oaks. He opens it to find Zavier standing there with a beautiful gold garment bag. The gold hanger causes Thian to squint as it flashes its expensive hook his way.

"Zavier! Come in!" says Thian cheerfully as he takes the garment bag from Zavier like it's a cotton ball.

Normally, Zavier would have the dress delivered by one of his appraisers or special courier, but since Thian is an Academy Award nominee and this dress is going to make Hollywood history, he wanted to ensure his place as front and center throughout the whole process. Even though he cringes at the thought of anyone knowing that a dress this size has his name on it, Zavier wants everyone to know that this is a once in a lifetime design he did as a huge favor for Thian. Like making a donation to his favorite charity.

"Oh, do be careful with that. It's not one of your movie props you can just swing around any kind of way."

"Yes, yes, of course. This is very precious!" says Thian as he gently lays it on his white leather couch.

"I would have been here sooner but I just wanted to

shroud this glorious gown in one of my special garment bags." *One that's free of footprints, tears, and shame.*

"I so appreciate that. I know you put a lot of time, thought, and magic into this. I can't wait to see it!"

Thian starts to unzip the garment bag.

Zavier stops him and says, "Don't you want to wait and see your lady in it on Oscar night and have that big wow moment together?"

"Heck no! She's already a wow moment in or out of this dress."

Thian is as giddy as a six-year-old at Disneyland.

"But it's bad luck to see the dress before she does."

"You're thinking about a wedding dress, Zavier. Relax. You're not afraid I'm not going to like it, are you?"

Zavier looks offended and catches his breath to maintain his cool bass.

"Offended? I have never been offended a day in my life. I was just trying to provide you with a special moment you and your love can share, compliments of me."

"Yeah, a very expensive compliment," Thian laughs.

Zavier prides himself on being the reason women felt good about themselves solely because they were wearing or owned a Zavier original, and this case was exceptional. He had not ever designed, conceptualized, or even fathomed making a specialty dress of this immensity. *Thian Rodgers, you should be grateful that I even considered making such a monster of a sized dress!*

Thian unzips the garment bag down to its full length. He stops and stares at it, still and speechless. Zavier watches intensely as Thian picks it up by the hanger and gently lays it full length across the couch like a sleeping princess. The canary yellow dress is stunning as the reflective crystals dance on the walls and floors. Thian shakes his head in amazement.

"Zavier, you are a true genius," he says with tears in his eyes.

Zavier is slightly touched by how humbly happy he has made Thian. *This is going to make a wonderful story for the talk shows after the Oscars. 'Famous Designer's Dress Brings Action Star to Tears Just Before Oscars,* Zavier thinks as he walks over and puts his anointed hand on Thian's arm.

"It was my pleasure. It was my honor," he says in his kind, condescending tone.

"She is going to look exquisite."

Unable to further verbalize anything positive about

Thian's choice of a huge mate, Zavier silently stands as he smiles and accepts his much deserved accolades. *No doubt she will. I can make any troll look decent, even one as massive as this one.*

"It's just so beautiful! She's just absolutely going to love it!"

Of course, she's going to love it, it's me!

"I wanna make a toast to the dress and the genius who made it. I'll get the wine." Thian says joyfully as he heads towards the kitchen.

"That would be great. I'll just put it back in the garment bag for you."

"No no! Leave it out. Let it breathe. I just want to look at it," Thian calls out from the kitchen. "I've got some wonderful bottles of red wine I've been saving up for a splendid occasion such as this."

Yes please! Bring all the bottles. Help me get over this monstrosity! "Thian, you are too kind. This is just what I do. My every day. My calling."

Thian comes back into the room with two glasses of red wine.

"Well I'm just so glad that your calling answered my prayers."

Both men smile at each other.

Thian hands the glass of red wine to Zavier's outreached expectant hand, then slowly pulls it back and pours it on the dress.

Zavier is thunderstruck beyond disbelief as the red wine absorbs mercilessly down the front of the dress as Thian pours methodically from one crystal glass and drinks merrily out of the other.

"You didn't really think I'd let Corrinne near something touched from filth such as yourself, did you?" Thian asks him calmly as he empties the last lazy drop of wine onto the dress. He sets both glasses on the coffee table.

All Zavier can do is stand there, unable to process that he is being spoken to with nothing less than high praise and reverence. He watches as if in a hypnotic state as Thian picks up the dress, drops it to the floor, then whistles. Out trots two happy German shepherds that play his sidekicks in his movies.

Suddenly, Thian yells, "Zavier!"

Zavier wets his very expensive Italian custom-made suit pants as the dogs growl, gnash their teeth, then jump on the dress. They tear it to shreds as crystals fly, scatter, and ping everywhere.

"You see, they despise evil in real-life as much as I do."

Thian looks at the dogs and yells, "Corrinne!" The dogs immediately stop, lay down, and roll on their back playfully. Thian kneels and rubs their respective tummies. "Now, Zavier, this is what's going to happen. You're going to take this piece of trash that has your disgusting name on it, get it out of my beautiful home and never speak of either of these meetings and what went down to anyone. You are never ever to speak her name, show her picture, utter an opinion, or even look her way." Thian stands up and walks towards a cowering Zavier. "Or I'm going to release footage of this whole thing, that is captured on my security cam, to the media. You got that?" he roars in full Rogan's Rage then puts his finger to his lips and says softly, "Shhhhh…Nobody has to know."

Zavier shakes and nods in submissive shock as Thian turns and commands, "Thank you!" the dogs get up and run out of the room as Zavier runs towards the door at the same time thinking the command was meant for him.

"Hold on Zero, you can't leave without this!" Thian picks up the mangled shredded, wine stained, once heavenly dress as hundreds of crystals still fall and dance across his marble floor and flings it at Zavier. It smacks him in the face as he turns around, causing him to stagger back.

Zavier awkwardly gathers the dress like he's wrestling an octopus.

“Now go!” demands Thian,

Zavier scrambles to open the door then trips over the dress and clumsily catches his balance down the front steps.

Thian closes the door then turns around and smiles as he looks at the thousands of crystals on the floor. He kneels and picks them up one by one and says with satisfaction, “And that ladies and gentlemen is why I am nominated for an Academy Award.”

Chapter Ten
Dressed to Confess

Three days later…

Corrinne is nestled comfortably in her luxurious robin's egg blue colored bathtub filled with lavender bubbles as she admires her engagement ring. She knows tonight is going to change her life forever. She is about to step out of the shadows and into the spotlight with the man she loves more than anything in this world. More than her anonymity, more than her fear of public scrutiny and size shaming.

Thian had been so patient, giving, and accommodating to her needs and desires by living in her sheltered world for so long, unable to live his life his way. She knew it was getting to be too much for him with the prosthetics, makeup, change of clothes and accent. He did everything it took to see her. It was time she started making sacrifices. She had hidden long enough and no matter what Hollywood and the public had to say about her, she was going to look fabulous!

Corrinne's cell phone rings. She takes it out of the waterproof case sitting on the tub's side.

"Hello?"

"Hey, on my way. You guys need anything?" Malinda asks.

"Yes, a plane ticket to Greece," answers Corrinne kidding not kidding.

"I've already got it as a backup," laughs Malinda, "Be there in a few."

"Okay thanks, bye."

They hang up. Corrinne sighs.

Malinda is coming over not only for moral support but to do Corrinne's hair and makeup for the Oscars. This was not going to be a big ordeal. Corrinne does not believe in hours on hair and makeup. She could hire a team from the most exclusive salon, but no one was better and more talented than Malinda. And it doesn't take a team to make Corrinne look flawless.

An hour on both hair and makeup will be more than enough time. Corrinne knows it doesn't take much for her to go from current wow to WOW! She likes hair and makeup worry and touch up free. She had decided early on to go to the Oscars as herself. She made her own gown and was going about her daily routine, pizza delivery and all.

"You sure you want pizza? It is Oscar Night. I'm sure there will be grapes," joked Malinda when Corrinne had mentioned it.

Corrinne never worried about bloating. She has one of those phenomenal bodies that is firm, curvy, and cellulite free. She always felt bad watching clients struggle with undergarments to give them the illusion of a figure they did not have as they pushed, pulled, smashed, mashed, tugged, broke nails, and sweated just to put them on. Then came the bruising and imprints left after a long day of deception. She never wore body illusion garments even at the begged request of her mother at age eight when her baby fat just didn't seem to grow up and leave the nest. Corrinne didn't like the idea of trying to fool people into thinking she looked like something she wasn't. She likes her body. And hopes to feel the same way after tonight.

Meanwhile…

Thian recites the off-the-top-of-his-head acceptance speech Dalton wrote for him in an email, "I am shocked and truly humbled to have even been nominated, let alone win. There are so many people to thank but first and foremost, I'd like to thank the person who is completely responsible for me being up here tonight and that is my agent, Dalton. (Point to me so camera can capture my sincere acceptance of your gratitude)." Thian slams down his laptop. "I'm not going to say this crap!"

Not even Dalton's relentless narcissism can contain Thian's excitement for tonight. Not because of the nomination but because Corrinne is going to be by his side.

"Hey Babe, do you want me to order the pizza now?" Thian calls from Corrinne's living room.

"That would be perfect. We can eat before Malinda does my hair and makeup."

"Yeah, and mine too!"

Corrinne laughs as she steps out of the tub.

"Everything on it?" Thian asks, always happy to inspire a chuckle from her. Especially tonight.

"Everything plus! We're going all out. It's Academy Awards night!" says Corrinne elated to have Thian there with her so they can get dressed, be nervous, and laugh together. She doesn't care about the pomp and circumstance of him seeing her for the first time in her dress when he comes to pick her up. She wants him with her, in her space, in her face, in her ear. She has an overwhelming sense of freedom knowing that they will no longer have to sneak around. She is going to enjoy this night no matter what.

Meanwhile…

Zavier admires his reflection as he gets dressed in his signature black fitted suit with a silk red shirt and black tie. The colors make him look powerfully sinister; like someone you'd be afraid to approach but hope he notices you. Zavier loves the dominance of intimidation and superiority. However, today, he's a little anxious about tonight after his encounter with Thian. He had never been so scared and shook up like that before. Zavier knew he angered people with his body image point of view but never to the point of one of his designs being destroyed by attack dogs in his supreme presence. Until that humiliating moment, Zavier thought he was untouchable, even invincible. No one had ever raised a whisper to him. He was always in control, telling others what to do, eat, and feel. But when Thian poured that wine on his precious one-of-a-kind design and those dogs went on the attack, Zavier saw his whole fashion line flash before his eyes. For the first time, he feels vulnerable, like the possibility is out there that others could stand up to him. *Shake it off! Impossible. You are Zavier. Don't let one beast of a brainless movie star ruin this for you! You are Zavier*!

Meanwhile…

Avery sits in a pink high back stool amidst a team of

beauty experts as she nibbles on frozen peas. She is being curled, pinned, lashed, plucked, painted, and sprayed. She still has no idea who her date for the evening is. Normally, she would be brag chatting to the envious workers about how lucky they were to be in this moment with her and how not many people are as fortunate as they are to be this close to fame but still not in it. Avery would have been telling them how much in love she and Thian are and that they would be hopping a plane to Paris right after the show. It was supposed to be hours of "Life is Great for Avery" in front of a live living room audience. But today is different, she sits humbly quiet, much to the pleasure of the beauty battalion.

Avery is deep in thought about who her date is. *Who will show up? Will he be famous enough? Will he be my next relationship? Could I fall in love with him? Of course, he's already in love with me.* Avery had been looking forward to this evening ever since Thian was nominated. She had visualized her and Thian gazing at each other lovingly as he holds the Oscar and how beautiful those pictures would look on television and in magazines. She had even practiced different poses, expressions, and pretty-cry faces for hours. Then Thian had to ruin everything by breaking things off. She can't imagine the woman he is taking is better looking than she is. *Doesn't matter. Yes, it does! There will be fan backlash and I can't wait.*

The headline about their breakup came out yesterday, "Avery Calls it Quits Just Before Oscars!" It has been the hot topic of all the entertainment and news shows. There were women all over the world weeping over the breakup and alleged accusations of Thian's cheating.

Everyone in the world will have eyes on me as they wait to see who I show up with, how I'm doing and how incredible I look in my gown, Avery reasons to herself. She doesn't have anyone to confide in and discuss the full truth with. There was no one to talk to about what to do next. There are eight people in her immediate reach and not a connection to be had. They all know, have their opinions, but can't say anything to her about it and cannot wait to discuss it amongst themselves afterwards. Avery would love to have some girl chat with any one of them, but they were instructed not to make eye or verbal contact with her beyond professional necessity. *I hope he loses.*

Meanwhile…

Corrinne, Thian, Malinda, and Thian's brother Dominic, laugh as they sit on Corrinne's living room floor and eat pizza. Thian and Corrinne are both in sweatpants and tank tops. Malinda, ever the fashionista, has on studded blue jeans with a red form fitting sweater.

"I think you should go as Gregge tonight," jokes Corrinne.

"Now why didn't you think of that sooner? I would have brought my costume," Thian riffs back.

"That would be epic! Everyone would wonder, 'Who is this construction guy? And how did he make it to the red carpet?' And just before they tackle you to the ground, you reveal yourself!" says Dominic.

"With that security? There will be no before they tackle me. It will be a tackled me trying to explain with a mouthful of red carpet and regrets."

They all laugh.

Meanwhile…

After seven long hours of hair, makeup, manicuring, pedicuring, spray tanning, and dressing, Avery is natural beauty ready in her extraordinary, exclusive, once-in-a-lifetime Zavier body hugging, gold sequined dress that shimmers from every angle. She is barely able to move gracefully due to the heavy and pretentious four-foot train that languishes behind her. It is heavier than she is. Avery practices her walk throughout her apartment to get used to the excess weight she has to carry. After a few laps and the faux gushing from the once silent glam brigade, who are now allowed to speak in order to spew needless praise on how phenomenal she looks, the doorbell rings.

Avery rudely orders Rella to answer the door. She wants to make a grand entrance for her blessed date and goes into her bedroom.

Twenty minutes later, Avery dramatically enters her living room as if she were appearing before a crowd of seventy thousand in a stadium. She stops short and almost tumbles forward when she sees a man of well under six feet dressed in a black suit, white shirt, and thick black tie waiting at the door. He is in awe when she steps in the room and immediately starts to sweat more. Not because Avery is so hot but because the room is due to all the placed movie lighting and mirrors so that Avery could see how she's going to look on television from every angle and to ensure she's sweat and melt proof. Too bad no one else in the room is armed with so much resistance. It looks and feels like the inside of a giant microwave set on high.

Avery cannot help but show her disappointment at seeing this nondescript being in her presence.

"Who are you?" she asks rudely, taking a little shine off her sparkle. "I know you're not my date.*" Because if you are, I'm going to kill Dalton and look fantastic in my mugshot*!

"Oh no, Miss, I'm just your driver," he replies as if speaking to royalty, "Your date's in the car."

Avery is apoplectic, "So…he's not getting out to escort me to the car? Does he know who I am?"

The admonished driver shamefully answers, "No, no, he is not and I'm sure he does, Miss."

Avery was supposed to overwhelm her date in full, to-be-worshiped standing length. Especially in the six-inch tower martini gold and glass heels that have already brought tears to her toes and ankles. She is an amazon of epic slim proportions that begs to be seen and revered in its entirety and best lighting, not through a tinted window for a few seconds then folded like an origami in order to get into the car. She should be admired for at least thirty minutes before the plan of attack for sitting down graceful and painlessly begins. She even had champagne on ice waiting for a quick drink, (for him, she didn't want to risk bloating), and a few (a lot) of photos were supposed to be taken of them to place on social and mainstream media. Nope.

She whips around to Rella and spits, "Why didn't you tell me it was just the driver? I wouldn't have wasted my entrance on him!"

Rella drops her head in shame and says in a barely audible voice, "I thought he was your date."

"You...You! You thought **this** was **my** date?! Seriously? Look at me! Look at him! Have you lost my reality?"

Rella's voice breaks in between nervous verges of tears and hiccups, "He said he was here to take you to the Oscars, so I thought..."

"That's why you don't get paid to think! You get paid to do! See what happens when you think?"

Everyone looks away wishing they were anywhere else but here.

After a long, cringing, silent brat standoff of disbelief and humiliation, Avery finally shrieks, "Whatever! Rella, get my purse!"

Rella picks up the tiny jewel encrusted matching purse that was sitting on an accent table right next to Avery. Avery snatches it angrily from her and inadvertently cuts Rella's hand. Rella doesn't flinch. She will just cry and tend to her wound after Avery leaves as she does after every encounter with her boss. The trick now is not to get blood on anything.

Avery stomps to the front door. The driver opens it in time for her to make a seamless exit. He skips in front of her to get the elevator door. They ride down the twenty-eight floors in awkward silence. Avery had visualized making out with her date as a gift to handsome him.

Instead, she is in the elevator with this nobody civilian who is just the help. *A double chili cheeseburger would be great right about now.* The elevator stops at various floors. Avery hides in the corner and commands the driver to close the door before anyone can get on. *I can't be seen alone with this schlub!*

They finally get to the lobby and out the door with Avery walking with her head held high and her sore feet held captive not making any eye contact but feeling all eyes on her. They can't help but notice. She looks fantastic, like a mystical siting, something you don't see every day, a legend, an icon, walking amongst the commoners on her way to a royal event that only a few get to attend. Actually, the only person in the lobby is the concierge and he is on the phone looking at the computer.

The sleek, gleaming black sedan that is parked in front of her building awaits her splendid arrival. The backdoor slowly swings open and a pair of well-dressed feet slide out. Avery's heart starts beating for the fortunate gentleman who gets to be in her presence for the evening, and possibly beyond if he plays his cards and looks right. The mystery steps out of the car and on to the sidewalk to greet Avery. It's Zavier. Though happy to see him, she isn't HAPPY to see him. All her expectations for the night and the rest of her life were dashed in that second of recognition.

"Avery! You look unimaginable!" says Zavier admiring his dress more than Avery. He was not happy with waiting so long but did expect it because he knew Avery and wanted her to look the best because she was wearing his dress.

"Zavier!" Avery squeals in false delight as she Hollywood hugs him in order not to smudge her make-up or snag a jewel. She must play nicer than nice because this is the man who continues to boost her career. This is a great match. She gets to walk in with the world's top designer wearing a gown he made only for her. No one else on the red carpet would be wearing a Zavier original. Sure, there were other designers, but everyone wants to be in a Zavier and Avery won. Being envied is much better than being loved. She learned that from Dalton.

Meanwhile…

Thian sits on the couch waiting for Corrinne.

"Babe, you almost ready? I've been waiting a whole five seconds!" he chuckles as he calls out.

"No, I'm not almost ready," she calls back then steps into the room, "I am ready."

One thing about Corrinne, she never likes to keep people waiting. Especially people she loves and respects.

Thian is speechless as she floats towards him in a bright periwinkle body-proud sleeveless Grecian-style gown that makes her look like a fantasy. Her curly hair cascades down her back while a bundle of curls in the front are tied and intertwined with diamonds to form a headband crown that holds back the force of her tresses, completely exposing every angle of her face. Her neck is bejeweled with periwinkle sapphire and diamonds that dance gracefully about her décolletage. The matching three-stud earrings round out her fashion performance spectacularly. Corrinne's make-up is flawless as it accentuates every feature to be appreciated without making her look like a wax figure. Thian is overwhelmed by how unbelievably beautiful she is and how lucky he is to finally be seen with her in public.

Corrinne can't help but notice how extremely handsome and happy Thian looks. It is a look she can't describe and will never forget. She feels safe, cared for, proud of, and loved. She feels sorry that she put him through so much just to be with her, and the fact that he did it for so long is a bit overwhelming for her. *This is the most handsome man in the world and he's mine. Look at him in this suit looking so sexy and looking at me in this dress. What more can I ask?* she thinks to herself as they meet in the middle and twirl for each other.

They laugh until they cry, knowing what a momentous

occasion this is. Thian is elated by her coming with him and wearing his ring. This is the day he's been waiting for. He would have been just as happy if she had gone with him for coffee. He is just happy to be with her, unrestricted.

"You look…you look…as beautiful as you always do. I'm just…I'm just so happy I get to have you with me as me. Thank you for taking this leap."

She puts her forehead on his chest then looks up at him.

"Thank you for being so patient and shielding me from all the crazy I've been trying to avoid. And whatever crazy is about to come my way, I'm ready for it because you're more than worth it."

"Oh my goodness! Step out of the soap opera already! You look great, she looks great, he loves you, you love him, blah, blahdy blah blah blah! We know, we know already!" Malinda chimes in, nauseous from all the sugar and sap.

Corrinne and Thian wipe away tears and laugh.

"Now get in that car and bring back an Oscar!" commands Dominic.

Chapter Eleven
Lean With Envy

Meanwhile…

Avery recounts to Zavier the situation with her and Thian, "So, I guess you know by now Thian and I are no longer a couple…"

Zavier shudders at the mention of Thian. If she only knew how much he knew.

"I was only with him to help his career. It was suggested by our agent. I never liked him anyway. He was way too into himself."

Yeah, can't have two of those in one relationship. Zavier thinks to himself.

"I wonder who this loser girl is anyway. Dalton says he doesn't know. Do you know?" she asks Zavier.

Now this is the billion-dollar question. Zavier is so startled by the inquiry, that he doesn't know which tone of "no" to answer. If he sounds as surprised as he feels he'll sound like he's hiding something. If he sounds indignant, he'll seem way too invested and this conversation will never end.

"No," he states casually. *Not only do I know, I designed a dress for your competition.*

Zavier's plan was to have both women come in his specially designed dresses and have a fashion dress off. A "Who Wore It War" between Thian's girls. Hosted by the media and cruel opinion polls. It was going to be scandalous, messy, and best of all, vicious publicity. But, at least now he has the golden child, the winner. He had already seen the competition and there is none. *She is the victor and she doesn't even know it.*

"Because you would tell me if you knew, wouldn't you?" Avery probes.

You are just one of my models, Honey, not my most bestie best friend! If you weren't wearing one of my precious gowns so strikingly well, you wouldn't even be in this car right now.

"Of, course I would," he tells her with a comforting smile. *Now shut up about it!*

"I would just love to embarrass them on the red carpet," says Avery.

Zavier's heart jackhammers. He wants nothing to do with Thian being upset and thinking he has something to do with it. Aside from feeling nervous, Zavier is stone-cold terrified.

"Why don't you just let it go. The situation will take care of itself. I'm sure there's no way she looks in the realm as stunning as you do. And that's all that counts."

Avery leans back and smiles at Zavier and says, "You are so right. So wise. So present. You must have read my mind. You know what they say, 'Grapevines think alike.'"

It's going to be a long evening.

Two hours later…

Thian and Corrinne are two blocks away from the red-carpet entrance and the hundreds of yowling fans who are stationed across the street. He and Corrinne are in the famous Rogan's Rage tricked out army green and yellow monster truck that Thian is driving. This unorthodox grand entrance was a special request made by the studio to help promote the movie he is nominated for. Thian would have much rather they walk the red carpet with quiet dignity, but he is obligated to promote the movie. He really didn't want her debut as his fiancée to be such a circus. Thian was hesitant to tell Corrinne about the arrival hullabaloo and deathly afraid she'd change her mind. To his surprise, she just threw her hands up, laughed and said,

"Let's do it!"

The crowd goes crazy as the giant monster truck rumbles down the street playing his movie's theme music. Even the reporters get caught up in the spectacle, leaving their posts and the secondary celebrities they were just gushing over to capture and be a part of whatever the commotion is that will surely be on everyone's mind and lips the next day.

On the ride there, Corrinne was anxious about how she was going to be received. Not only did she not physically fit what a superstar is expected to date, she is also the one he chose over a world-famous model. They may hate her as they perceive her as the reason for his and Avery's breakup. *What if they boo me? What if they call me fat? What if the reporters shun me? What if they make fun of my dress?* She then took a deep breath and looked over at Thian who was talking and laughing with such exuberance while driving and holding her hand. *And what if they do? What if all that happens? I'll still be Corrinne Mayars. I'll still be I-can-do-whatever-I-want-in-this-world-rich, I'll still be one helluva designer, and best of all, I'll still have him. Let's do this Girl!*

Thian pulls up, parks the truck, and kisses Corrinne.

"I love you, Baby," he says to her, barely able to contain his emotional excitement.

"I love you, too," she tells him, barely able to contain her chattering teeth.

"You ready?"

"For you, always."

They kiss then take a long deep breath.

Thian suddenly realizes how jarring this situation is and feels that he may be asking too much from Corrinne.

"Are you sure you want to do this?" he asks her.

"Well it's too late now!" Corrinne laughs.

He looks at Corrinne and says sincerely, "It's never too late. I'll drive this thing straight down the street and back home if you want."

"Listen, I did not get this fine and climb into this monster truck not to be seen in this dress! If you don't get out first, I will!"

Thian laughs, feeling more secure in this decision.

Corrinne is overwhelmed that he would be willing to miss his big night just for her comfort. She is ready for anything.

Thian does his famous hero exit from the monster ride. Pandemonium doesn't begin to describe the reaction from the fans. Extra security is called to stand in front of the cement barriers. Thian runs over and waves vigorously to the fans, touches fingertips, and blows kisses. The sound barrier is broken. Thian then runs back to the passenger side of the monster truck where hundreds of reporters and camera crews are waiting for Corrinne's exit.

Corrinne sees the mob of cameras and flashes as she waits for Thian to escort her down. They look like hungry zombies ready to take a bite out of her. *Maybe I should have done this with baby steps. Be seen with him at a coffee shop, the grocery store, or even a movie theater. Not this! What were you thinking, Corrinne?* The door swings open and there stands her hero. *Go big 'cause you can't go home!*

A gust of fame sweeps through as flashes and voices join in on the mayhem of the Rogan's Rage theme. Thian presses a button and a set of stairs and a railing unfolds from the passenger seat to the ground. Corrinne elegantly steps out of the famous vehicle and glides down the steps to the sidewalk. Suddenly, there is silence, all flashes cease, and all cameras come down so everyone can make sure they are really seeing what they think they are. No one like her had ever made such an entrance. Thian takes and kisses her hand. The flashes go crazy. They stand to get their picture taken in that moment. Corrinne's first thought is to run back up the steps and into the truck, but the steps are already gone, and the hired attendant has started driving off.

They turn around and face the fans as they are revealed on the jumbo screen. There is a collective gasp then a hush as the fans catch sight of the two of them holding hands. They are not sure what to think. This is so unexpected. *She's not a model, an actress, social media star, who is she? How is she?*

As the monster truck roars further down the street, the silence from the fans grows louder until one woman's voice rings out, "What's your name?"

"Corrinne!" she calls back as she waves a firm arm towards the voice.

Another voice rings out from the fans, "Corrinne, who made your beautiful dress?"

Corrinne confidently points both thumbs to herself and yells proudly, "I did!"

The crowd goes nuts. She gives them all two thumbs up.

Thian hugs and kisses her. Like a thunderstorm, applause, whistles, and shouts rain down from the fans as they capture this monumental moment on their phones.

Meanwhile…

Avery and Zavier's car pulls right up in front of one of the jumbo screens that lines the blocks for all the fans standing out to see what's happening. Zavier is on his phone watching the red carpet live. He sees a close-up of Corrinne and is taken aback. *She is absolutely breath-taking! And that dress.* Even though he is a sizeist, Zavier does know pure fashion and beauty when he sees it and is mesmerized by her. *That picture definitely didn't do her justice.*

Avery squints then presses her face against the window just as Thian and Corrinne break away from their kiss. "Is tha…is tha…IS THAT HER?!" Avery screeches.

Zavier jumps, sending his phone flying across the backseat floor. As he searches for it, Avery goes on a verbal tirade.

"She's fat! I mean huge! This can't be real! She must be some charity survivor, winner of some contest, or a practical joke he's playing on his fans!"

Zavier coughs and chokes on his own spit at the mention of a practical joke, jolting Avery away from the window. She rubs his back in comfort as he coughs and turns red.

"I know, I know, this must be extra hard for you, especially since you're allergic to people of that size."

Meanwhile…

Corrinne and Thian turn around to face the barrage of press and flashes as they make their way to the first entertainment reporter they are supposed to talk to. The rest of the press scramble back to their assigned positions and comment as they wait anxiously, hoping Corrinne and Thian come to them.

Thian holds Corrinne's hand tightly which makes all this mayhem all right. He constantly looks over at her to gauge how she's doing. The two are so in sync, that whenever he looks at her, she looks at him. He knows when she's putting on a fake smile and muddling through situations, just from the many dinners they've endured at her mother's house. When she smiles up at him, he can tell it's real and that she's happy to be there.

Corrinne has been to many awards shows and celebrity gatherings, but never in the middle of the cameras, craziness, and curiosity. Thian's strong protective grip on her right hand and the engagement ring on her left gives her a sense of being grounded, that there is life after this moment, that this is just an instant of fantasy fun. The real celebration has been going on for over a year since they met and will continue well after tonight. Every time he looks at her, Corrinne can feel his shield of love surrounding her. She is able to breathe and thoroughly enjoy this with him.

Their first stop is on the famed orange couch with the number one morning television talk show gossip host and most tanned human being, Syte Walker, from "Syte On Scene." His show always gets the first word, verse, and chorus on what's happening in Hollywood. He is known for getting "The Elusive Exclusive" on everything.

Thian and Corrinne step up to his platform that is perched well above everyone else's. They are greeted with warm hugs and a kiss for Corrinne. Syte eyes Corrinne curiously and can't believe what he's seeing. Having had the heads up that Thian would be debuting his new and allegedly improved girlfriend, saved him the embarrassment of asking if she was his aunt or former nanny. Such a snob, this one.

"So, welcome to Syte On Scene! I am Syte Walker the Best Talker and here on the couch with me is Oscar nominated for best actor, Thian Rodgers! And this stunning human of a being is his latest lady love, Corrinne!"

"Uh, let me clarify something for you and your audience." Thian takes Corrinne's left hand and kisses it, making sure the camera and Syte pick it up, "That's last lady love."

Syte is sucker punched with surprise and sheer delight.

"You heard it here first, people, from Syte on Scene! Thian Rodgers is engaged! Congratulations to you both!" He does his signature, 'just between us' lean in, "So, tell me, what happened to you and Avery? How does she feel about all this?"

Thian smiles that smile of charm and charisma that will swaddle anyone's heart. "Well, let me tell you, Syte…"

Meanwhile…

Zavier has found his phone and is finishing his second shot of vodka while Avery scrutinizes her image in her compact mirror and continues to babble on.

"I can't believe Thian is actually dating her! She doesn't fit into our world. Hell, she barely fits into the world period!" Avery laughs at her own cleverness then turns to Zavier and says soberly, "You and you alone have worked soooo hard to keep people like her away from people like us. Now look what's happened! You let one in then that opens the door to possibly two, then they'll start having children and we'll have to see chubbies almost every month!"

Avery works herself into a fiery froth as Zavier quietly pours himself another shot.

"I'm going to say something about it. How wrong it is that he's dating **her** and bringing **her** to our events where we are free from such visuals."

“NO!” Zavier shouts involuntarily just by the sheer terror of being part of anything that mentions Corrinne being shamed, blamed, or even named.

Avery jumps and says, "What? Why not?"

Think fast Zavier! “Because Princess, negative talk will ruin my dress and that’s not something you want to do. Do you?” he says in a soothing tone with a dash of threat.

Avery gets it and calms down. She had gotten so wrapped up in Thian and his date that she forgot she was being es-corted by the man who could end her career.

“You’re right, Zavier, Thian is my past and this dress is my present and future. “I’ll say nothing about them.”

“That’s my girl,” says Zavier as he kisses her on the cheek.

Zavier smiles and comfortably takes the last sip of his drink.

The door swings open and the deafening sound of cheers and camera clicks fill the car.

“Unless they ask me.”

“What did you say?”

Avery alights onto the red carpet. Zavier follows.

Meanwhile…

Thian and Corrinne make their way to the various news and entertainment reporters and show off Corrinne's awe and jaw dropping-inspiring ring and their bliss. They are very well received as the shock wears off and Corrinne seeps her witty way into their hearts. She is complimented to the hilt but not in a condescending way but in a fascinated "We've never seen or met anyone like you, and we like it," kind of way. They are refreshed, like the new cool girl has arrived at school with her own mind and style.

Thian has never felt so much joy to be at a Hollywood event before. It feels like his first time. When he waves at a fellow celebrity, handshakes, and hugs them, he really means it when he says, "It's so good to see you!" Everyone is fascinated to meet Corrinne as they literally size her up and are captivated by her hair, face, and dress.

A couple of actresses ask her in a sweet, curious catty way, "Who's hair are you wearing?" Knowing that they can't come right out and mention her size, but something must be pointed out to wipe away that irritating confident look of being engaged, happy, beautiful, and having regular meals.

She just looks at them and smiles sweetly, "Oh, it's a little family secret called, Born With It."

Meanwhile…

Avery and Zavier are on the couch with Syte. Avery is ready to let loose on what she thinks of Thian and his hot mess of a girlfriend. Syte looks at Avery like dessert after a four-week fast and can't wait to talk to her after they hug and kiss. Zavier sits next to her cool as a cucumber on the outside and hot as a jalapeño from anxiety on the inside. *What is she going to say and how can I get away?*

"So, Avery, my stunning! Thian told me everything!"

"Oh, did he?" says Avery with a raised eyebrow that has an attitude all its own. She throws her head back and sticks her tongue in the side of her cheek and looks at Syte with renewed determination, "Well did he tell you…"

Zavier braces himself.

"Yes he did…" Syte always likes to be the one to repeat a story first in order to prove he has the information before the other person tells it. "He told me what a good friend you were to him and Corrinne to help keep the paparazzi and reporters from finding out about their relationship. And how you put your love life on hold so that they could live theirs until they were ready to tell the world. They both think the world of you and consider you the hero of the night."

Avery and Zavier have the same shocked and confused look as they lean in closer to Syte and say in unison, "He told you that?"

"Word for word," Syte looks into the camera, "And he told it to me first." He looks back at Avery, "You seem surprised."

Avery tries to gather her thoughts. This was the last thing she expected.

"Well, yes…yes I am. I…I…I just thought this would always remain our little secret, that's all." she replies, very proud of herself for thinking so fast.

"Really, well what were **you** going to tell me?" Syte asks in an instigating tone.

"Oh, that doesn't matter! All that matters is now everyone knows the kind of person Avery truly is." Zavier chimes in, relieved to have that verbal catastrophe averted. *That Thian Rodgers is a genius! Not only did he fool the world into thinking he was dating a superior model, my superior model at that, then he makes her look like an angel when he turns up with a fiancée behind her back! I love it! Now I can enjoy my evening!*

Thian and Corrinne came up with the scenario a few weeks ago when they realized Corrinne was going to be perceived as a homewrecking side-chick to the world's most beloved love stories. Knowing what an attention clown Avery was, they decided it best to make her the hero of their story. As much of a narcissistic pain Avery has been to them, they still did not want to see her hurt or embarrassed because of them. Corrinne and Thian rehearsed it several times like an audition for a movie role and had perfected it by the time they were all sitting and eating pizza before getting dressed that afternoon.

It finally lands on Avery that she looks like the good guy in this scenario. She's the star. Everyone wants to hear from her. She's not to be pitied but praised on a pedestal where she belongs.

Avery puts on her most humble voice and states, "It's just that I had no idea they were going to tell everyone about it. I really just wanted to see them happy and anything I could do to help them was never too much. Plus, I got some free dinners out of it!" She laughs with humble humor sprinkled with generosity.

Syte overly laughs with her.

Zavier smiles. *Okay and let's just leave it at that.*

Loving the attention, she so rightfully deserves, Avery continues, "You know, so I figured, if that's what he wants to date then who am I to not help."

Zavier squirms and can feel the panic pulling in. *Here we go.*

"I mean, can you blame him for wanting to keep that a secret?" Avery asks.

I can't! Zavier stealthily slides away from Avery and off the couch.

Syte is so enraptured by Avery's uncouth candidness, he doesn't even notice Zavier's slithery exit.

"That's a little harsh, don't you think?" Syte asks her.

"That's a little true, don't you think?" Avery lobs back with a conspiratorial wink.

Oh, how Syte loves a good sound bite with a bite.

Chapter Twelve
Twist of Weight

The next morning Avery wakes up from her post Oscar food coma of fried chicken, waffles, tacos, and rocky road ice cream feeling good about herself and the night before. Thian won the Oscar, announced his engagement to Corrinne and thanked Avery for making it all possible. Everyone kept telling her she was the real hero of the night and jokingly asked her to match them up with their soulmate. *Maybe I should have my own matchmaking business or show.* She thought on her ride home without Zavier. He was pretty scarce last night and barely would be seen with her; which worked out fine because the spotlight was on her and there was no need to share it with him.

Meanwhile…

Zavier just wants to stay in bed, hoping to sleep the day away. He doesn't answer the phone, read any texts, or watch any entertainment reports out of fear and exposure after Avery's ridiculous, but true, comments about Thian and Corrinne. *Some truths are just meant to be kept to oneself or only spoken in private with the like-minded.* On post awards nights, Zavier's favorite thing to do was watch all the entertainment reports and count how many times his name is mentioned. He would jot down the glowing words used for his designs then have them printed and framed with the name of the show and the year it aired. Not this one.

Zavier did everything he could to avoid being seen with Avery after her statement to Syte. He was shaken all evening wondering if word had gotten back to Thian that he had somehow been a part of it. He jumped whenever someone tapped him on the shoulder or leaned in for a kiss or whisper. This was a night he usually looked forward to, reveled in, but instead it was riddled with anxiety and paranoia. He cringed when Thian won Best Actor. He just knew he was going to expose him, but he didn't. He was grateful, gracious, and gregarious. The audience loved him and Corrinne. The cameras were obsessed with her all evening. Not a bad angle or awkward moment as she and Thian held hands, whispered to each other, laughed at jokes, cried at acceptance speeches, and participated in the silly antics of some of the presenters. Zavier was a non-factor in this equation and for the first time he was happy about it.

Thian was so overwhelmed with joy and gratitude for

everyone who voted for him, believed in him and enjoyed his work when he accepted his Oscar, but most of all, he was jubilant at having Corrinne there with him. He was already having the best night of his life before the win. It was life-giving to have her with him and moving through his world effortlessly. He didn't have to protect her, prompt her, or anything. She was grace, humor, and beauty on full throttle. Corrinne had an unscripted mind, personality, and spirit that shone through to everyone who encountered her. He became at ease the moment she walked down the steps from the monster truck. He could feel her confidence when she took his hand. Thian knew right then and there Corrinne was in it for real and for the long haul.

Corrinne was so proud of Thian. She knew how much work he put into Rogan's Rage and was so happy when he was recognized for it. Though everyone was nice to her face, she knew there were going to be major comments about her the next day. She was okay with that because she was with the man she loves and celebrating his accomplishment. That's what real people in real love do.

Thian and Corrinne laughed throughout the show about the third person on their date, the camera. They even named it Joe. "Ope, here comes Joe again." "I'm starting to get a little jealous. Didn't you tell him you were with me?" "Here he comes again. I think he's got a major crush on you." "There's stalker Joe just waiting for your reaction," Thian was saying under his breath throughout the show which gave Corrinne the giggles and made everyone wonder what they were talking about. When Thian announced their engagement during his speech, there were raucous cheers amongst applause, and ear-splitting whistles. Corrinne knew he was going to do it but didn't expect such a huge reaction.

Now that the ring was out of the box, Corrinne had to figure out how to explain to her mother that she has been dating Thian all this time while bringing "Gregge" home for dinner once a month for the past year. Yet another scenario for them to work out and rehearse while eating pizza on the floor.

Meanwhile…

Avery checks out her post Oscar face and body in her bedroom mirror. Satisfied, she grabs the pail of Prime Chicken from the floor with four pieces of a twelve-piece deal left in it and hops back into bed and turns on the television. Nothing like cold fried chicken for breakfast while watching glowing entertainment reports about yourself. She was out too late last night party hopping and cramming her face to catch any of them before now.

The first show she turns on is "Syte On Scene." Her favorite because she knows she's his favorite. First thing that pops up is a picture of Avery looking glorious. Syte sits on his signature orange couch, in studio, next to the picture and says incredulously, "Can you believe she said that? And she said it to me first!"

Avery drops her chicken thigh in surprise. "Wait! What did I say? What did I say?"

"Remember this?" he says with a smirk as he turns to the large screen behind him. Avery's image from last night of her sitting on his couch pops up with an awkward freeze-framed expression then plays.

Avery's voice rings out over the background noise of cheers and bullhorn announcements, "You know, I figured, if that's what he wants to date then who am I to not help? I mean, can you blame him for wanting to keep that a secret?" The footage stops on an unflattering shot of Avery about to laugh that makes her look like an evil movie character.

Syte is appalled.

"What kind of a friend is that?"

A stunning picture of Corrinne pops up on the screen.

"I'd date her…You know, if I weren't… married." Syte-gives his famous up-close sly smile.

"That's not what I meant! Well, yes, it is what I meant but I didn't mean for you to make it look bad." Avery grabs her phone and greasy dials Dalton.

A dry and disappointed voice answers, "Avery."

He called her Avery. This is bad. Dalton never calls her by her name. She was always Doll, or Super One or Number One, but never Avery. She was feeling the pang of a shamed child about to be scolded after tracking in mud on just scrubbed floors.

"Avery, Avery, Avery, what were you thinking?" Dalton asks as his stock in her drops rapidly.

Think Avery think! WWDD? (What Would Dalton Do)

"I didn't mean it that way. I meant, you know, like, she was so beautiful why **would** he want to share her with the world," Avery explains trying to sound confident.

"You called her a 'that.' Even I can't spin **that**. And you know what? I don't want to."

"Oh, come on Dalton! You can't think I'm wrong in this. She's not up to our standards."

"Hey, I'd do her. Checking now to see if she has a sister. Oh, by the way, did you know she's the heiress to the billion-dollar Mayars Majestic Materials?"

Suddenly feeling vindicated, Avery jumps up on the bed

and yells, "That's why he's dating her! For her money! I knew there was a reason!"

"Well you're the only one who feels that way."

"What do you mean?"

"You should be getting a package from me soon. You'll see."

"What should I do? Should I call into some radio shows and do some interviews? Have you sent out a spin release?"

"The last thing anyone wants is a comment from you."

He's gone.

Avery deflates and sinks back onto her bed. Dalton had never sounded so professional. This was bad. She unfreezes the t.v., changes channels and lands on "Chews 'n' Views." The ladies are sitting at the counter eating their way through their comments.

"She really stuck her foot in her mouth this time!"

"She should've stuck a sandwich in it!"

"What a bottom feeder! She's just bitter because Thian chose bigger and better and she couldn't hide her peanut butter and jealousy."

"You think this is going to make America hungry for

more, Avery? Well think again!"

The audience applauds.

"I thought her dress was pretty."

"Look at her face, so full of herself, so smug."

"That's just Resting Hunger Face."

Avery turns off the television.

"Who cares what you cows think! Mooooove on to something else."

The doorbell rings. Unless it's a seven-layer burrito, she doesn't want it. Avery goes to her door and opens it. On the floor there is a special delivery box. She picks it up, puts it on the coffee table, and opens it. There is a handwritten note that reads:

"You better get on board quick! Dalton"

Avery looks in the box to find a stack of entertainment papers and magazines hot off the press this morning. Some have covers with Corrinne and Thian holding hands and smiling at each other with a red circle around her ring, the epic shot of him kissing her ringed hand, them kissing each other, them talking to the press, them talking and laughing secretly in the audience, a single candid shot of Corrinne lovingly watching Thian give an interview, Corrinne with a reporter laughing, and on and on and on and on. Then there are the unflattering pictures of Avery looking scorned with her mouth open as if shouting at Thian and Corrinne, (when in reality, she was saying hello to someone across the carpet), and the now infamous evil shot of Avery with Syte Walker. Her famous pouty pose is now regaled as jealousy and resentment.

Avery starts to feel sick as she reads the headlines.

"The New Trend Is Corrinne!"

"That Was Thin This Is Now"

"Two Big Wins For Thian Rodgers!"

"Thian Rodgers's Fiancée Is A Plus

In Her Own Designer Gown!"

"Meet America's Hottest Couple: Corinthian!"

Avery remembers back when it was "Thievery" because she and Thian had stolen the world's heart. It feels like it was just the day before yesterday. Because it was!

At the bottom of the box are tabloids with headlines that read:

"Bitter Avery Starved For Attention!"

"Slim Chance Avery Comes Back From This!"

"Skinny Is The New No."

"Icon-Ick!"

"Waist Not Want Not"

There are side by side comparison pictures of Avery's sublime column figure next to Corrinne's perfect hourglass shape. Now unflattering pictures of Avery, the press held back as a favor to Dalton, are splashed all over these periodically friendly periodicals.

This can't be true. Dalton must be trying to teach me a lesson. He doesn't like it when I speak without being told what to say and that's why he's doing this, Avery rationalizes as she grabs three caramel coated ice cream sandwiches from her freezer. *He's just trying to teach me a lesson. That's it! I get it! These stupid magazines aren't even real!* Avery laughs as she unwraps the first sandwich and walks back into her room. She turns the t.v. back on and switches the channel to "Wake Up America" where there are reporters from all over the world on four split screens reporting from newsstands that are filled with the same magazines Dalton sent her.

"Thanks, Dave, as you can see, I'm standing out here in front of one of the largest newsstands here in Vegas where the cover on the street is all about Thian Rodgers and Corrinne Mayars and the unfortunate Avery…"

"Unfortunate? I'm now an unfortunate? Look at me! I'm nothing but a fortunate!" Avery yells at the television as she sits on her bed with a pail of chicken on one side, two ice cream sandwiches on her lap while eating one with chocolate and caramel dripping down her chin and arm.

Meanwhile…

Corrinne rolls out of bed, flawlessly make-up free, wearing boy short panties with a tight crop t-shirt that reads: "And The Winner Is…," she designed, and walks into the bathroom. Her face tells the story of satisfaction and glory. The night before was magical. She can't believe how much fun it was and is feeling no fear of gossip, backlash, or being considered a figure don't. Thian comes up behind her in all his bare-chested splendor and wraps his strong, muscular Oscar winning arms around her waist.

"Good morning, Mr. Rodgers!" Corrinne says as she nestles into his broad manliness.

"Good morning, Mrs. Rodgers!" he responds with glee. "I just can't believe my incredible win!"

"Well you deserve that award. You worked really hard for it" Thian looks lovingly at Corrinne and says, "I wasn't talking about the award."

They made their union official right after the Oscars

in a posh hotel room in Santa Monica. It was quite the covert affair, once again, with Corrinne, Thian, Malinda, Dominc, and a minister. The five of only seven people on the planet who knew what was to ensue. Corrinne and Thian had planned this the same night he proposed. Thian wanted to run off that evening but Corrinne talked him out of it and compromised with the morning after the Oscars, 3:03 a.m. to be exact.

They had the tiny but elegant and meaningful ceremony after doing all the rounds for Thian's post Oscar win interviews for every news and entertainment outlet. They were just as interested in talking to Corrinne as they were Thian. She willingly obliged, telling fun, quick little stories about Thian that gave them great insight into what a wonderful and caring person he is which made the world fall in love with him in a whole new light. They had timed it perfectly by setting up the minister in his own private suite. Corrinne knew her beautiful Oscar dress had the potential to appeal to other women, but it was also to be her wedding gown and any knock-off dresses that were to be manufactured had no idea how truly priceless and precious that gown really was.

Malinda and Dominic decorated the suite next to the minister with aqua, white and gold draping with lavender and pink tulips in crystal vases throughout the room. Corrinne's bouquet of periwinkle dyed roses matched her gown. Malinda and Dominic had thought of everything,

"All you have to do is show up," they told Thian and Corrinne.

After Thian and Corrinne left for the Oscars, Malinda and Dominic raced to Santa Monica to ensure everything had been delivered and was in place. They decorated, ordered dinner, watched the Oscars, made out several times, then got dressed and waited for the couple and Oscar to arrive.

When Thian and Corrinne arrived at 3:01 a.m., the room took their breath away. It had been completely transformed into a Grecian dream. The minister was standing under a draped canopy with Dominic to his left and Malinda to his right. Dominic started the voice command music as soon as the door secured them in.

Corrinne and Thian walked down the sea-blue carpet stripped aisle together to "I Only Have Eyes For You" by The Flamingos. Their favorite song. It was playing in the banquet hall at her father's gala when they decided to date. The wedding was beautiful, filled with tears of joy and vows from the heart. Afterward they sent the minister back to his room with a hefty donation to him and his church with an extra night's paid stay. The four of them stayed up until 7:00 a.m. laughing, talking, and planning the future over Thai food and a beautiful small five-tiered chocolate wedding cake that read: "Congratulations Cori and Gregge." That's exactly who they are in their real world, Cori and Gregge. Corrinne and Thian belonged to the rest of the world, but Cori and Gregge belonged to each other. Malinda and Dominic had no idea just how much that touched both of their hearts.

By 7:15 a.m. all was still and quiet in Beverly Hills and Hollywood. Corrinne and Thian were packed up and ready to go. After multiple hugs and kisses goodbye, Malinda and Dominic took down and packed up all the decorations so as not to leave a trace of any type of ceremony. They secretly left the flowers by different doors and headed out to the second part of their mission, which was to play decoy for the newly married couple in Europe.

Corrinne and Thian decided to elope because they knew the announcement of a wedding date was going to start a family and fame frenzy of paparazzi, what gown, who's catering, what flowers, my mom wants this, have it at this venue and so on to eternity. Corrinne and Thian just wanted to be married without all the unnecessary stress of planning their special day for other people. Now that they are married, they can relax, laugh and enjoy the mayhem as the wedding of the century gets underway. They would prefer going without all the hoopla, but will do it for their mothers, who will have no idea they are already married. They laughed about how they were going to be guests at their own wedding. No matter who doesn't show up, what catering arrives late, what venue has a flood, and who won't sit next to who, they're still married. At this point it's just going to be pure entertainment for them.

Corrinne's phone has over a thousand texts and voicemails from her mother and sister after seeing her with Thian last night, which is like a dinosaur siting because they never communicate in between their obligatory monthly dinners. Priscilla only likes to have these dinners for appearance sake to the staff and anyone who may ask the latest on Corrinne.

"I can't believe it!" "Why didn't you tell me?!" "When are we going to meet Thian?" "Is he coming to this month's dinner?" Let's make it tonight!" "What does he like to eat?" "We should start having weekly dinners, or every night." "We need to spend more time together." "Can't wait to see you!" "I love you!" "Is he there with you right now?" etc…ad nauseum.

Corrinne just answered, "Crazy night, right? Surprised me too! Let you know."

Now Corrinne is interesting to them, very interesting, which makes them super interesting to others. It was killing her mother and sister that they couldn't be in her presence as picture proof of their connection. Corrinne knew her mother was fielding calls, both made and received about her having a daughter who snagged a superstar. She was going to go over-the-top crazy with the wedding plans. Although it sounds exhausting, Corrinne is secretly looking forward to seeing her mother make a fuss over her like Lorrinne had gotten all these years.

"How long before we land?" Corrinne asks Thian.

"We, my wife, have another eight hours."

"Think it's enough time to…?" Corrinne looks at Thian and smiles.

"More than enough time to…" he responds enthusiastically and gently guides her back to the bedroom.

The luxury private plane Thian chartered will be landing in Volos, Greece where they will kick off their unplugged from Hollywood honeymoon for the next four weeks and return when all the shaken dust settles.

They boarded the plane at 8:30 that morning. Corrinne was aware they were going to Greece, but she had no idea they were flying private and in such luxury with just the two of them and one attendant with all their favorite amenities. Thian had thought of everything. The plane is palatial, like a house in flight, complete with a dining room, living room, theater, bedroom and two bathrooms. Throughout their flight they will enjoy movies with popcorn, candy, and soda, dine on the finest meals and lounge and love before they land for the continuation of Life is Grand.

Meanwhile…

Later that day, Zavier managed to pull himself, his hair and his wardrobe together and head downstairs to his store. What should have been a glorious day of victory with a line of no less than 250 starving women waiting anxiously to attempt the impossible and fit into the glass encased dress Avery wore to the Oscars, turns out to be a group of women of all shapes and sizes outside of Zavier's store protesting with a line of food trucks by eating nachos, hoagies, burritos, burgers, fries, ice cream, cupcakes, you name it. News crews are parked outside interviewing the women.

"It looks like a revolution is taking over the country! Women are eating again!" announces large toothed, large haired, large personality, Wyatt Kannbe. He shoves the microphone in one of the former desperado's face and asks, "What is going on?

"We're taking our meals back! Getting back to what we're supposed to be!"

"And what is that?" he asks dramatically.

"Fed!" The woman screams into his microphone as she takes a big bite of a Philly cheesesteak sandwich and chews in between words, "Because fed is beautiful!"

The other women cheer and chant, "Fed is beautiful! Fed is beautiful! Fed is beautiful!"

Zavier watches the whole circus from inside the blackened windows as if seeing it on television. His loyal, unfed staff stands on either side of him watching as well in stunned silence.

This isn't real! They hate me! How could this happen? Damn that Avery! If she had only kept her mouth shut like she did to fit into my clothes! Look at them, eating like their life depends on it when they should be living to fit into my Oscar dress.

There is no coming back from this. Or is there?

Chapter Thirteen
Image Scrimmage

Zavier, staring straight ahead says in his monotone matter-of-fact cadence, "You're all fired."

His appraisers all stand there for a second in shock then a wave of relief comes over them one by one as they obediently single file towards the side exit.

"Your final checks are being delivered to your homes, so there's no need to come back," Zavier tells them.

As they approach the door, it opens like the release gates of prison and the much-missed smell of food wafts through the building. In steps a line of curvaceous Corrinne size-alikes with long dark hair slicked back into severe ponytails wearing tight red dresses. The line of women eye each other as they pass. Once the old appraisers leave the building and into the light of reality, they each run to different food trucks and order huge amounts of food.

The red dress crew stands on either side of Zavier as he smiles, knowing that he's ahead of the revolution.

At first, he thought he was defeated and made plans to pack his bags and leave the country, but then he remembered who he is, Zavier, "The Reigning King of Fashion Behavior." *There's no running from that! I start revolutions, not run from them.* So, with that egotistical thought speech he returned to his pompous circumstance and made some calls that he knew would change everything in an instant. He designed that incredible dress for Corrinne once, he can do it again thousands of times over. When you're as rich and powerful as Zavier, any idea is just a breath away from manifestation. And boy did he have an idea. *If you can't beat 'em, feed 'em. Let them protest, they have no idea of the publicity they're giving me. Ordering those food trucks, yet another stroke of genius on my part.*

Once he saw the crowd's reaction to Corrinne, Zavier could feel the alteration coming. There was no way he was going to be caught with his scissors down. After Avery's comment at Thian's life-preserver explanation, Zavier no longer wanted anything to do with her, not because it was the right thing to do but because it was the career thing to do. So, he slid off the couch, mingled a bit, made phone calls and headed back to his store to mastermind his next fashion religion. While everyone was on their razzle dazzle tour of deal making, friends faking, money raking, interview taking, and hangover waking, Zavier was busy gathering a team for photo shoots, sewing, printing, and publicity. Luckily, he kept Corrinne's dress pattern. Even though he despised making the dress, he was too cocksure to get rid of any whiff of brilliance he had created.

His narcissism works in his favor, as usual. He easily visualized and sketched beautiful clothes for Corrinne's body type and had prototypes made for the photo shoot. Within hours he had a warehouse full of top-notch seamstresses making sample jeans and gowns. He knew his audience and how much they crave to be like someone they couldn't and shouldn't be, and he would be right there to ensure they wouldn't be. The desire to aspire to something unattainable is what has kept Zavier on top for over four decades. Now there will be a different group of women trying to fit his line of clothing.

He even had the doorway widened with specific instructions on the inches that the body type must fill in order to enter his kingdom to vie for the exquisite replica he designed for Corrinne. The soon to be coveted electric yellow gown has secured its encased place and levitates gloriously. Of course, the measurements are skewed so that no one will ever fit into it. The new perfect size perfect. Designed to decline.

Look at them, traitors! You followed and worshipped me and after one night you turn on me? Such pathetic pigeons, hungry for attention, hungry for acceptance, hungry for relevance, and just hungry. You throw them a crumb and they gather and wait for more. I tell you what to do. You don't tell me. Eat! Eat up! You'll never ever fit into any of my dresses!

Zavier no longer feels the full anxiety of Thian's possible public wrath. After seeing how much he loves Corrinne, he knew Thian would never reveal his brutal reaction to her size because it would crush her. However, he decided to still tread lightly and hoped that this switch would be viewed as an homage to Corrinne.

The women continue to gather and digest in protest as busloads more get dropped off to join in. One very thin woman with a pastrami sub sandwich in her hands yells into a reporter's microphone, "Come on out, Zavier! You coward! Come on out! You told women for years not to eat in order to fit into one of your idiotic unattainable sized dresses. Well we're fed up!"

Everyone cheers.

A sudden hush slams the crowd as the door opens, and Zavier confidently steps out. The once hostile air dissipates as the electricity of excitement and fear floods the crowd as he enters their mediocre atmosphere. They never expected him to come out. Heck, they didn't expect him to be there. They were brave to the point of him seeing them on the news, not in person.

Zavier steps into their view like a king addressing his subjects as his image projects gigantically against his glass building. Cameras flash as all food drops down to everyone's side. Even the food truck providers make their way to the top of their rolling restaurants to witness this moment. So few have been fortunate enough to be in his presence, and here he is. The crowd is bewitched. Some cry, some stare, and most smile broadly forgetting their anger, resentment, and years of hunger pains because he is right here in the flesh. Tall, powerful, immaculately dressed and oh-so handsome. Look at him, he has every right to tell them what to do.

He speaks with mesmeric command into the battery-pack microphone that blasts his words for blocks, "Ladies! Eat and turn up the volume! Be devourful!"

Suddenly a sexy rift of music plays and the black glass building flashes on like a colossal television. The crowd is seduced as they watch the commercial of a size fourteen red-headed model in dark-wash jeans and a body hugging indigo blue tank top, in different slow-motion poses and close-ups to the musical beat. It ends with her tossing her head back then looking straight into the camera and saying, "Size Up Your Competition." The picture freezes and the words, "Zavier Zaftig Zipper" fades in as the music dissolves. A collective look of hope crosses over the faithful followers' faces.

"I would like you all to meet the new waist of fashion, Tassidy!"

Out of the doorway struts stunning size fourteen, twenty-year-old, Tassidy Parker, with her long wavy scarlet hair pulled up in a high ponytail that accentuates her emerald green eyes. Her makeup is light and carefree. She is wearing the same soon-to-be iconic outfit from the ad. Tassidy stands next to Zavier like his queen. She waves to the peons as they delight in her arrival that will save them all from starvation and self-loathing. Cheers and tears erupt as the tyranny of fashion famine has been lifted. Zavier gently takes her by the hand and escorts her to the awaiting car through the cleared path to the opened door. The crowd goes crazy as they applaud and shout out Zavier and Tassidy's name. He is now back in their good graces because Tassidy is the girl, the body, the image to be. Tassidy gives one last wave and gets into the car.

Zavier turns to the crowd before getting in and says, "Glad you came out and are enjoying the food. It's all on me until 2:30 this afternoon."

He removes the microphone, hands it to security, waves and disappears into the car.

The women melt with gratitude as they have been granted permission to eat freely and shamelessly. A new goal has been set.

Tassidy Parker was in a deep sleep at 1:17 a.m. when her phone rang. It was her agent, Martina, from Ample Savvy Agency yelling on the other end, "Wake up! Wake up! You have a photo shoot for Zavier!"

Tassidy did not respond because she thought she was hallucinating. Her dreams for modeling were never set that high. The most she hoped for was some plus size catalog work to earn a little extra money to supplement her customer service job at a bookstore.

"Did you hear me? You have a photo shoot for Zavier!" Martina screeched.

That last statement is what fully shook Tassidy awake. This must be real because hallucinations are not this loud. Tassidy laughed, "Hey Martina, funny thing, for a second there I thought you said…"

"I did and I am! You have a photo shoot with Zavier!"

"What?" Tassidy jumped out of bed and started pacing back and forth in short steps like a trapped chicken in her single room apartment. She stopped suddenly as reality started to sink in. "Wait, Zavier who? He's not one of those knock-offs that spells Zavier with two s's or something, is it?"

"No, Hun, this is it! This is for real legit."

"Wow. Wow! I mean WOW! I can't believe it! When is it?"

"A car will be there to pick you up in 20 minutes."

"Excuse me?"

"No excuse. Are you waxed?

"From face to toe. Is this really real?"

"As real as really gets. Now get off this phone and go be a star!"

Inside the car, Zavier and Tassidy watch the crowd of women as it pulls away from the curb. They wave at the self-reflective tinted windows and shout out praises. Some run alongside as if that's going to stop the car for an invitation for them to hop in and become best friends.

"How does it feel to hold the self-esteem of women in the palm of your words?" Tassidy asks Zavier as he looks out of his window.

He is struck not only by the sound of her voice but the audacity to ask such a bold question. All the models he has ever granted access into his personal space know to just sit, be pretty, and wait for orders.

He slowly turns away from the window, gives Tassidy a stern look and asks, "What did you say?" in that rhetorical tone where one knows not to repeat what it was they just said.

Tassidy has always been bold and outspoken. As the

youngest of seven children, five girls and two boys, Tassidy grew up in a household of meek females and domineering males. Her mother is a homemaker and extremely subservient to her father. He wanted her barefoot (during the day and heels on at night), pregnant, cleaning, cooking, beautiful, happy and waiting on him at all times. After all, he was a very successful architect. He went off to work every day while she stayed home and homeschooled all stair-step born children with no help at all. When her father got home, all the attention was to be paid to him since they all had the day to spend together. So, the kids had to be fed, bathed, ready for bed, and occupied by the time his car pulled up and his dinner was to be hot and plated. This was not an abusive relationship by any means. These were the terms they had agreed upon during courtship and they both seemed to be happy. Never was there a day when she saw her mom visibly upset, but Tassidy knew this was not the life she wanted to lead. While her sisters fell in line with this lifestyle being their future, Tassidy wanted no part of it. Her brothers were deemed the little princes of the palace and the sisters were their scullery maids. But not Tassidy. She fought the submissive role all the way in-spite-of punishments, stern talks from her father, pleas from her mother and dirty looks from her sisters. She liked the way her brothers were being treated and wanted that lifestyle. She questioned everything. Her first words were not mama and dada, but, "how come?" College and career were never an option for the girls. It was just a given that the boys would go off to college while the girls were groomed for wifedom by age eighteen.

Tassidy's tenacity had gotten so out of hand that she was sentenced to attend public school when she turned twelve. She pretended it was a punishment but secretly loved it. She thrived as an A student and was very popular. It had been her parents' goal to have as many children as the womb would provide, but after Tassidy, her mother went on birth control and her father had a vasectomy out of fear of more children like her.

She left home as soon as she graduated high school. It was Tassidy's goal to go to college, work, graduate, and become a teacher. Keenly aware of her exotic looks, she signed up with Ample Savvy Agency for Plus Size Models to pick up some modeling or commercial gigs to help pay for an apartment and car. Her fearlessness is what landed her where she is today.

"I said, how does it feel to hold the self-esteem of so many women in the palm of your words?"

Zavier looks surprised. He can't believe she repeated it.

"Well, I've never looked at it that way before."

Of course, he had. This was the power that fueled him,

his career, his fame, his empire. *Why am I even answering her?*

"I find that very hard to believe," she tells him, looking Zavier in the eye with a smirk.

For some reason he is amused. No one has ever challenged him. *Who does she think she is, me? I will not give her the satisfaction of my interest.* "Believe what you want."

He turns away dismissively and checks his phone.

Tassidy is unfazed by this.

Any other model would have been left out on the curb with a call to her agent never to be heard of in this business again. She wouldn't even be able to work as a cashier at a fast food restaurant. Zavier knew he was in trouble the moment Tassidy walked into the photo shoot early that morning.

Chapter Fourteen
Curve Appeal

Once his eyes adjusted to her size, Zavier secretly and reluctantly had to admit to himself she was quite captivating. But Tassidy's confidence was what really threw him for a loop. She was supposed to be shaking, crying, grateful to have a face to face let alone be his next spokesmodel. But she was cool, calm, collected as she leveled up to him by shaking his hand and looking him right in the eye. Most models averted his steel-gaze, but she gave as good as he did. He could feel the floor fault beneath him. This had thrown him off. He liked the feel of her hand in his even though it was a cordial contact. She was only supposed to be a face and a body. Not a human, not three dimensional. He was accustomed to being in the presence of beauty, but this was something else. Usually he checks out the model before the shoot to be sure she came with all the parts he ordered then leaves the set. Not this time, he felt compelled to stay.

"From now on, you're going to go by the name Luxe," Zavier told her matter-of-factly.

Tassidy tilted her head and replied without a beat, "That's okay, I'll stick with Tassidy. But thanks for the…upgrade."

She had said it so sweetly with such an affable smile, he

couldn't challenge it without sounding like a bully.

"Okay, what are you all standing around for? Get her ready! Time is running out!" he yelled trying to regain some of his sunken power and remind her and everyone else who the boss was around there.

Why wasn't she afraid of him? Why did he even want her to be impressed? Zavier had never been in the presence of someone this size and acknowledged them. *Where is her gratitude? The worship? I always name my models.* Avery was the only one he hadn't named because she had come to him with a recognizable one.

The photo shoot got underway and Knyfe barely had to give Tassidy direction. She was a pro. She knew her angles, her body, her appeal. The jeans fit perfectly and felt good. She looked great in them and she knew it. And so did Zavier.

"That's great. Now turn left and put your hands on your…um…those…um…," Knyfe couldn't find the word.

"Hips?" asked Tassidy.

"Yeah, those."

What an idiot, she thought.

From that moment on, Tassidy directed herself and not a single bad shot was taken. Zavier toggled between watching her on the monitor and up close. He hated that he was so drawn to her. Usually he just waited for the photos to be sent to him where he could dress down, critique the model, and hate every pose until he found "The One." He delighted in this power game. But because there was so little time and so many good pics, he didn't have the luxury of belittling anyone for any length of time. When the photo shoot was over, Zavier went through the photos on the monitor. Tassidy comfortably came up and peeked over his shoulder. She knew he liked her. She could just tell.

"This must be a big adjustment for your company," she said.

"A **huge** one," he responded laughingly, hoping to temper her confidence.

Knyfe and the rest of the crew laughed loudly, wanting to please the emperor and shame the serf who had the gall to so boldly stand so close, and to speak in his exalted realm.

"I wouldn't say huge. More like luxe," she quipped back, daring not to be intimidated. Everyone stopped in shock, waiting for the wrath of Zavier to engulf them all.

He ignored her but thought to himself, *Touché My Dear, touché.*

Chapter Fifteen
Waist Management

Meanwhile…

Avery is still in bed after collecting her delivered Chinese food and New York cheesecake. She is glued to the television and can't believe what every channel has to offer. All Thian and that large girl he proposed to. That was supposed to be her proposal, her ring, her moment, even if it wasn't real. She deserved it, was entitled to it. Not some double digit sized basic! She had worked for this! Not her! The only mention Avery receives is the comment she made about Corrinne and it's being played repeatedly, pausing on the same ugly expression she had in mid-cackle.

Why do they have to stop it right there? It makes me look so ugly and evil. Just one frame more and I'm beautiful again.

"Hey Morons! There were more important things going on last night than those two fools!" she yells at the television, "Like how phenomenal I look in that dress! Ugh, people are so petty!"

She flips back to "Chews 'n' Views" as all the women

are still eating and talking.

"They can't still be yammering on about me."

"Two buns up to Thian Rodgers and Corrinne Mayars!" says Liza as she bites into a croissant.

"Did you see that dress! It was absolutely to eat for!" Bloom chimes in, dipping eight french fries in ranch sauce.

"But today's catch of the day is Zavery! Yes, the buffoons of the night! Order up!" yells Sharla enthusiastically while waving a churro.

The women swivel around and watch the big screen. Up pops Avery and Zavier on the now infamous couch with Syte.

The audience boos.

The women comment throughout the segment.

"Look at Zavier! Sliding off the couch like a fried egg on a Teflon pan," laughs Deanne now on her second cup of cocoa and breakfast sandwich.

The audience laughs.

"More like a scrambled egg!" Sandy blurts out mid chew of bacon.

Audience laughs harder.

The segment ends and the audience groans.

"Oh wait, there's a second course! Check please!"

Zavier and Tassidy's image appear on the screen from that morning's impromptu press conference in front of his store. When the segment is over the audience boos loudly. The women are grill fired up and in a feeding frenzy of banter.

"Caaaaan you believe this man? I can't! And what I really can't believe is, why people are still epicureans for his ginger snap judgment trends."

"Right? He's just now caught up to what we've been saying and doing all along. Why doesn't anyone make him eat his words?!"

"I think he's annoying. I can't stomach him anymore!"

"You have to admit he is a quite a tasty morsel."

"Oh please! Now don't you go soft serve on us!"

Bloom is now surrounded by plates of Thanksgiving foods. She gnaws ungracefully on a giant turkey leg not caring at all that she's on t.v.

"What do you think, Bloom?" asks Liza.

Bloom doesn't look up as she dips her spoon into a luscious gooey bowl of mac and cheese with her mouth still full of turkey.

"He's my hero."

Avery angrily changes the channel and lands on "Excessive Hollywood."

"I know they'll have my back. They were always the first to all my exclusives."

She settles on her bed confidently and eats orange chicken from the container. Suddenly, a size fourteen blonde crowds the screen.

"Good morning, Everyone! And welcome to a special post-Oscar extreme edition of Excessive Hollywood where everything is larger than life as we make something bigger than what it is then blow it up even more! I'm Kytelin Monroe, and sitting atop Hollywood is none other than legendary, world changing trend-getter, Zavier!"

There Zavier sits with Tassidy, who is wearing the now iconic Zavier Zaftig Zipper jeans and tank top.

Avery fumes as she yells at the television, "What the full size?! That should be me sitting there next to Zavier! Not her! Especially not her! What is happening here? And where did they get that tank of a host?"

"Hello Zavier, and welcome once again to Excessive Hollywood!" cheers Kytelin excitedly.

"Thank you, the pleasure's all yours," responds Zavier with an air of disdain. He hates the fact that a trend was born without his hand being the first to touch it. He's taken aback that the show had already hired a plus sized host before he had a chance to shame them into doing so.

"Of course, it is. And who is this you've brought with you today?"

Zavier opens his mouth to speak when…

"I'm Tassidy."

Both Kytelin and Zavier are surprised. Didn't she know models are never to speak for themselves or to others before, during, or after Zavier speaks? This is **his** interview, not hers.

"Come on, Zavier! Really? You sell out! Don't you have a mind of your own? You idiot!" Avery yells as she scarfs down pork fried rice.

"Uh, okay, well, very nice to meet you…Tassidy," says Kytelin uneasily, chagrinned as this exchange is not on her conversation prompter. "So, Zavier, why Zaftig now and so suddenly?"

Zavier doesn't bother to make eye contact with Kytelin out of such annoyance with the whole situation. He is out of his element and feels out of control as he's grasping to appear to have the reigns.

"Because I felt like it. I became bored with the cookie cutter severely thin look and decided to change it up. Way up."

"So, does that mean you're going to join in on your growing trend and put on a few pounds yourself?"

What a stupid question! Did I become extra thin for the last one? "I don't participate, I dictate," he answers her curtly.

There it is! The sound bite she was waiting for.

"Dictate, hmmmm…a very interesting word for fashion." Suddenly Kytelin turns from sweet humble golly-gee-nice-to-meet-you-sir host to prosecutor with Zavier on the witness stand defending his crime. "Because that's what you do, don't you, Zavier? You dictate to women what they should wear, how they should look, what they should eat, and how they should be in order to have any tiny bit of worth in everyday life. You take advantage of those who enjoy your gift. You have all these followers who adore you, spend their money on you, keep you relevant and all you do is belittle them."

Zavier tries not to look shocked as the camera zooms in for an up-the-nose close-up of his reaction. *Who the hell does this heifer think she is, talking to me in that tone? Your opinion doesn't count Sweet Tart! Just sit there and try not to eat between syllables! A day ago you wouldn't even have been considered for this job, let alone the opportunity to be in my presence with permission to speak. It's because of* ***me*** *that you can eat in public now and not* *be ridiculed. It's because of me there will now be fashionable and trendy clothes for you to wear. It's because of me you are now allowed to even be seen in public void of scorn and shame. You're on top! So yes! Yes! I do dictate and you better be damn well happy that the dictation pendulum has swung in your favor! So, shut up and take it to your nearest hamburger drive-thru and enjoy it! For now.* Zavier inner rants as he feels his neck getting hot and the sweat gland damn beginning to burst. He doesn't have a defense. She nailed exactly what he has been doing all these decades. He did train women to hate themselves and want to be anything and anyone other than who they were. They weren't good enough and never will be no matter how hard they tried. He sets the standard and he loves it.

Who is she to try and take that from me?

"So, if he tells you to burn yourself up and you do it, that's his fault?" Tassidy pipes in.

For some odd reason, Tassidy feels protective of Zavier even though he is a narcissistic prick who deserves every bit of backlash he gets. But still…there is something about him that makes her not appreciate the ambush. She can feel the pulse of his embarrassment at being verbally toppled. He wasn't prepared not to be worshipped.

Once again, Zavier and Kytelin are taken off guard.

Kytelin gets flustered, "Wha…Wha…Well no. Of course

not! Of course, I wouldn't even…

"Then why would you or anybody starve themselves to fit into one of his stupid dresses then blame him?"

Kytelin grits her teeth and hate smiles Tassidy. *Come on, Girl! We're supposed to be on the same side! Work with me here! This is my big gotcha moment and you're ruining it!*

"Well, that concludes this interview. Thank you, so much Zavier for being here." Kytelin shoots Tassidy a smirk of contempt, "You too, Assidy." She turns back to the camera.

"It's Ta...."

"Thanks for joining us, Everyone. See you tonight as well at our regularly scheduled time."

Zavier and Tassidy look out of their respective windows as they leave the studio and the ambush interview behind them. After thirty minutes of silence, Zavier finally breaks the wall of sound as he continues to look out of his window.

"You really didn't have to come to my defense, I can handle myself."

"I know," she answers still looking out of her window.

"Then why did you do it?"

"Because I could tell she was trying to make a name for herself at your expense. She doesn't care about women's self-esteem and how they perceive themselves through the eyes of others."

"And how would you know that?" Zavier asks thinking she sounds childish.

"Because she's from the same modeling agency I am, and she has been trying to diet herself down to fit into one of your dresses for months. She thought she was too good for plus size modeling. But she could never get small enough to be good enough for one of your designs. She's a hypocrite and that's number one out of a thousand things I can't stand."

"You really think my dresses are stupid?"

"Yes…Only because I could never fit into them. Now I think they're divine!"

Zavier smiles slightly.

"Then doesn't that make you a hypocrite?"

"No, I've just had a change of heart. There's a difference."

"Sounds the same to me."

"The difference is, I never tried to change myself to fit

into your world. I kept being me and now you've come to mine."

Zavier is struck by this statement and looks over at Tassidy and says, "So does that make me a hypocrite?" *Why do you care what she thinks?*

Tassidy can feel his eyes on her and turns to face him. She looks at him for a long time then finally answers, "No, that makes you smart."

Zavier unexpectantly smiles in relief. He didn't know what he would do if she had said yes. He's vulnerable and doesn't know how to handle it.

Tassidy can see that he is sinking in the quagmire of humility and it's up to her to pull him out. She quickly turns and looks out of her window and says, "And what kind of a name is Kytelin, anyway?"

Zavier turns and looks out of his window, "What kind of a name is Tassidy?"

"A damn better one than Kytelin!"

"I can't believe she called you Assidy."

"She wishes she had this Assidy!"

Zavier laughs out loud. It feels foreign. He can't remember the last time he laughed a genuine laugh in public. He can't remember when he enjoyed a car ride home. He can't even remember feeling like he had company while working. This woman is no object.

Chapter Sixteen
Weight For It

After two weeks of self-disciplined binging, Avery had only managed to gain three pounds and was only up to a size zero and a half, an absolute disgrace two weeks and three days ago. It looked like she was making progress towards a greater goal, but it wasn't happening fast enough.

Worried about his client, and even more his twenty percent, Dalton stepped in and secured a multi-million-dollar deal with "Weight Wanters," a national weight gain program that was established a week ago and has taken off like a roadrunner since Avery signed on as their hoax-person. Her inspirational commercial guaranteed America's suffering thin that she can and will gain and maintain ten pounds a week just by following the simple uncalibrated, non-nutritionally endorsed, high salt, high fat, high sugar, high risk, of at least eighty-five hundred calories a day program, complete with weekly weigh-ups, group support, and passive shaming.

The commercial starts with Avery sitting alone at a window with rain pelting the pane. She is surrounded by her iconic magazine covers. A soft clap of thunder starts the slow depressing music that plays under Avery's voiceover, "I have been an under-eater ever since I can remember.

Even though I have a glamorous modeling career, lots of money, beautiful and expensive things, in reality, I hate myself, how I look, and the way clothes don't fit me." A picture of Avery wearing a size fourteen pair of jeans that are ridiculously too big for her appears. She drops to her knees and sobs. "I am so empty inside, empty of self-worth, empty of love, all because I am empty of calories."

Avery slowly looks into the heart of the camera with tears flowing from her eyes and says, "Why? Why me? Why can't I live a full life as a full person?"

She cries in despair when notes of optimism play as a size fourteen woman, Araya Sulluvyn, dressed in dove white flowy clothing appears like a summoned angel. Her waist-length charcoal hair is parted straight down the middle and her ice blue eyes make soulful contact with all who need her. Avery looks up at her in reverence.

She speaks in a soothing elixir of hope, sympathy, and condescend, "Well Avery, if that's what you want then you're wanted at Weight Wanters, where the weight is over for wanting a better life."

Avery finds her way to her feet and gratefully hugs Araya, who swaddles her with her blessed wind-blown wardrobe.

Araya looks into the camera and declares, "You too can be me if you eat hard. Come, gain pounds in no time."

Avery breaks away with confidence and says, "Follow and gain weight with me as I take on the pounds. Because if I can do it, any fool can!" Triumphant music plays as she fades out.

Avery hated every second of filming that commercial, especially when they squirted the onion juice in her eyes to create the painful tears she was unable to conjure up on her own. When she fell to the floor out of excruciating pain, it made for an authentic effect no one had expected. The redness and swelling in and around her eyes were just extra presents under the tree. However, she was being paid a lot of money to do it. Well, she will be paid a lot of money. She was paid twenty five percent of the agreed upon price up front and will be paid the remaining seventy-five when she becomes a complete success story. This was an incentive to complete the program and make "Weight Wanters" the champion. It is also part of her contract to shoot commercials throughout her journey (only if she's making progress), until she reaches her size fourteen goal and seventy-pound gain.

Avery despised Araya's pity of her as she watched Avery's every move on set. She kept offering her food from the catering tables and stood close to make sure she finished every bite then would offer her another. Avery was very happy to eat but she didn't need a food nanny to babysit her every chew and swallow throughout the day. Everyone on set would shake their head and look away whenever Avery made contact in their eyeline as if not wanting her to see their embarrassment for her. She was used to people avoiding eye contact with her when she was working, but that was because **she** demanded it out of respect and power. She was the one in control and better than everyone. The underlings desired to look at her and couldn't. But this was different. They didn't want to look. It pained them to look. This was lonely. Even her browbeaten assistant, Rella, had more confidence and was giving her more attitude than servitude. Avery felt like the spectacle no one wanted to see. And on top of that, she had to admit to the world that she was a lesser than, unacceptable, defective to society and struggling to fit in. She was accustomed to making others feel this way, not feeling this way herself.

The "Weight Wanters" commercial plays all day every day and because of Avery, a massive weight list was gained.

So here's how it works: There is a one thousand dollar monthly membership fee that accepts twenty inducted Wanters at a time for each session who are granted weekly weigh-ups in front of everyone (because they're all family here), a two hour group support eating where they sit at an over-sized round-table and scarf down food and their feelings about their weekly progress. Should a Wanter gain a considerable amount of weight and hit the one-size-fits-all gain of eight pounds a week, they are granted one cheat day of smoothies and salads only. There are three different sessions daily, seven days a week. For those who cannot make it there in person, an online version has been created. The Gold Membership.

The Gold Membership costs a mere five thousand a month. It includes weekly private in-home one on one sessions with a certified (two-week trained) Caloriesta where they receive personalized counseling, weigh-ups, and a specialty house brand brownie (purchased from the bakery next door) each time. Avery is not privy to the private counseling as she is the public example for the everyday woman who walks through those doors of gaining weight, confidence, and their life back.

Food is not included and for an additional cost of twenty-eight hundred dollars a month, the Wanters can have hot food delivered to their home from the "Meals on Meals" food program exclusively prepared from restaurants, "Carb," "Gorge," "Starch," and "Satiate." These eateries are former health conscious establishments that saw which way the lazy Susan was turning and hopped on board.

The "Weight Wanters" menu choices consists of:

Breakfast One

Two Bagels, Butter Cream Cheese, Ham, Three Eggs

Breakfast Two

Four Buttermilk Pancakes, Bacon (eight strips),

Four Eggs, Toast, Fried Potatoes

Breakfast Three

Two Bear Claw Sausage, Egg, Bacon, Cheese Sandwiches, French Toast

Breakfast Four

Four Donuts, Two Hot Chocolates, Three Hot Links

Breakfast Five

Chicken Fried Steak, Waffle Biscuits, Gravy,

Hash Browns

Lunch One

Triple Patty Double Cheeseburger, Chili Fries,

Sixteen Ounce Soda

Lunch Two

Sixteen-Inch Lasagna Sub, Parmesan Cheese Chips,

Sixteen Ounce Soda

Lunch Three

Two Burtacens – Burrito Stuffed with a Taco Stuffed with an Enchilada, Beans and Rice, Sixteen Ounce Soda

Lunch Four

Three Foot-Long Butter Sourdough Bun Hot Dogs,

Bacon Fried Chips, Sixteen Ounce Soda

Lunch Five

Six Cheese Tuna Melt, Breaded French Fries,

Sixteen Ounce Soda

Dinner One

Two Barbeque Beef Rib Racks, Five Macaroni Un-salad

Dinner Two

Whole Loaf Meat Loaf, Pastrami Cornbread, Butter Cream Smashed Potatoes, Sixteen Ounce Soda

Dinner Three

Eight Short Ribs, Macaroni and Cheese Stack,

Sixteen Ounce Soda

Dinner Four

Four Garlic Bread Stufffed Pork Chops, Dumplings,

Sixteen Ounce Soda

Dinner Five

Seven Pieces of Fried Chicken, Cheese Grits,

Sixteen Ounce Soda

Desserts

Nine Layer Say a Prayer Chocolate Cake

Peach Cobbler Gobbler

Triple Chocolate Chunk in the Trunk Cookies

Caramel Pecan More Please Cheesecake

Go Bananas Pudding

Get to Stuffin' Cream-Filled Muffin

Better Butt Butter Cake

Don't Ask Why Ice Cream Sandwich pie

Chocolate Chip for the Hips Cheesecake Brownie

Lemon Found a Pound Cake

Araya wasted no time turning her extremely successful wellness center, "Just By Chants" into "Weight Wanters" when she saw the need for the underweight to succeed. Not many people can afford the program, so houses have been remortgaged, college tuitions aborted, bills resorted, extra income not reported, all because body image, once again, has been distorted.

Today is the day Avery dreads most, Weigh Day at "Weight Wanters." She wishes it was Go Away Day. This is her third week and her pre-repulsion of being greeted by the phony plastered smiles of encouragement and stares at her still slim frame fiasco is at its peak. Food isn't even fun anymore. It is a chore, a source of punishment, a burden. Avery has yet to meet her astronomical goal of gaining ten pounds a week and her weekly non-progress is shared and announced immediately all over the world for support, of course. But today, Avery has a few tricks up her sleeve for the scale. She has been following the food plan to a tee but just needs a little something to boost her up.

Dressed in bulky, oversized sweats and a matching long sleeve jacket, hoping to fool everyone into thinking she's larger than last week, Avery pulls up to the "Weight Wanters" parking lot in the strip mall consisting of a quick dine-in/take-out, a bakery, a mini-mart, and a nail shop to see a group of fifty or more women waiting out front, as usual. Some have signs of support for Avery and some are just on-the-fly reporters recording her on their phone and telling their followers their opinion of her situation. Avery is sure most of them are the same "Aters" sending her ate mail telling her what a loser she is, and that obviously she's choosing celery over spaghetti. They offer their fatty food recipes and weight gain techniques then request she mention them in her daily updates. She does neither.

Avery takes a deep breath of dread and inhales the delicious smells of baked goods, barbeque, and burgers that are falsely piped out to the public to induce hunger. As she walks to the glass front building where Rella is waiting loyally, Avery gives a slight wave as the women shout her name. Rella opens the door. Avery stops and does something she's never done before. She notices Rella. *Is she gaining weight?*

Unbeknownst to Avery, Rella has been secretly following the "Weight Wanters" program and is now up to a size twelve.

Her fellow Wanters eye Avery as she enters the yellow walled room with its large pictures of delicious fattening meals and desserts as the new a la mode to victory. Doctored before and after posters of slim make-up free women wearing "Why bother?" clothing next to their counter-part larger size with the slogan, "This Could Be You. You Choose," line the walls as well. These nineteen other women are the fortunate ones to have the same appointment as Avery. She gently nods, as friendly as she can, in their various states of weight gain success direction.

Avery is greeted by one of the five Caloriestas, Tillian,

a bouncy, happy size fourteen, twenty something donning the "Weight Wanters" yellow doctor-like coat with her name printed on a plastic tag in the shape and likeness of a scale. She is so happy to be the one to greet Avery personally since she used to be such a big fan (now she just pities her). Tillian is most excited because she gets camera time as the film crew captures Avery's every weigh-up. After she signs in on the community clipboard that displays everyone's progress, Avery is compassionately escorted into the weighting room by Tillian. The camera crew surrounds them while the nineteen other Wanters follow closely behind, competing for face time with the camera.

The weighting room is also yellow with more pictures and slogans of ingestion inspiration. The yellow cushioned high-backed chairs are placed in a circle, surrounding the digital medical style scale that stands high and mighty in judgmental solitude. The Wanters eagerly volunteer to be weighed and are applauded and praised as they dramatically make their way to the steel machine that decides their day's disposition. They each stand in breathless anticipation then shake in surprise and relief at their positive result, even though they weighed before coming. Nonetheless, the histrionics are effective.

Avery feels the hard pinch of envy as the women who are fast tracking their weight hike are cheered on by everyone when their gain is announced. Truth be told, most of the Wanters started off at a size ten. Araya always makes it a point to be there when Avery comes to weigh. She sweeps into the room, igniting gasps of hero sandwich worship from the Wanters, to give Avery the hug of life and pounds. The cameras and the already weighed Wanters watch Avery's every move as she is lovingly escorted by Araya to the scale while she whispers words of encouragement throughout their pilgrimage. This is the most annoying and creepy walk Avery has ever taken. Tillian frolics ahead to set the scale to zero before Avery steps on. A camera is fixed on the result screen, Avery, Araya, and the breathless in-the-round congregation to capture all the results, expressions, and reactions for the live viewers who subscribe and tune in weekly for her weigh up.

It has been quite a loss the last two weeks for Avery since she's only managed to gain three pounds a week. According to Araya, she should at the very least be up eighteen pounds by now. Oh, the accusatory looks of undereating from Araya, her team, and the Wanters when Avery has stepped off the scale and declares she did her best. She even showed them the food diary she's been required to keep and share each week along with her food attitude.

"Well, just because you're writing it doesn't mean you're eating it!" Wanter Evyn Elise pointed out, in her bossy I'm-a-week-away-from-my-goal tone, at their last meeting where Avery wanted to wipe that priggish look off her face with the heel of her foot. Everyone agreed and all she could do was sit there and take it.

Avery finds it humiliating to have to talk about something so basic and personal then have it picked apart by strangers like a fresh desert carcass. *Whatever it takes to stay relevant.*

There is palpable excitement as Araya gives Avery the warm hug of a mother sending her first child to preschool then releases her to the cruel world scales. Avery approaches the scale and steps on it. The numbers dance and interchange as they play hide and seek with her results. Even the scale is on the drama team. The numbers land and show that Avery has a twelve-pound gain for the week! Everyone cheers and tears for Avery.

Araya embraces her and cries, for it was her healing power that brought Avery back to life. When she releases her, Araya lifts Avery's left arm like a prized champion fighter. Suddenly everyone freezes in quiet horror. Still feeling the love and admiration in the room, Avery puts her other hand to her face and begins the contrived cry of "I couldn't have done it without Araya and Weight Wanters" speech when she notices everyone's look of sheer disappointment and anger. Araya and Avery simultaneously follow everyone's eyeline up to Avery's raised wrist where the gangly appendage reveals a one-pound weight.

Araya over-horrifies as the grey weight looms heavily over both their heads. She yanks Avery's arm down with the velocity of slamming a car hood. Araya immediately raises both of Avery's sleeves to reveal weights on both wrists. The Wanters clutch their pearls. Araya lifts both of Avery's baggy sweatpants to reveal bright pink five-pound weights wrapped around each ankle. The Wanters are overcome with a cocktail of shock, grief, disbelief, and delight in Avery's deceit and embarrassment. She was the one, just over a month ago, they wanted to be and now she's cheating to try to be them. This tasted more delicious than the hot fudge lava cheesecake they had all eaten for breakfast in a last-ditch pitch for an upward pound on Weigh Day.

Avery quickly pulls down her pants legs and sleeves in hopes that everyone didn't really see what they just saw. She could explain them away as weight gain therapy bans or the latest fashion accessory that is only exclusive to her and she was coming to share it with all of them, her new friends, her family, her sisters in weight.

Before the lie could travel from Avery's brain to her tongue, the voice, formerly known as kind and loving, roars, "How dare you! How dare you! Who are you to come into this sacred space of growth and expansion with women who are trying…trying so hard to improve their looks, their self-esteem, their worth in society, and you…"

Araya pauses dramatically and leans back to give Avery and the camera the full scope of her disgust as if she just realized she hadn't actually stepped barefoot in mud but in a pile of St. Bernard shit and points, "You…you…you just come in here and mock their progress, my process, all for your false success!"

Avery tries to center herself as she stands, stupefied and speechless, in front of All Mighty Goddess Araya whose head is about to spin off its axis in rage.

"I cannot and I will not condone or forgive such a blatant act of disrespect and repugnant actions to filth up my name and this establishment of wellness!"

The Wanters cheer their leader and bathe her in grateful applause and tears. Araya spreads her arms as if embracing each Wanter individually. She then clenches her fists and drops her head in a deep contemplative fashion then raises one finger. The Wanters hush in unison and look expectantly for her next words of wrath. All Avery can hear is the dismantling of her dignity. The only thing she wants to do in this moment is evaporate and reappear in her car. The daggered looks being shot her way are physically painful. Avery doesn't dare move or interrupt Araya's 10.5 lexiconic quake. She can tell Araya is reveling in her soon-to-be fame.

Araya continues as she raises her head in self-propelled

slow motion and opens her arctic blue eyes. She viciously stamps them on Avery. Her once pitied expression is now one of pure disdain.

"So, Avery, your weight is under and you are no longer wanted."

Araya storms elegantly out of the room with her long yellow cotton duster billowing dramatically behind her. The Wanters clap thunderously in vindication. If they had dinner rolls on hand, they would have fast pitched them at Avery.

Avery feels both humiliated and relieved as she makes her way out of the circle of purgatory. The vicious snarling pack of disciples hope for eye contact so they can pounce. Avery isn't about to give them the satisfaction of her shame. They are still followers and she is still better than all of them combined.

Some of the Wanters yell, Eater Cheater!" 'Scamburger!" "Bod Fraud!" "Scaleure!"

They follow her out of the weighting room and into the lobby, still yelling. The camera is right in her face as Avery fumbles for her dark shades that are in her jacket pocket as she wades through the gauntlet of insults. Her weighted legs feel like she's walking on wet sand. *What happened to all the support? The love? The we are in this together?*

She finally makes it out of the building only to land into the net of the crowd of women waiting outside who have been watching the live weigh up on their respective phones. Within that time, they had already come up with protest chants. Three claps of the hands and they're off,

"Hamburger, shakes fries, we won't stand for your lies!"

Three more hand claps and,

"Cookies, ice cream, chocolate cake,

Avery you're such a fake!"

You look like the rejects from the rejects for cheerleading tryouts! Avery wanted to yell as she vigorously fights with herself to not give them all the finger individually. How would that look on the front pages and top news story when she's trying so desperately to squeeze her way back into the world's good graces? Dalton would be so disappointed. Again. So, she refrains and scurries to her car and speeds away. Avery barely misses hitting the awaiting cameraman who captures her post weigh-up ride home for private insights as per the agreement. He was supposed to ride along with Avery for a few blocks to get her take on the day's weigh up and the group eating for all the fans.

Avery speed dials Dalton on her dashboard.

"Hey Doll."

“What the hell, Dalton! What happened? That is not how it was supposed to go down!”

“Yeah, change of plans.”

“What do you mean change of plans? Nobody told me!”

“That was the plan. Had you known the plan it wouldn’t have looked as authentic. You should see your face! Priceless! You’re the only and everything in the headlines, breaking news, and soon to be late night comedy sketch!”

Last week when Avery had barely gained three pounds, Araya had a fit and wanted to fire her because she was not making her program nor herself look legitimate. So, Dalton suggested to Araya that Avery cheat the scale for the week to increase faith and membership. Avery agreed. She was tired of Araya’s aggressive passive-aggressive attitude towards her which spilled over to the Caloriestas and Wanters. Araya had a whole internet chat room devoted to Avery’s progress called “Fat Checker.” The hundreds of thousands self-anointed food sleuths did not believe Avery was taking in and keeping all the foods and calories necessary to be successful and thought she was only in it for the publicity, which made “Weight Wanters” look thin on integrity.

What Avery wasn’t privy to was that Araya had contacted Dalton the night before to tell him she no longer wanted Avery to represent "Weight Wanters."

"She just doesn't have the substance I'm looking for. I'm done."

She wanted a new and better spokesperson to represent her and her mission. Dalton had to think quick and met Araya at her office. This was not something Dalton usually did but he liked Araya's cutthroat ruthlessness to get ahead. He saw it in her eyes when he suggested cheating the scale a few days before. He had braced himself for all righteous fire and fury to spew from her, but instead he got a half smile. By the time he had arrived at her office, Araya already had a plan. She suggested that Avery be exposed for the fraud which would prove that her program really works and it's just that Avery doesn't.

"She's not ready to fully commit to changing her life and what better way to prove it than exposing her trying to beat the scale in front of everyone?"

Dalton signed Araya on as a client right then and there.

"Great! So now everyone hates me even more!"

"The publicity will be great for you. I already booked you for the newest weight gain reality show, Losers At Gaining. It airs live in two weeks. So, lose some weight so you can really show a huge gain for the show. Forget about

Araya. It'll all be in your past in ten and a half days."

He's gone.

Dalton hangs up and lets out the heavy sigh he had been holding in as Araya continues to nibble his ear and neck. He tosses his phone callously over his shoulder and kisses her passionately. Dalton had been sitting in Araya's office all morning like an obedient puppy trying not to wet the floor, knowing a treat is on its way. For Avery's exile, Araya promised him an even better meeting if all went well.

Araya first met Dalton during Avery's contract negotiation. When it was over, she stood up, shook his hand, pulled him close, and whispered, "Once with a fourteen, you'll never go lean."

From that statement on, Dalton has been obsessed with her.

They delight in the excitement of her staff and the Wanters being just a few feet away from her unlocked door as they have unbridled sex on her desk.

By the end of the day, every news, entertainment, talk, television, radio show, podcast, online blogger and the public had something to say about Avery's fraudulent weigh in. Even magazine and tabloid headlines are featured for the next days' exclusive inside look at Avery's desperation. The Aters have their five milliseconds of fame as they shame, blame, and aim everything that is wrong with society, the children, the environment, war, and long lines at public bathrooms on Avery's scale chicanery. It's being called "Weight Gate," "Avery's Depravery," "Scale Fail," and "Weigh Out." These all come with film footage from the time Avery walks from her car to the "Weight Wanters," door then meticulously time-lined, broken down and analyzed second by second through to when the wrist weights are exposed.

"What was she thinking?"

"Did she really think she'd get by with this?"

"She's sick. She needs help."

"Avery is spiraling out of control."

"Think she'll do time?"

"They should take her to food court!"

The ladies on "Chews 'n' Views" have their take on the situation:

"Looks like Avery just can't catch a cake as she tries to fool us all with an imaginary weight gain."

A teary-eyed Araya appears on "Views 'n' Chews" the next day to tell her devastated side of the bamboozlement, "I did everything I could for Avery. I took her under my wing and taught her how to eat and eat big. I counseled her, poured my heart out and into hers so that she could live a well-rounded life as a well-rounded person. And this… this is what she does to me! To me! She almost ruined my reputation, my business, my life, and the lives of all the people who come from everywhere to be part of Weight Wanters. I just couldn't believe it when I lifted her frail yet heavy arm and saw that monstrous wrist weight staring down and mocking me! It was devastating! I couldn't eat for hours…"

Araya makes sure to drop a tear as the camera moves in for a close-up. She then pulls herself together and announces that the "Weight Wanters" new coax-person is go-ing to be Avery's now ex-assistant, Rella.

Instead of following Avery back home for some good old-fashion ego pumping and you-still-got-it-they're-just-jealous talk, Rella hung out back at "Weight Wanters" by Araya's car. What she didn't expect to see was Araya and Dalton heavily making out by the dumpster then Araya giving Dalton an intimate squeeze before gliding to her car. Rella stopped Araya and sob storied to her about her own struggles with past non-weight and how the program has helped her get on track. But most important, she has major inside embarrassing dirt on Avery that she would gladly share with her exclusively. For a price, of course. Rella sparingly dished out tiny morsels of what it's like to work for Avery which intrigued Araya.

Because Rella was such a skittish creature, Avery mistook her fear and adulation for eternal loyalty and didn't bother to have her sign anything preventing the scaring up and making up of stories. So, Rella is free to say what she wants about Avery.

Araya loved the idea of getting revenge on Avery (even though Araya is the one who double crossed her). And with that, Rella became the next face of fullness. But she had to agree to only share those shocking inside stories for "Weight Wanters" commercials, blogs, and internet chats. Araya made sure to get that in a written agreement which also states that if Rella betrays her in any way, shape or form, Araya reserves and deserves the right to destroy her life.

Because of this vengeful shift, "Weight Wanters's" and Araya's popularity grows exponentially to the point of her announcing that sixty more centers will be opening across the country in the next two months. Avery's false weight gain is the best thing to happen to Araya…and Dalton.

Chapter Seventeen
Table Manners

Corrinne and Thian have just returned from their month-long heaven on earth honeymoon in Greece and it is now time to serve their sentence…dinner with Priscilla.

"Think she'll be mad at us?" Thian asks Corrinne as they drive to Priscilla's house as they have so many times before as Corrinne and Gregge, but now for the first time as Corrinne and Thian.

"I think she'll be too enamored with a superstar being part of her DNA."

"That sounds incestuous."

"Oh, just you wait."

Thian gives her a playful look of fear. Corrinne laughs and gives him a sweet supportive kiss on the cheek.

"How are you going to explain dating Gregge?"

"Won't need to."

Corrinne knew that Gregge barely existed to Priscilla, as did she for the most part, but Corrinne continues her daughterly duties to help Priscilla maintain her image of being a good mother, not only for the outside world but for her soul. As beautiful and powerful as Priscilla has always been, Corrinne always saw her frailties and insecurities. They are complete opposites.

Corrinne is thoroughly enjoying Thian's preoccupation with this evening's dinner.

"What if I slip up and say something that lets her know that we've met or that I've been there before?"

"It could be that I told you."

"Think she'll recognize my voice?"

"She never pays attention to any man's voice under a certain register…cash register, that is."

Thian laughs unexpectedly. He raises Corrinne's hand and kisses it.

"I love you."

"I love you, too."

Corrinne feels a tingle of excitement about introducing Thian to her mother and seeing how this was going to play out. For once, she was going to be the special one.

Thirty-five minutes later, Corrinne and Thian quietly stand, dwarfed by the tall ornate double doors of her family home, which today feels as if she's visiting it for the first time. Corrinne rings the bell. She has been ringing this doorbell since the day she moved out at eighteen. Thi-an holds her hand in a super-hero rescuing a cliff dangling climber grip. His heart beats to the rhythm of a drum roll. Corrinne always looks forward to being greeted by Morganna, Priscilla's lady-in-waiting, as she still likes to call her.

Morganna had been living at the Priscilla Palace ever since Corrinne could remember. She eventually moved up to Estate Manager as she was the only person Priscilla really trusted. Morganna came to them through a prestigious agency in England where she was trained to serve those the likes of royalty and high-profile celebrities. Priscilla was neither but she had married into money. She was very specific with the agency that her lady-in-waiting was not to have nor will ever develop any sex appeal, personality or ambition. Her life was to tend to Priscilla's life until either life ends. She made sure to choose the most humble and somewhat homely lady-in-waiting so as not to have any competition with her husband or any other men who worked at or walked into her house. Priscilla must always be number one when it comes to beauty.

Morganna's real name was Esme but Priscilla had a hard time rolling it gracefully off her lazy tongue and felt that it lacked sophistication for the life she led. So, she changed her name to Morganna. Priscilla loved calling Morganna's name where it echoed from room to room to hall to hall. Esme did not mind as she was such a young girl of eighteen and so excited to be moving to the United States, especially Los Angeles where all the stars lived.

Always the curious one, Corrinne, at age six snuck up to Morganna's third floor attic-like bedroom (where she was not allowed) to learn more about this mysterious woman as they rarely interacted but lived under the same roof. It was there that Corrinne discovered Morganna's incredible talent for making jewelry. She peeked through the cracked door and was fascinated. Corrinne watched her for over an hour make a beautiful necklace just from thread, seashells and colorful aquarium pebbles. When Morganna suddenly got up and walked towards the door, Corrinne quickly shifted out of sight.

"Time to go to bed, Sweet One," said Morganna as she closed her door.

"Corrinne? Bedtime!" her nanny, Franny, called out from the second floor. Corrinne scurried away but came back night after night. From that night on, Corrinne requested beads, gems, and jewelry making materials for her birthdays, Christmas, and just because. When she would see Morganna in the hallway, Corrinne would slip beads and wires in her pocket. A few days later, a beautiful piece of jewelry would end up on Corrinne's vanity table.

She wore every earring, bracelet, necklace, barrette, and brooch Morganna made. Everyone just thought Corrinne was making jewelry as well as clothes.

Corrinne was always friendly with the staff, helping them out by making sure not to leave a disrespectful mess for them to clean up, or having unreasonable demands for them to follow up on. She left that nonsense to her mother and sister.

Priscilla often joked (not joked) about Corrinne being born to be a servant after one evening at a dinner party with three other couples, and their children, Corrinne, age eight, started helping the staff clear the table of dishes. It just felt wrong to her to have people doing the simplest things that one could do for themselves. Priscilla was so outraged and embarrassed that she reprimanded and shamed Corrinne in front of everyone. It wasn't so much the act itself but the fact that her peers had witnessed it. *Oh! What they must think of my mothering skills!*

"You want to act like a peasant then you'll be treated as one! Is that what you want? To be like them? A servant? Ignored by society? Just someone in the background?"

Corrinne was mortified as she burst into tears and hung her head. She just wanted to disappear. Her father started to get up and comfort her, but Priscilla shot him ocular bullets that froze him in his seat.

"Go up to your room! And no dessert for you this evening! You could stand to miss a few anyway."

It was at that moment Corrinne knew she never wanted to be anything like her mother. Lorrinne thought it was hilarious and slightly hid her glee behind a linen napkin.

Although the guests were flabbergasted, Priscilla felt proud of the way she handled the situation and quickly recovered to her sweet self-centered pedestal and carried on like nothing had happened.

Corrinne ran upstairs and curled up in a ball in her padded windowsill and cried quietly. Only her hyperventilated breaths and shallow sniffs could escape from her broken heart as her tears flooded her face and soaked her green party dress. After an exhausting twenty minutes, her category five storm of tears had simmered to a category three when her door opened. Corrinne peeked up slightly from her folded arms on her curled-up knees to see a blurry figure place something on her vanity table and leave. She blinked away a tear just in time to catch the distinctive outline of Morganna exiting her room as she quietly shut the door behind her. Corrinne wiped her eyes to see what she had put on her table. It was the biggest slice of chocolate cake with a heart design in Belgian chocolate syrup.

On their tenth birthday, Priscilla fired their nannies and

proudly gifted Corrinne and Lorrinne with their own ladies-in-waiting. Lorrinne was delighted because her only ambition in life was to please and emulate their mother. Corrinne refused hers, much to Priscilla's offense. So, as a punishment, she made Corrinne give away all the birthday gifts she received from friends and family.

"I'll take them!" Lorrinne volunteered greedily.

This punitive measure didn't shake Corrinne at all. She had more than enough games, dolls, and toys.

"Fine," said Corrinne as she shoved her enormous amount of gifts down the long dining room table to Lorrinne.

Priscilla was not okay with how okay Corrinne was with giving up her gifts. The only thing that secretly broke her heart was giving away the enormous jewelry making kit her father had given her because she was planning on giving it to Morganna.

Lorrinne joyfully picked through Corrinne's gifts as if she were at a boutique. She shoved the jewelry kit down the table and spat, "I don't want this, it's too much work!"

Priscilla saw the flicker of relief in Corrinne's eyes as the huge kit slid towards her. Priscilla reached out her perfectly manicured hand and stopped it in mid-slide and said, "She gets nothing back." Priscilla looked down the table and delighted in Corrinne's crestfallen expression. Corrinne knew how to play the game. She had to let Priscilla think she broke her in order to avoid any further repercussions.

All Corrinne ever wanted was fabric and material to make clothes and accessories to make jewelry. She knew her father had her back on that. Corrinne made sure Priscilla never knew how important any of this was to her to avoid it being taken away from her permanently.

After Lorrinne picked through all of Corrinne's gifts, she folded her arms and pouted.

"There's nothing good here! I don't want any of this stuff! This is the worst birthday ever!"

Priscilla immediately got up and consoled Lorrinne and yelled at Corrinne, "You see what you've done! You ruined your sister's birthday!"

The doors open in a grand manner as if trumpets should be playing and uniformed guards should be marching out in unison for their formal entrance. Corrinne had expected to be greeted by estate staff, but instead Priscilla prances into sight. She should have known there was no way in her bank account Priscilla would allow anyone else to be the first to greet and welcome Thian Rodgers into her home.

Corrinne stops short and is astonished by what she sees. Her mother is wearing a billowing periwinkle maxi-dress with her boobs hoisted to the brink of taking flight. Her once straight hair is curly and almost identical to Corrinne's and she looks like she's packed on about twenty pounds.

"Cori! Baby! My most beautiful engaged angel baby girl!" Priscilla hugs Corrinne like a long-lost pet as she strokes her hair, kisses her nose and speaks baby gibberish.

Corrinne is taken aback and not sure what to do. She knew her mother was going to put on an act, but she didn't expect so much affection.

Thian is quite amused with her theatrics. Priscilla steps back and looks at them with tears of societal pride in her eyes that a bonified Oscar winning superstar wanted something that she produced and was going to be part of her family. She looks at Thian with lustful admiration and shakes her head.

"Welcome to the family! I feel like I know you already!"

She throws herself on him, bosom first, and languishes in the engulfment of his bionic biceps. Thian gives Corrinne a helpless look as she stifles a laugh. They smile at each other as the hug lingers uncomfortably long.

"Mom? Shall we go in?" Corrinne asks.

Priscilla takes one more deep breath, inhaling Thian's masculine essence, then slowly releases him as she caresses his arms to his wrists before interlocking her fingers with his and leads him into the house.

"Here we go," Corrinne says under her breath wishing they were exiting instead of entering.

"Where's Morgana?"

"I gave her some time off. Poor girl works so hard."

Corrinne was so accustomed to Morganna greeting her at the door, she still felt disappointed even though she saw her that morning for breakfast at her father's house.

Morganna and her father had been secretly dating for the past five years. Corrinne was overjoyed when they broke the news to her and Thian a couple of months ago at one of their weekly dinners.

Instead of one of her father's staff bringing the main entrée, Morganna walked in with a platter and set it on the table. Both Corrinne and Thian hiccupped in surprise.

"You work here now?" asked Corrinne.

"No, she lives here now," answered her father as he kissed Morganna's hand.

Before Corrinne could think to blink, she was on her

feet hugging them both. They plan on getting married next year. Her father made Corrinne and Thian promise they would not let her mother know that they know about his and Morganna's "arrangement" because Priscilla wanted to tell everyone when she was ready. It was that same evening Corrinne and Thian told them of their plan to elope. Two exciting announcements and two more secrets that must be kept from Priscilla. So, Corrinne must pretend she thinks Morganna still works for her.

Priscilla took the news like she took out the trash. Not at all. She remained bullet-proof armored in reasoning to herself, *Well at least now he's finally dating within his league because Morganna is not and will never be as beautiful as I am.* Even though she didn't want him, she did want him to want her.

Priscilla didn't want anyone to know that someone she was once married to had fallen in love with a household domestic. Not even her children. She told Lorrinne that Morganna was on a very long vacation. The same thing she told her why the Tooth Tooth Fairy stopped visiting after all her baby teeth had fallen out.

Done with daughter time chit chat, Priscilla whisks Thian away for a personal grand tour of the house. She never gave Gregge a tour of the house. Since he was just a blue-collar construction worker, from a blue-collar family who could add nothing to her social resume, there was no need for him to see past the informal dining room and eat on informal china. If she hadn't been allergic to the notion, they would have eaten on paper plates. Now Thian is the hostess's hostage of hospitality. Corrinne's amusement over this show of affection and Thian's comical over-the-shoulder look of sheer terror while silently begging for help sends her into hysterics…until….

"Corrinne!"

Part two of the circus begins as Corrinne looks up to see Lorrinne barreling down the right side of the double staircase like a cat chasing a bell-ringing ball. Corrinne can't quite lock down her impression of her sister's appearance in the ruffle-collared orange and green striped, knee-length voluminous baby-doll sundress, frantic vintage movie star make-up, and matronly bun. It's obvious their mother had dressed her.

Whenever Priscilla wants to assure her space as the most attractive in the company of men, she dresses Lorrinne as a special mommy favor. She never bothered with Corrinne because Priscilla never viewed her as a physical threat. She also knew Corrinne was too savvy to fall for it. But opinion-free, voiceless Lorrinne would do and say anything just to be in Priscilla's presence and acknowledged. Today Priscilla pulled out all the jacks-in-the-box including her famous line, “Ignore the mirror, it’s about how you feel in this outfit.” And Lorrinne bought it like the hottest stock on Wall Street.

As much as she tried, with the help of her mother, Lorrinne just couldn’t gain any weight, much to the joy of Priscilla who managed to make her way up two sizes and is excited to keep going. So, Lorrinne wears large dresses to hide her fault-finding form.

Lorrinne looks like she’s preparing for a comical pratfall as she whisper-yells in excitement.

“Where is he? Where is he?” She is beside herself with fandom.

“Where is who?” Corrinne whisper-yells back just to get under her skin.

“You know who!”

“You mean Robert?” Robert’s the estate landscaper. “I think he’s…”

“Shut up, Corrinne, you know who I’m talking about!”

She makes it safely to the bottom of the stairs.

Now if Corrinne could just get to the bottom of her stares as she takes in Lorrinne’s absurd appearance.

“I can’t believe **you’re** engaged to Thian Rodgers!”

"Awwww, thanks, Sis. And I can't believe you're wearing that dress," Corrinne counters wishing her eyes would shut every time it comes into view.

"You like? Bet you wish you thought of it first!"

Lorrinne sneers, then twirls like a pretty princess, loving every ounce of her sister's envy, completely missing the sarcasm.

All Corrinne can do is choke back an ugly and cruel laugh in the guise of a deep quivering sigh.

"That's what I thought," Lorrinne states, victoriously tossing her head back and flouncing off.

Corrinne holds onto the banister as she quietly releases her laugh while the orange and green run-away bouncy house with legs makes its way to the formal dining room.

The dinner table is lush with every high-end, high-calorie food there is including fried calamari, truffle macaroni and cheese, wagyu steak in garlic butter, duck confit, just to name a few. Priscilla put together the menu herself and made sure everything was flown in fresh. A fact she makes sure to mention every time a bite is taken. Corrinne had never seen her mother eat so much, especially in front of other people. She has a glow that is two parts being in Thian's presence and one part eating again. She seems happier, prettier and natural. Priscilla is seated at the head of the table in her plush tufted red queen's chair with Corrinne to her left and Thian to her right. Thian's seat is considerably closer to Priscilla than Corrinne's. Lorrinne is seated next to Corrinne, bumping her out of her first-class seat.

The dinner also consists of Priscilla prattling on about her favorite subject…Priscilla. Lorrinne sits in rapt attention, awe, and right on cue laughter as if she had never heard these stories before partly out of loyalty and partly out of surprise due to the outrageous embellishments. Thian reacts in shock and fascination. He laughs heartily, smiles endearingly, and asks the right questions at the right time. Priscilla never shared these stories with Gregge, so he was genuinely amused with a sprinkle of overacting.

Corrinne is shaken out of her mindless nods and auto-pilot laughter when Priscilla reaches over and grabs her hand. She is startled then steels herself for the reprimand, put down or criticism that is to follow as she looks expectantly at Thian. He had heard them all before during the many dinners he had there as Gregge.

"But this girl, my girl, right here, has always had a strong will and her own mind. She never wanted to do what was expected of her, especially by me. Nope, she had her own passion, her own talent, her own path and always chose to take it and follow it."

Here it comes. Corrinne braces herself for the low blow to hit. She can feel Priscilla's squeeze tighten like a vice. This gets Corrinne's full attention. She turns to look at Priscilla whose eyes have teared up.

"And I admire that. I always have."

As Corrinne looks at Priscilla, for the first time she can see her. A real person. A happy person. She is startled by this revelation and has no idea how to react. Everything she has known and come to expect from her mother has now dissipated. Corrinne has to start all over again getting to know this new woman.

Priscilla wipes away the tear swiftly that has hit her mid cheek and summons her voice back.

"She used to make her own clothes because she didn't like what I picked out for her and Lorrinne. At age six, she started and would make the cutest things! She had this talent for designing and sewing from such a young age and wouldn't let anyone stand in her way. I can't say I was always supportive of what she was doing but I sure thought deep down inside, I wish I were that brave, that bold, that driven to do my own thing. And with that said, I want to give you a special engagement present."

Priscilla gets up from the table and brings over a beautifully wrapped box and hands it to Corrinne. Corrinne is not sure how to react as she takes the box.

"Go ahead, open it."

Corrinne unwraps the beautiful gold wrapping carefully and as daintily as she was taught when she was two-years-old.

"Oh, for goodness sake, Corrinne, let it rip!" Priscilla yells playfully and laughs.

Where is my mother? Who took her and replaced her with this well fed, clear thinking, fun loving creature?

Thian laughs which helps to ease Corrinne's bewilderment. He can tell Corrinne is confused, touched, and out of sorts.

Corrinne laughs then noisily rips through the beautiful and expensive wrapping paper causing Lorrinne to wince and flinch in pain as if her very own skin was being torn off. Corrinne removes the top of the beautiful aqua blue box to find a velvet periwinkle photo album inside. She takes it out and opens it. The inscription inside reads: "Dear Corrinne, When I see you, I see me, Love Forever, Mommy."

Corrinne tries to hold back her tears. She sniffs and tries to shake it off. She turns the page to see a picture of her chubby self at age six and a picture of little girl who looks exactly like her next to it.

"Oh my gosh! Is this you, Lorrinne? I never knew we

looked this much alike when we were kids!" Corrinne laughs, grateful to break the tension in her heart and brain.

Lorrinne frowns an indignant and putrid frown and says, "I was never fat!"

Thian visibly cringes at Lorrinne's bitter outburst.

"No, Corrinne, that's not Lorrinne, that's me," says Priscilla completely ignoring Lorrinne.

"What?!" Corrinne and Lorrinne say at the same time. The only time they've ever been in sync.

"Oh, this I gotta see!" says Thian as he gets up.

They all gather round the photo album. There they are. Corrinne and Priscilla. Identical twins. The only difference is the texture in picture richness due to the twenty-five-year difference. Wait a minute, are those tear and burn marks on these photos?

Priscilla had never shared these pictures of herself because she was so ashamed of her appearance and desperately tried to hide all evidence of her past look life by cutting and burning them up. Her mother managed to rescue them each time by fishing them out of the trash can and fireplace, gluing them back together and eventually hiding them. Priscilla always wanted to give the impression she was born slim and beautiful. So, she created a new identity, a new story, a new physical outlook and did not show pictures of herself until she starved herself into the body she hungered for at age thirteen.

Priscilla regretted getting rid of those pictures the second Corrinne stepped out of that monster truck with Thian that fateful night. The next morning, she went on an eating spree and scavenger hunt at her parents' home for any proof that she looks like Corrinne. She went there with a catered breakfast under the pretense of looking for her mother's wedding dress to pass down to Corrinne (the same dress she wouldn't even want to see her worst enemy buried in). Lucky so lucky for her she found the pictures hidden in the attic in a box marked literature. Her parents knew she would never look there. She knew they thought she'd never look there too.

As Corrinne slowly goes through the album in amazement, she savors each photograph searching and seeing the eerie similarities from how they look to how they stand, and how they naturally cock their head to the right when posing. All these years her mother had blamed Corrinne's excess weight on her father's side of the family. Priscilla proudly shares a cute story for each picture about herself and Corrinne. She remembers everything that was happening on the day a picture was taken of Corrrinne and the things she said and what she was doing during that period of time. The pictures were from age six to twelve. Corrinne is touched that Priscilla had cared enough to make up all these stories.

When she is done, Priscilla abruptly closes the photo album, puts it aside and announces, "Okay, enough of that! Now, we have a wedding to plan!"

Suddenly Corrinne feels guilty about eloping…until…

"We have eleven months to put together the biggest, most extravagant, luxurious wedding anyone has ever seen! I have already called the florist, the baker, the chef, and movie director, Thyme, to film this epic union like a movie from start to finish, I've already booked the most amazing venue and wait 'til you see the menu. We also have to…."

And she's back!

Chapter Eighteen
Let The Shames Begin

Avery arrives at the set for her stint on a new weight gain reality show where she hopes to regain and boost her fan base and leave behind all the negative publicity. Dalton told her this was the best path to take and the fact that she will be paid fifty-thousand dollars for each week she stays on the show was a great incentive…for Dalton. The incentive for Avery is to not be the most hated underweighted woman in the world.

As per the producer's instructions, she has been waiting patiently then impatiently in the car for the past hour to be called inside. There are no trailers or assistants or any special celebrity treatment. Just Avery and a driver parked outside with a few security guards milling about. One of them finally approaches her car and taps on the window. Avery lets it down.

"Okay, they're ready for you, Miss."

"It's about time!" she says already in a bad mood, already not wanting to do this, and ready to go home.

Avery waits for the driver or security guard to open the door. Neither budges. She sighs, annoyed at the lack of service she's accustomed to then opens the door herself.

She steps out and reaches back in to grab her tote bag. The trunk pops open and Avery looks at the security guard expectantly as he looks at her expectantly.

She rolls her eyes and says sarcastically, "Oh, no, no, I'll get it."

Avery walks angrily to the back of the car and unloads her two suitcases and garment bag. She situates herself clumsily as she has never had to lift, carry, roll, or even acknowledge luggage until it was in her room and unpacked. The security guard follows her up the walkway and steps to the two-story pine green building. He hops ahead just in time to open the door for her. She pauses to look at him then shakes her head and enters. Avery walks through the entryway where a bright light and a camera appears out of nowhere. It has begun. The camera follows her as she looks around and sees the well-lit staging area with seven other people standing side by side. They all turn around when they hear Avery's heavy bags roll unevenly across the floor indicating her struggle to keep them straight.

"Aaaah…finally, the princess has arrived, Everyone!" A booming male voice calls out as Avery approaches the group. "You're late. See these people here? They were here on time. That means they're serious about their weight gain. Are you?"

Avery can now see the chastising is spilling out of the

mouth of an extremely muscular, tall, and handsome early thirties man in shorts and a barely-there muscle shirt that looks as if it fit him as a toddler. He is standing next to a very curvaceous size fourteen long curly-haired blonde in her early twenties who is wearing an uncomfortably tight, sleeveless white dress that hits her mid-thigh with five-inch red and gold striped stilettos. They are a stunning pair as they stand side by side sizing up the contestants. Avery takes her place next to her competition. The other contestants, who are dressed in bulky figure masking clothing, look her up and down in disgust as she has the audacity to wear form fitting jeans and a tank top (exactly what she was told to wear). *Doesn't she know that it's unacceptable to walk around exposing such flaws in public?*

Out of the ethers of Hollywood, steps a man in his early fifties with molding clay black hair that is combed and whipped high to the left of his part. He is wearing a well-tailored eighties' prom blue suit with all the fixings for attention. His smile is that of two mouths in one as it spreads across his face and almost to the back of his head. Avery recognizes him immediately.

It is Creign Kitchell, the number one game show host in America. He stands next to the man and woman and loudly announces in his signature revved-up game show host voice, "Hey Everybody! As you already know, I'm Creign Kitchell, and welcome to 'Losers At Gaining!' I will be your host for the next eight weeks while these pathetic slim beings compete to gain their dignity back!"

A woman off camera signals for the contestants to clap and cheer. They all follow suit.

"We are filming live here at zip code renowned all-you-should-eat restaurant, Sodium, where these society shunned souls will have to out eat, out-weigh and outfit each other in order to win!"

They are signaled to cheer again.

"Now, each week we will watch as they eat, sleep, drink, and sit their way to victory in order to achieve that elusive perfect size fourteen. Each contestant has brought with her a dream outfit she would love to grow into for the final reveal reception and yearned entry to public acceptance. They will be coached, berated and humiliated by their oh-so beautiful and perfect mentors, Davannah, the ultimate example of what all women should look like and strive for. And Worthy, the man all women who look like Davannah are entitled to have. You can be her, Ladies!"

The women cheer in hopeless hope and desire. Avery goes along because, once again, it's in her contract. Davannah and Worthy pose proudly and wave to them like grand marshals in The Rose Parade.

"Each day, you will have the opportunity to gain as much

weight and increase your dress size by following the free-for-all non-dietary compliant, unplanned meal plan and mantra that is designed specifically for this show which is, 'Eat All You Can Eat To Avoid Defeat!' You will have access to the twenty-four-hour Canal of Cuisine that is located right here."

A bright light appears over a long silver island that stretches the length of the room.

"Go ahead, Ladies, take a look."

The women slowly walk over and feast their eyes on the mile-long trough with every greasy, salty, cheesy, meaty, fatty, starchy, saucy, sweet and gooey decadent food you can think of.

"Welcome to the holy grill of grub!"

A couple of the women start to wretch and air vomit at the sight of the food. Three others start to cry and declare that this is already too tough.

"That's okay, Ladies, let it out! That's just hunger leaving your body!" Worthy yells at them.

Avery is excited. *I can have my cake and the bakery too!*

"Well, now that I've gotten you off to a miserable start, I'm going to now hand your journey over to your mentors and I will see you at your first comp**eat**ition. Once again, you know I'm Creign Kitchell and this… is 'Losers At Gaining!'"

The upbeat theme music plays as Creign Kitchell dances his way out. Each contestant's headshot and name appear on the screen along with who they were before public imposed self-loathing brought them here.

Timber: The Nanny *(aspiring second wife to current client)*

Solar: The Yoga Instructor *(aspiring actress)*

Seebra: The Dancer *(aspiring reality show star)*

Falerie: The Organic Caterer *(aspiring trophy wife)*

Kennon: The Fashion Student *(aspiring clothes designer)*

Tivanny: The Art Teacher *(aspiring girlfriend of Worthy)*

Vivi: The Dog Trainer *(aspiring rich widow)*

And

Avery: The Disgraced Former Model and Scale Cheater *(aspiring not to be here)*

Worthy claps his hands twice to get the ladies' attention. They stop mid-tears, dramatic pacing, and heaving to listen to His Fineness.

"Gather around Ladies!" They all scamper quickly around him and Davannah.

"Now, this is how it works," says Davannah in her sympathetic cheerleader tone as she reads from the cue card trying to seem engaged and interested in their plight while feeling fortunate not to be them, "Each day you will be given a challenge to complete that will give you an advantage on Judgment Day at the end of the week."

"In the meantime, you will have to eat and maintain a minimum ten thousand calorie a day diet of sodium, sugar, fats, and carbs that are all provided for you here at the Canal of Cuisine. It is up to you to get in your four meals and five snacks. At the end of each week, we'll have a flaw-exposing scale and measure up ceremony to track your growth and magnify your failure where you will either stay in place or be disgraced," explains Worthy.

"The person with the least amount of weight gained and measurement increase will be the Loser at Gaining and tossed like a salad out of here," Davannah tells them.

"The winner after eight weeks will receive the coveted title of Winner at Gaining and fifty-thousand dollars!" they both announce enthusiastically.

"Not only that, you'll also win an exclusive Zavier Zaftig Collection knock-off wardrobe from the store, 'Seams Like It!' Which I am wearing right now!"

Davannah struts and poses.

The women jump up and down as they watch their future selves on the make-believe catwalk. Avery can't muster the level of enthusiasm the other women can. She's been there, worn that. The original at that.

"I see some of you, or should I say one of you, don't seem that excited. And that is just the kind of attitude that's going to keep you being a Loser at Gaining!" preaches Worthy as he stares Avery down.

This is the part where the hosts stop reading and speak from their heart, mind, and desire to have the catchphrase they can trademark. They both know Avery doesn't belong there. He thinks she thinks she's too good for this kind of show and she knows she's too good for this kind of show.

Everyone gives Avery a side glance then flips their hair as if flicking away her negative energy. What good is a feel-good show if nobody feels bad?

"Don't let anyone's negativity complicate your progress," Davannah states in a profound tone.

The contestants cheer. Avery knows good and hot ham well she will not make it in here eight weeks without being brought up on murder charges.

"Are you ready to see where you'll be living for the next eight weeks? Well, at least two of you will make it to eight weeks," says Davannah.

The women laugh and cheer, desperately wanting to catch her eye and be her favorite for extra close-up camera time and maybe best friend after the show. Avery manages a half smile.

"Then follow me!"

The women "woo hoo" and follow Davannah up the fifteen stairs to the second floor which has been changed from an additional dining area into living quarters consisting of puke peach walls with shameful before (now) pictures of each contestant make-up and hair combed free in a skimpy bikini to showcase their perceived flaw and insecurity. The women recoil when they catch sight of themselves. Beneath each picture is a twin bed indicating where each victim is to sleep with a small nightstand filled with sweet and salty snacks.

During their individual photo shoot, a week prior, each woman was instructed to portray themselves as downtrodden and ashamed of their body. The producer of the show, Doss, reminded them of the non-life they were leading as a non-bodied woman and how they were viewed as society's under fed underdog, and that no man would ever find them attractive (even though six and a half weeks ago they were proud and loving life in the skin they were in). It worked. The pictures are pitiful with their gray background and broken spirit poses. Avery's, on the other hand, looks like a defiant mug shot. All that's missing is her giving the camera the middle finger. She just doesn't buy into her looking so bad. But she'll play along to ensure her place back on top.

Against one wall are four binging machines. One houses candy, one houses chips, another with pastries, and the last one, sugary sodas and drinks. Then off to a corner, on its own, is a bright binging machine with only fruits, water and low-calorie snacks for the purpose of temptations and punishments. Another wall is dedicated to an enormous flat screen television and eight Slug-A-Lounger chairs in front of it where they are required to sit and watch for at least ten hours out of the day. The chairs have a built in tush timer that counts the hours one has spent in the chair. Each chair is counted and recalibrated remotely every time someone gets up. The television is only programmed for selected movies and nothing from the outside world. This will make for good fights over what to watch.

Davannah delights in explaining their room like a game show hostess revealing prizes to anxious button-pounding-ready contestants. The women fawn over the slightest reveal as if this were their first time seeing anything ever.

Suddenly Worthy pops up and announces after he claps his massive hands two times for their undivided attention, "Okay! Okay! Enough of the niceties! It's time to go to work! Get changed and meet me downstairs in five minutes."

"Let the shames begin!" Davannah says happily as she throws up her arms.

The women cheer anxiously and run to their appointed bed to change into the outfit that is laid out for them.

Davannah carefully makes her way down the stairs, with the help of Worthy, for an enviable wardrobe change.

The outfit the contestants are to wear is a black spandex leotard. All panic and mayhem are released in the form of shrieks, tears, and fears as they gasp in horror then bawl while Avery makes her way to the public style bathroom to change her clothes.

"Oh no! I can't wear this! Everyone will see how skinny my thighs are!" cries Solar.

"What about how flat our stomachs are!" howls Timber.

"The arms! What about the arms?!" bellows Seebra

"And it's black! Black is so slimming!" wails Falerie

"This is so going to embarrass my family!" bawls Vivi.

"My boyfriend is going to be so ashamed and ridiculed! He's probably going to break up with me!" sobs Kennon.

"I could lose my job!" whimpers Tivanny.

Avery casually strolls by, fully dressed for combat in the black leotard and sneakers which causes the women to stop, look, and pretend whisper.

"Oh, my goodness! Look at her."

"She's so thin!"

"She looks terrible!"

"At least I don't look that bad!"

"Neither do I."

"Me neither."

These, the same women who were killing themselves to be her just a couple of months ago.

Having heard every word, Avery remains calm.

"You know Ladies, the time you've spent crying, pissing yourselves and shitting on me, you could have been dressed and ready to change your life. You've got two minutes left," says Avery as she folds her clothes and places them in her suitcase without looking at any of them. She zips it up. "See you downstairs." Avery heads towards the stairs.

The women look at each other and scramble to get dressed.

Although she'd rather eat a burger from a skunk's butt than be here, Avery is a fair and fierce competitor and loves a good challenge.

One and a half hours later…

After the mortifying and demeaning starting point of weigh-ins, measurements, and what-the-hell-is-wrong-with-you's, Avery and the other contestants are standing on the edge of a blue covered pool at a non-disclosed location (somebody's backyard) for their first competition. They arrived by a tinted window party bus complete with double decker sandwiches filled with mayonnaise and fatty meats. Avery was able to eat two while the others could only get one third the way through, collectively. Worthy is dressed in tight orange board shorts and no shirt where he voluntarily involuntarily flexes while Davannah dons a pink sequin one-piece bathing suit and pink five-inch stilettos.

Creign Kitchell makes his over-the-top entrance wearing a lifeguard uniform complete with whistle and red torpedo buoy. Everyone laughs and applauds. Avery reluctantly plays along with enough of a titter to pass for being a team player. He climbs animatedly up to the lifeguard chair and speaks obnoxiously loud into the bullhorn the instructions for the competition. When the cover is removed by a touch of a button from Worthy, it reveals the pool divided into eight lanes filled with four feet of chocolate pudding. The women jump back in fear, all except Avery, she has filled her tub with chocolate pudding many times and just grabbed a spoon.

"Are we going to have to eat all of this?" asks a horrified Vivi.

"No, but you will have to eat all of that!" answers Creign as he points to the other side of the pool where each lane has two buckets. One is full of chocolate pudding and the other one is empty. The object of the game is for them to make their way through the pudding to the other side, eat the whole bucket of pudding with a teaspoon as fast they can, grab the other bucket and fill it up with the pudding from their lane and bring it back to the other side empty having finished eating it on the way back.

"First one back with an empty bucket wins ten tokens to the binging machines. Last place loser has to eat only from the salad bar for the rest of the day which may affect your weight gain for the week. Now…are you ready to play… Pudding On The Ditz?"

The contestants cheer. Avery is not looking forward to getting sticky and gross.

Dalton had assured her that the show was going to be just about living in a big house with seven other people (possibly celebrities) who are also trying to gain weight and all they have to do is sit around all day, talk, eat, and get weighed while the world watches. Avery packed her cutest clothes, shoes, and attitude. She even practiced pretty-eating fattening and sloppy foods from every angle in her mirror so she would look good while stuffing her face. The world had never seen her eat before and she was going to make it look fabulous. This was going to be epic. So many firsts for her, a fresh start as a real and likeable person. Avery was led to believe that she would only have one roommate in a luxury suite whom she should bond with to show that she is capable of being human. Avery had no idea she would be living in a restaurant, sleeping in a twin bed (she hadn't slept in a twin bed since she was eight), in the same room with seven other people and subjected to such belittlement and humiliation. Over what? Over weight.

"All righty, on your mark, get set…slow!" Creign Kitchell bellows then blows his whistle to start off the game.

The women slowly and squeamishly ease into the ooze.

And so, the week carried on with silly costumes and messy games like "Pie-Man Says," "Musical Eclairs," "Tic-Tac-Donut," "Rump Rope," and "Follow The Eater." All designed to debase, demoralize, and demolish any trace of dignity the contestants came in with. It was well orchestrated to cause a buffet of fights and dissention amongst them while well-groomed, well rested, Davannah and Worthy yelled endearing encouragement such as:

"Come on! Do you want to be slim forever? An outcast? A no body?"

"You can do this! Get outta your head and into that bread!"

"You got yourself into this dress, now eat your way out of it!"

"Do you really want to go back to that sad life of lettuce, kale, and quinoa? Huh? Do you?"

Despite all the odds, participants, and mentors against her, Avery thrived in the competitions and swept all the tokens to the bingeing machines and other advantages for herself and teammates. Her competitive nature kicked back into high gear as she followed all the rules, rallied her teammates for certain competitions and led them to victory through encouragement and strategy. She was feeling strong and in control of her life again. She wanted to stand out and be that leader she was when she played soccer and baseball as a kid. Avery was starting to enjoy the other ladies (some of them) and her time on the show. *Another seven weeks here might not be so bad.*

Avery was sure she was the top fan favorite and that whole Oscar madness was behind her. She could tell she was starting to gain weight and was visualizing fitting into her dream dress as she stands victoriously as the winner at the end of the show. This was turning out to be an unexpected positive journey for her. Some of her competitors took to her and would ask for style and makeup tips while others would try to start fights with her over silly things hoping to get a rise out of her and a rise in their popularity, but Avery wasn't having it. She was focused on the prize and making it to the end without any further battle scars.

After an exhausting week of sitting and eating, the first Judgment Day has dawned to gauge how the participants are progressing and who will be sent home. Avery is excited about her progress and hopes no one she likes leaves today.

All the women are barefoot, dressed in black barely-there spandex shorty shorts with the letters LAG (for "Losers At Gaining") emblazoned on the back and a skimpy black bikini top. As per the director's command, there are many shots of the logo as they walk in a straight line eating their last chance meal (Avery chose two large pieces of chocolate cake and a large meatball sandwich) on their way to "The Lunchroom." The location is on a soundstage in Hollywood that was built just for this show. The contenders reach the door to the ceremony and it is opened by a crew member who is given the signal through his earpiece. They walk in and the first thing they see is a giant, round, neon pink seven-layer prop cake on the main stage with the words "Losers At Gaining" on it lit up in bright green. The rest the set looks like a school cafeteria.

Out of nowhere thunderous applause and cheers suffocate the soundstage. The contestants are startled as they turn and look up to see an audience of three hundred people yelling, jumping up and down and waving their arms. They have their favorite contestant's name on homemade banners with hearts, encouraging words and high calorie foods they cut and pasted themselves. The women wave back, look for banners with their name on it and blow kisses towards that section. Avery searches the crowd for the banners with her name. For some reason it is important to her to be cheered on.

Before she can glimpse her section of fans, Creign Kitchell takes center stage on a platform in the shape of a lasagna and orders the ladies to take their plates. Which means standing on the bright green light on the floor that is shaped like a plate with their name on it. Avery's plate is right in the middle. She is disappointed to not have seen her name in the audience. *I didn't have enough time to look, anyway. So much confusion and excitement I couldn't even focus.* Avery is annoyed with herself for even caring.

Davannah and Worthy sit in roomy cushioned elongated high-back emerald green armchairs next to the giant cake to cheer their protégés on. They are fashionably dressed like they're ready to go for a couple's night out. Davannah in her yellow tube dress and Worthy in his tailored eggplant purple suit and no socks with Italian leather loafers. When taping is over, Davannah is going to hit the gym and fast for the rest of the day and weekend. Worthy is going to pick up a vegan meal for his wife and three kids.

"Thank you all so much for being a part of this delicious occasion! What you are about to witness are eight brave and desperate women who are as unhappy with their bodies as we are with their bodies and decided to do something about it, for all of our sakes!" declares Creign Kitchell

The crowd goes wild.

"After seven grueling days of eating, sitting, napping, watching television, drinking sugary beverages, and snacking, these women now stand curvelessly before you, exposed and defenseless to find out if it's been a smooth ride or a crash and burn on the road to their re-binge bodies!"

Solar is the first one up and she has gained a disappointing three pounds for the week. One after the other, the women step on the scale to disappointing numbers from three pounds to eight pounds and hopelessly decry they did everything they could. Worthy and Davannah assure them that they didn't.

"Did you sit for the assigned ten hours a day? Because your tush timer says different," Davannah points out to them accusingly.

"Did you eat the minimum ten thousand calories a day you were supposed to?" asks Worthy angrily.

Davannah dramatically slides towards the edge of her chair and states, "And… there is secret footage of two of you eating from the salad bar instead of the Canal of Cuisine for a meal!"

The audience wheezes in utter repugnance as if she had said they were caught eating kittens.

Worthy has had enough and jumps passionately out of his chair and rushes towards the contestants, yelling as he cries and points at each of them, "You're going back to your under-eating habits and it's killing you! This week! This week in particular! You all should have gained double digits! What…do…I…have…to…do…to…get…that through to you?"

He buries his face in his hands and sobs.

The tear-soaked audience applauds his compassion.

Davannah leaps out of her chair and carefully hurries in her six-inch camel colored stilettos to Worthy and puts her arms around him, thankful she managed to gather enough tears on her way over for them to pool within her eyes but not enough to mess up her flawless closeup ready makeup.

She looks at each contestant intensely and declares, "We only humiliate and belittle you pitiful people because we care and hold nothing but contempt for you in our hearts!"

The audience cheers again.

Creign Kitchell gives a loud wet sniffle to bring the camera back his way just in time to capture him wiping away tears from his eyes.

"As you can see, there's a whole lotta love for attention in this studio. Such a bond has been sealed just over the past week! This is amazing!"

The women love circle around Davannah and Worthy and apologize for being un-ateful and not totally utilizing all their expertise, time, and godly wisdom. They weepily exchange I love you's, gratitude, and pledges to do better. Avery tries to get a place in the love circle but there are no openings and she is awkwardly left out.

"All right, everybody, whew! Looks like that was just the breakthrough breakdown they needed. Let's bring it back to the real reason we're here. To find out who the true Loser at Gaining is!"

The audience stands, claps and pulls themselves together as the contestants and the mentors start to pull themselves apart.

"We have one more contestant to denigrate…And that is Avery!"

Scattered polite applause can barely be heard. In her mind, Avery thinks the reason she can't hear the applause is because her heart is beating so loud. She steps on the platform that is shaped like a cake slicer and is lifted to the top of the cake, which is the scale, as dark dramatic music decorates the mood.

"As you can plainly see, there is no place for her to hide any **extra** weight!" jokes Creign Kitchell. "We also had round-the-clock security guarding this scale to ensure no pounds were added for this one." He points at Avery with his thumb.

Everyone laughs, more out of contempt for Avery than Creign Kitchell's catchy humor.

Avery steps off the cake slicer and onto the middle of the cake where the weight calibrator is anticipating her arrival. Everyone watches as Avery stands and faces her judges like a towering cake topper. It is obvious her face is slightly more round and her body seems a teeny bit fuller. Creign Kitchell reveals her previous weight as the jumbo screens displays the scale's configuration. The giant numbers dance up and down tauntingly then settle complacently on their final judgment. There is a collective gasp. Avery can't see the number and has no idea. She turns her head slightly to be clued in with the rest of the crowd because a stunned Creign Kitchell has missed his cue.

"Avery has gained twelve pounds this week!" he finally calls out with disbelief and feigned excitement.

Her competitors and mentors are crestfallen. The audience reluctantly applauds her. In her mind, everyone is as ecstatic as she is. Avery can't believe it! *I did it! I really did it!* The swelling of pride in her heart brings her to tears. *I'm going to win this thing and win my life back!* She has not felt this good and proud of herself since she made her first meringue pie at age seven. It's all too overwhelming.

"You can step down now, Avery, congratulations." Creign Kitchell tells her. He tries to mask his disappointment because one of the contestants he's been flirting and having off-camera secret feel-up sessions with is in danger of going home.

When Avery returns to her spot, she is met with half-hearted hugs from the ladies and tepid congratulations from Davannah and Worthy. They are all shaken and dismayed by this unexpected stomach turn of events. They shouldn't be surprised. Avery followed every rule, won all the competitions, took advantage of all her advantages at the bingeing machines, and did extra sit downs.

The results have bumped Timber and Seebra down to last place where it will be up to the remaining participants to vote on who stays and who leaves. Timber and Seebra sob at the prospect of what is to come. They stand side by side facing their judges as they hold hands in anticipation.

"Hold your courses, Ladies! As with all games, especially ones played on t.v., there is a cruel cinnamon twist!" says Creign Kitchell enthusiastically after being handed a note.

This must mean there's going to be another competition that gives them a chance to come back or that no one goes home the first week. I hate to see anyone go home the first week since we've just started. Avery's delight over her victory has left much room for compassion.

"Ladies, please take your place back on your plate," Creign Kitchell instructs Timber and Seebra.

They hug each other happily and run over to their assigned plate.

"Instead of your friends deciding which two of you will go home today…the audience gets to decide who out of all eight of you has to leave today!"

"WHAT?!" Avery yells before she could think not to. She is thunderstruck.

The audience stands and cheers as Timber and Seebra are the most popular players on the show.

"That's right! Audience, now Fate Holders, feel under your seat and pull out the remote-control mechanism that has been placed there."

The audience quickly sits and searches under their seats for the power wielding mechanism. Meanwhile, Avery is beside herself saying to the mentors, "But I won! This isn't fair!"

"Hey, it's unreality t.v., nothing's fair," Worthy tells her nonchalantly.

The audience is now anxiously ready to vote. On instruct, they press the corresponding button to the contestant's name they'd like to see leave. The jumbo screens dramatically blaze the contestant's name and picture as their percentage of votes come in. They all look at the screen as they shake and cry.

Avery is grounded by two-parts fury, one-part confidence, and one-part uncertainty. *They can't still hate me after I've done so many embarrassing things to prove that I'm a human just like them.*

The cameras are focused on the face of each contestant as the calculation takes an exorbitantly long time to reveal itself. All that is heard is the manufactured sounds of rhythmic beeps to indicate the formulation of a solution. Finally, there is movement on the screen as the percentages are revealed.

By ninety-eight percent, the audience has chosen Avery

to be voted off the show. The only reason it isn't a hundred percent is because two devices malfunctioned.

Avery is at a loss for feeling as Creign Kitchell announces in a profoundly sad host voice, "Avery…I'm sorry, but you're still a Loser At Gaining. Please pack your lunch and go."

And just like that, the light on her plate goes out and Avery is escorted out of the soundstage amongst cheers and jeers without so much as a good-bye from anyone.

The sunlight strikes her eyes like a prize fighter's punch. Another set of camera crew is awaiting her shameful exit as she angrily stumbles her way down the steps to find her suitcases waiting for her.

The producer, Doss, itching for a statement to make the day's headline, stands gleefully next to the invasive window to the world's prying eyes and asks, "Avery, any comment?"

Avery stops, looks at her, takes a long quivering breath, incredulous, her voice trembling, "I won! Fair and square. I followed your rules, did everything I was told to and you still set me up to fail! When is everyone going to stop punishing me?"

Doss is speechless as she didn't expect this reaction, if the show weren't streaming and airing live, she would have cut this part out.

"How do you feel?" another voice from behind the camera rings out, picking up where Doss dropped off.

Avery opens her mouth to respond but nothing comes out. She tries again. Then tears up.

"How are you supposed to feel when the whole world hates you?"

Suddenly the blaring sound of a horn blasts through their conversation and a rickety, smoking, and rattling food truck pulls up.

"Uh…so...this is your ride home, Avery," says the abashed producer now regretting such a disrespectful and ridiculous send off.

Avery looks at the white and orange paint peeled truck as it arrives on four donut wheels with the words "Loser at Gaining on Board." It pulls up and comes to an exhausted, smoke sputtering stop. She stands in utter disbelief that this is where her life has landed, even after playing by the rules.

Something clicks. Avery snatches her pride back and gives the producer a withering look and asserts, "I'll walk!"

She turns and angry walks down the street with her designer suitcases in tow as if she had trained them on how to be in lockstep with her.

The camera watches Avery go down the street until she turns the corner. An intern, at-the-ready to make his bones in this business from someone else's skin, takes out his phone and yells, "I'll follow her!" and takes off down the street.

"Rocker!" Doss calls out.

The intern stops and turns around.

"Let her go."

Chapter Nineteen
Fed Up

Realizing, after four blocks, that she is barefoot and barely dressed after stepping on a rock that painfully shakes her back to civilization, Avery ducks into an unnamed, exclusive, nine-star hotel. Everyone in the lobby turns to look due to her speed, attire, and the rumbling suitcases.

"Give me the biggest ass suite you have!"

Having seen what happened to her on "Losers At Gaining" while watching the live-feed on her phone, the stunned and sympathetic front desk clerk orders Avery's bags be handled immediately and a blanket to cover her with.

As Avery rides up the private elevator with the sworn-to-privacy assistant assigned to her by the hotel, Avery's anger simmers to pain and hurt feelings. She knew the booing and chanting at "Weight Wanters" was a result of her cheating but this time she legitimately won, and America still wanted her gone. Everyone hates her and she doesn't know how to process it. Her phone rings, chimes and beeps with Dalton's calls, texts, and alerts about her latest events; something she used to look forward to. Now she can't stomach to look at her phone or even herself in the invasive reflective glass door that houses the image of her wrapped like a lost child after a storm waiting for someone to rescue her.

Eleanor, her personal assistant is a petite woman in her late forties with a stern gives-no-for-an-answer face and only accepts yes ma'am as a response. She is wearing a brown business skirt suit and two-inch heels and stares straight ahead, prepared to handle anything on the other side of this flying box.

The doors slide open to a plush and beautifully furnished four-bedroom apartment suite. All Avery wants to do is take a long bath and crawl into bed for the next six months. A basket of imported and exotic fruits, chesses, and a menagerie of petit fours await her pickings. Right now, she can't even think of food after the last seven days she's had of mindlessly gorging herself for that stupid show.

Eleanor moves into action as if reading her mind and runs a hot bubble bath in the enormous bathroom. She sets the water timer to a certain temperature and depth and leaves the room so as not to be in Avery's way. She stealthily moves about the apartment like a ninja on a secret mission. Her feet barely touch the floor as she sweeps from room to room to prepare the atmosphere to one that is homelike.

Avery's phone rings again and her anger begins to gain

momentum as she decides to get this conversation over with.

"Hey Doll!" calls out the soul-free elated voice on the other end before she can even say hello.

"Once again, Dalton, what the hell?!"

"What the hell? What an exit! The best in unreal reality show history!"

"But I won that round by a frickin' molten cake mud-slide! And they still kicked me off! How is that possible?"

"You gotta read your contract, Doll. On page five hundred eighty-six, it clearly states in microscopic print, 'Rules are subject to change at whim of producer as it may benefit the show no matter how much it may hurt, harm, or humiliate the participant.' And you agreed to it."

Dalton already had that page dog-eared and highlighted the day he thoroughly read the contract and knew he'd have to regurgitate it to her, as he does for most of his clients because they do not read their contracts completely, if at all. They just take him at his word. Big mistake.

"Yes, but..." she gives up. There's no winning here.

"Forget that! Bigger news. After Zavier saw you gain so much weight so fast and fill out, he's willing to bring you back as the new face of his new sizeable line of dresses called, Drezz to Exzezz.' That is, if you can get to a size fourteen in three weeks for the re-launch of your career. I tell ya, Doll, after today's incredibly embarrassing and pathetic performance, I almost shed a tear, and I don't have any! You have a chance to be on top again, bigger than ever, literally!"

It was Avery's plan to disappear for a while and maybe quit the business. But now her competitive appetite is once again spurred.

"You really think so?"

"Absolutely! People love to see the rise and fall and rise then final fail of their icons! Right now, everyone loves dejected bargain basement Avery."

"They love me?"

"Yes! Who couldn't love someone who falls flat on their ass, arms flailing, legs akimbo, and underwear-free in such a public way…twice?"

Not quite sure if that makes her feel any better, Avery takes a moment to think.

Moment over.

"I'm in!!"

"Great! Now get back in there and order four pizzas and be ready to meet Dr. Fillupps tomorrow at 11:00 a.m."

"Dr who? At what time? For what?"

"I made an appointment for you to meet Dr. Fillupps. He's a drastic surgeon at the Weight A Minute Clinic. He can have you plumped up in a day and healed up in a week. Plenty of time before the launch."

Avery's head is spinning. "So…"

"I'll text you the address. Let me know how it goes."

He's gone.

"Oh, how I love to hear you spin and grin your clients while we shop," purrs Araya seductively as Dalton slowly unbuttons the high-end, high-hemmed, skin-tight, black dress she has just finished modeling for him.

He smiles proudly and nuzzles her neck.

"Will you be taking this dress also?" asks the salesgirl.

"Definitely," confirms Dalton. He reaches into his pocket and pulls out a black card, "Just put it on this. All of it."

"Great," says the salesgirl as she looks around the elegant outer dressing room area at the twenty-three dresses, eight dress pants, six purses, ten blouses, thirteen pairs of shoes, and five coats.

"I'm uh…going to need help getting out of this," says Araya helplessly.

"Oh sure, no problem," the salesgirl responds.

"That's okay, I've got it," Dalton tells her as he snaps off the price tag of the dress and hands it to her, "You can start ringing these up."

Araya leads Dalton into the private dressing room by his tie.

Avery's outrage and lament has less of a sting as she gets on with the business of erasing the day. She thinks about her vengeful comeback as she detaches herself from the body disgracing "Losers At Gaining" costume and steps into the long deep tub with pink iridescent bubbles. The temperature is perfect as she sinks down into the comforting fluid that envelops her embattled frame. Eleanor set the tub timer to reheat the water every fifteen minutes for the next four hours so that Avery can luxuriate without lifting a finger while she unpacks her clothes and hangs them neatly in the huge walk-in closet/dressing room. Eleanor sets a tray of food by the bed when she hears Avery stir from the tub. Eleanor's cozy and average lifestyle room is across the hall from Avery's. It is the Assistant's Quarters that consists of a living room, bedroom, bathroom and a kitchen. She is to be on call twenty-four hours. There is a button in every room of Avery's suite where she can ring for Eleanor as well as a hand-held device that sits by her bed.

Avery presses the button on the rim of the tub. After a light ring, Eleanor answers the device that is clipped on her ear,

"What can I get for you?" she asks lightly.

"Please order me two Big Burden Burritos, three Maxed-Out Nachos, five Champ Churros, the One-Ton Taco, and an extra-large colossal Double Sugar Delight soda.

"Consider it done."

Avery leans back in the tub, closes her eyes and visualizes her comeback outfits and statements.

The next day, Avery arrives at Dr. Fillupps' office at the "Weight A Minute Clinic" in West Los Angeles fifteen minutes early. She looks at all the cliché success story posters on the pale lavender walls with the gratuitous before and after pictures of slim, disheveled women who are miraculously introduced to cosmetics, ironed clothing and a brush after they have gained their desired weight. And it all can take place in a matter of weeks. Just what Avery needs.

A size fourteen twenty-nothing receptionist/greeter/goal for every poor soul who walks in, wearing the office uniform of tight white pants and snug white t-shirt that reads: "Plus and Highly Favored" and black high heels, (obviously, a choice Dr. Fillups made), sits behind the counter. She sees Avery and unnecessarily gets up and comes around the front; standing, posing, dazzling, the proverbial after picture eager to welcome and be envied. Even though Avery is wearing yoga pants, a hoodie and dark glasses, Miss Perfection recognizes her.

"Hi Avery, and welcome to the Weight A Minute Clinic. I just need you to sign in with the time you arrived and the time of your appointment."

Perfection walks back around to her chair after being fully assessed by Avery. She watches Avery very closely, half not believing her one-time idol is here and half at how bad she looks.

"You can have a seat anywhere and Dr. Fillups will eat with you soon."

Avery sits in a wide barstool style blue beanbag chair that feels like a pile of mashed potatoes.

"Can I get you anything while you wait, soda, candy, cake, pasta, marshmallows?" asks Perfection solicitously.

"No thanks."

"Well Dr. Fillupps is going to change all that," Perfection tells Avery in her best encourage-the-down-and-out tone.

Avery half nods wishing she would just shut the hell up and disappear. Just when it couldn't get any worse, Perfection 2.0 enters through a side door, in the same attire, with a clipboard.

"Avery, you can come this way."

Avery struggles her way out and down from the mushy clutches of the chair and makes her way to Perfection 2.0.

As they walk down the long corridor Avery asks, "So, are you one of Dr. Fillupps' success stories?"

Perfection 2.0 laughs, "Oh no, I was born this way. Just one of the few lucky ones, I guess."

If it weren't against the law, Avery would have kicked her legs right from under her.

They arrive at the monster.

"Okay, let's check your weight to see where we're starting from. Please remove your jacket, glasses and shoes so that we may get an accurate reading."

Avery follows directions. Her heart races in recollection of every time she has stepped on a scale, as it has been riddled with horrible outcomes. *Why is there always an audience when I get weighed?* What she really wants to do is run out of there, forget the whole thing, and try on her own to regain some modicum of dignity. Reluctantly, she steps on the scale and braces herself. When her weight registers, Perfection 2.0 gives an involuntary gasp. Avery quickly steps off.

Perfection 2.0 moves back as if she were contagious.

"Ummm... You can go into room three, change into the dressing gown and Dr. Fillupps will be in shortly after."

Avery makes an ugly face at her when she turns her back.

Ten minutes later, Avery is sitting on the examining table shivering in a noisy tissue paper dressing gown that opens in the front. Dr. Fillupps, a short stout balding of a man with the eyes of a crow enters the room followed by Perfection 2.0. *Oh no! Not her again!* Avery doesn't want **her** here during such a vulnerable moment. She hands him Avery's chart and steps back to observe.

"Well, I definitely see why you're here. Take off your gown and let's have a closer look," he states matter-of-factly with a hint of disgust.

Avery stands and removes the gown, vulnerable in her panties and bra. She can feel Perfection 2.0 staring at her in a happy-I'm-not-her way.

Dr. Fillupps scrutinizes Avery from all sides and angles as if inspecting a used car. He shakes his head and sighs as he looks at her chart.

"It says here you weigh a hundred twenty pounds. How

did you get so out of control?"

"I've tried everything," Avery's voice cracks as her throat becomes dry with shame, "That's why I'm here, Dr. Fillupps. My career and social life depend on it."

Dr. Fillupps picks up a marker and draws on Avery's body as he talks, "We'll start here by rounding out your cheeks, chin, and jawline. You definitely need breast implants and fat injections in your arms, stomach, sides, hips, back, thighs, and calves. Stretch marks will be an extra fifteen hundred a mark, for the look of an authentic weight gain. As far as your rear, you will need a separate procedure called a buttoctomy."

"A what? What is that?" Avery asks incredulously.

"It's where I surgically attach a pair of bodacious buttocks from a deceased patient who generously donated theirs for this type of emergency."

Avery, looking like a graffitied wall from face to ankles, asks in disbelief, "You mean I would have the ass of a dead person?"

"Do you want perfection or not? Let me know now because we are in limited supply and there is a long waiting list. I'm bumping your rear up from the bottom as a favor to Dalton."

"It...it just sounds like I wouldn't be me anymore,"

Avery tells him.

"Isn't that the point?" Dr. Fillupps asks flippantly with a raised eyebrow, clearly unaccustomed to resistance.

Avery's head is spinning, "Yeah, I guess but…"

"Okay, well, you can go a more natural route and have drastic surgery which is a gastric no-pass where I go in and widen your stomach to the size of a large watermelon in order for your body to catch and hold all the fat and calories you put in without the threat of any of it ever being burned off during activity."

"Will it stop at a size fourteen?"

"You will stop gaining once you hit four hundred pounds. How you manage where and how you want to stop is totally up to you."

Avery shakes her head and looks up trying to decide which plan is best for her.

"I do have one last option and that is to put you on the Upsyzeum pill."

"What will that do?"

"Each pill is three thousand calories and will quadruple your appetite."

"That option sounds perfect. Let's do that."

For the first time during this visit, Avery feels hopeful and smiles. J*ust to take a pill and eat? Nothing could be easier and less painful.*

. "Great. I'll send over a prescription and you can pick it up next door." Dr. Fillups sits down at his desk and types as Avery puts back on her gown. "Each pill costs twelve-hundred dollars. I'll start you off with a two weeks' supply. You need to take one pill with three large scoops of butter pecan ice cream three times a day before each meal. Now, if you have any peanut allergies, are lactose intolerant or just have plain common sense please do not take this."

"I have none of those," Avery says happily, only hearing that this is the solution to all her problems.

"Perfect. I'll start you on it today. For the first three days, for the pill to completely be effective, you must do as little activity as possible. If you can, have someone prepare and bring your food. Only get up when absolutely necessary, like going to the bathroom or if there's a fire. Make sure to read the side effects so you'll know what to expect during this treatment." Dr. Fillups turns around and stands up. "Good luck on your way to dignified living."

"Thank you Dr. Fillups, this is just what I needed," Avery says as she tears up.

"You're very welcome, Avery," he responds as he shakes her hand.

"Do I need to come back for a follow-up?"

"Only if you're a success."

Dr. Fillupps leaves the room and Perfection 2.0 tells her, "You can get dressed now. Oh, and use the Wipe Aways to clean your face. The rest of the marks will come off in the shower. Good luck." She leaves the room.

Avery gives her the finger out of pure jealousy of her not having to do anything to walk this earth looking like that. It is then that Avery catches a glimpse of herself in the full-length mirror where she sees her face completely marked up with circles, arrows, lines, and dots. She opens her gown to see the same marks all over the front, side and back of her body, like the blueprint for a non-existent building. For the first time ever, Avery feels disgusted and ashamed of her apparent imperfections.

"That's okay, perfection is back on its way," she tells herself trying to shake it off, because if she doesn't, she won't be able to leave the room.

Chapter Twenty
Food Awakening

Two hours later…

Avery is back at the hotel, showered, and happily propped up in bed with the television remote control, ready to start the pill perfecting program. She decided to stay at the hotel for the next two weeks since she has the convenience of built-in accommodations, no paparazzi, and Eleanor at her beck and call. Avery called Eleanor ahead of time with a list of all the foods she will need and how the week is to play out.

Avery pulls out the Upsyzeum Pill bottle from the bag to read the instructions. There is a separate folded sheet of paper titled: Side Effects. She unfolds it and reads:

Side Effects May and Most LikelyWill Include:

DRY MOUTH

CHAPPED LIPS

STUFFY NOSE

WEIGHT LOSS

DOUBLE VISION

DIZZINESS

SHORTNESS OF BREATH

ITCHY SCALP

SCALY SCALP

RASH

DIARRHEA

CONSTIPATION

INSOMNIA

BACK PAIN

JOINT PAIN

MUSCLE PAIN

MUSCLE WEAKNESS

MIGRAINES

GINGIVITIS

ITCHING

LETHARGY

HEADACHES

FAINTING

SWOLLEN GLANDS

SORE THROAT

GALLSTONES

HIGH BLOOD PRESSURE

LOW BLOOD PRESSURE

DIABETES

HIVES

DEHYDRATION

KIDNEY DAMAGE

LIVER DAMAGE

CRAMPS

GOITERS

ANXIETY

WAXIE EARS

CHILLS

HOT FLASHES

COLD SWEATS

NIGHT SWEATS

SWEATY PITS

SWEATY PALMS

SWEATY FEET

HIGH CHOLESTEROL

TUBERCULOSIS

RAPID HEARBEAT

LOWERED HEARTBEAT

MOUTH SOARS

MONONUCLEOSIS

CHICKEN POX

SWELLING

SPONTANEOUS COUGHS

SNEEZING

INFLUENZA

JOINT STIFFNESS

HEMORRHOIDS

NERVE DAMAGE

RUNNY EYES

RUNNY NOSE

RUNNY STOOLS

MEMORY LOSS

ASTHMA

ACNE

LOSS OF TASTE

LOSS OF LASHES

ARTHRITIS

FACIAL TICS

FACIAL PARALYSIS

VERICOSE VEINS

VISION LOSS

HEARING LOSS

BLEEDING GUMS

TOOTH LOSS

NAIL LOSS

HAIR LOSS

RINGING EARS

EAR-ACHES

BLOOD CLOTS

BLOTCHY SKIN

WELTS

HERPES

YEAST INFECTIONS

URINARY TRACT INFECTIONS

EXCESSIVE EAR AND NOSE HAIR GROWTH

VOMITING

NAUSEA

NIGHTMARES

DAYMARES

MEASLES

MUMPS

ANEMIA

RICKETS

SHINGLES

LOCK JAW

LOWERED IMMUNE SYSTEM

HEART ATTACK

STROKE

PNUEMONIA

FIBROIDS

NUMBNESS

SENSITIVE SKIN

LOSS OF APPETITE

VEGETABLE CRAVINGS

FRUIT CRAVINGS

HIGH ENERGY

SPONTANEOUS DISCHARGES

CHLAMYDIA

FORGETFULNESS

LIVER FAILURE

STREP THROAT

NIGHT TERRORS

SLEEP WALKING

SLEEP EATING

SLEEP CONFESSING

SLEEP SCREAMING

SLEEP SHOPPING

SLEEP DRIVING

SLEEP DRESSING

SLEEP FIGHTING

LOSS OF SEX DRIVE

RESTLESS LEGS

NARCOLEPSY

EPILEPSY

DRY SKIN

SCALY SKIN

BLOODY NOSE

EXCESSIVE GAS

EXCESSIVE HICCUPS

TUMORS

HALLUCINATIONS

HALITOSIS

FALSE PREGNANCY

PREMATURE MENOPAUSE

HYPER THYROID

HYPO THYROID

WHOOPING COUGH

SCARLET FEVER

PSORIASIS

BRONCHITIS

BRITTLE BONES

LOSS OF SMELL

PARALYSIS

DEPRESSION

INTERNAL BLEEDING

EXTERNAL BLEEDING

SWOLLEN JOINTS

NEUROPATHY

ULCERS

RHEUMATOID ARTHRITIS

DIFFICULTY SWALLOWING

NECK STIFFNESS

CHEST PAINS

HEPATITIS

ALOPECIA

SCARRING

MOOD SWINGS

IRRATIONAL DECISIONS

IRRATIONAL THOUGHTS

IRRATIONAL ACTIONS

RECKLESS BEHAVIOR

TREMORS

PSYCHOSIS

LOSS OF BALANCE

LOSS OF JUDGEMENT

LOSS OF PRACTICALITY

LOSS OF COMMON SENSE

LOSS OF INTEREST

LOSS OF RELATIONSHIPS

LOSS OF DREAMS

LOSS OF AMBITION

But at least you'll have the body you want

Avery tosses the paper aside, opens the bottle, pops a pill in her mouth and starts to eat the large bowl of butter pecan ice cream. She scrolls through the hundreds of channels on her television where all the programs reveal their obsession for weight gain and weight shame; how to do it, where to get, why you should, how you should and where you should. Avery is quite interested in these shows as she is now part of the growing population and will be having her own masterful reveal soon.

"Welcome to the Dr. Mel show! Today's shame-filled topic is 'Weight Loss After Marriage and How it Ruins the Sex Life.'"

Click.

"Coming up, after the break, on Mary Stringer, we'll talk to Morris who has a strange fetish and serious dilemma."

A man in silhouette sits behind a screen, fidgeting as he speaks, "Mary, I love thin women. Please help me tell my family!"

Click.

"Tune in tonight for Skylar Barrie's Love Thigh Neighbor."

Click.

A beautiful countryside cascades the screen with tranquil lakes with swans, beautiful trees with leaves dancing in the breeze as the melodic tune of birds sing happily. A sprawling mansion reveals itself with a pool, bar, cozy lounge chairs, cabanas and towels beckoning for the viewer's company. Buffet tables, filled with the feasts of seven holidays, creates a gastric maze throughout the property as a soft sympathetic voiceover croons, "Are you tired of being underweight, overlooked, underwhelming…an after-thought in society? Well come to Upscale and feed your face while you feed your soul." Words scroll across the bottom of the sumptuous foods, "Upscale, where your weight can finally be over."

After finishing her dosage, Eleanor brings Avery two foot-long double meat and cheese pastrami sandwiches, two large orders of steak fries and two slices of red velvet cake, all to be washed down with a liter of orange lime soda. Avery continues watching as she eats the sloppy and decadent meal from a tray in bed with the excitement of the dream body that is in store for her. After flipping through a few more channels, she settles on "The Nora Gintry Show," where beloved Nora has been struggling with her weight for the past six weeks and talks about her big life changing reveal to making it to a size fourteen as she holds up a size two pair of jeans.

"Girl…I remember wearing these to hang out with the President on casual day at the White House and thought I was looking fine!"

A picture of her and the President two months ago appears on the massive screen next to her. The audience, made up of mostly size fourteen women with a smattering of slender ones, gasps then laughs uproariously. The camera makes sure to focus on the shame of the slender women. Nora is joyous in her victory then turns on the insightful somberness.

"I presented like I was so confident, strong, self-assured, when in reality, I had no right to be. I felt like a failure. Look at me! I was a mess. I can't believe I even passed the security check. They really should have sent me home."

The audience applauds in agreement.

"Right after that, I was so distraught I slipped back into the abyss of under indulging and not being able to resist my love for tomatoes and sprouts."

The audience wipes away tears as some relate, feel pity, and inspired to see their sacred idol having issues and trying to put her life back together. The strugglers uncomely cry and are comforted by the victors via back rubs and head pats.

"But this is it for sure. If you ever see me eating somewhere with less than sixty-five hundred calories on my plate, you call me on it!"

The audience jumps to their feet and chants her name. Nora stands up and addresses her nation, "I will never ever go down another dress or pants size again! Thanks to Araya and Weight Wanters!"

Click!

Avery slowly opens her eyes. Her vision is blurry from a deep and dizzying sleep. She blinks several times and looks around the room. It is unfamiliar. She moves her arm to wipe her eyes and feels the pinch of the I.V. needle.

"She's waking up!" exclaims a familiar voice.

"Oh, thank goodness!" says another familiar voice.

"Hey, we're right here. Wake up and talk to us. Let us know you're okay."

Avery looks around and is finally able to focus then realizes she is in a hospital room. She tries to sit up but the hatchet splitting headache knocks her back.

"Whoa, take it easy, Soldier."

Avery looks to her left and sees Dalton then looks to her right to see who is holding her hand. It's Thian. He looks at her with relieved teary eyes and caresses her forehead and hair.

"You gave us quite a scare," he says, choking up.

"Wha…what happened?" Avery asks weakly.

"You passed out during the photo shoot. Don't worry, we captured it all and it's been breaking news everywhere. They have been playing it all day, over and over and over again. Free publicity magic!" declares Dalton in delight.

"How did I pass out?"

"You were dehydrated and lost all circulation from those jeans you were entombed in. The paramedics had to cut you out of them," explains Thian.

"That didn't make it to the news. Zavier would have had a complete fit," says Dalton then laughs to himself at his own unintended joke, "A designer having a fit, that's good. Gotta work that in somewhere."

Avery looks under the covers in horror and cries weakly, "Noooo! Do you know what I had to do and how long it took me to get into those jeans?"

Her head is pounding.

Thian calms her down and places the covers up to her neck.

"Don't worry about that. Just concentrate on getting better. Your health is more important."

"Yeah, don't worry, we got the shot," Dalton tells her as he's texting.

A nurse comes in to change her I.V. bag. Avery panics.

"How many calories are in that?"

"I already checked it out. You can afford two more for the day," Dalton assures her.

Thian simmers, "Dalton, she needs to be on solid foods."

"Fine, but don't overdo it with the carrots. You still have the Oscars coming up."

Thian rolls his eyes then turns his attention back to Avery.

"You were having some scary bouts of hallucinations about winning at gaining and having to be a size fourteen."

"Yeah, it was quite scary. For a moment there, I thought we were going to have to have you put down. Some things should never come out of one's mouth, dehydration or not," says Dalton.

Thian gives him a look of disdain but Dalton is preoccupied with his phone.

"Listen, her heal…"

"Gotta go. Press is downstairs waiting for a statement."

Dalton leaves the room then pokes his head in the doorway and says, "Hey Doll…"

Avery looks over at him and smiles sweetly, anticipating his words of comfort.

"Fix yourself up a little, you're gonna be live from here in five minutes. Your fans have shut down the city waiting to hear about and from you."

He's gone.

Avery slightly shakes her head and smiles at Thian as he looks at her lovingly.

"I still have fans?"

"Of course, you do. And your biggest one is right here."

"My biggest most handsome one."

They smile at each other.

"Wow! That was some dream. It all felt so real."

"Baby, our whole life is a dream. And it is real," says Thian as he leans in to kiss her.

Avery giggles, "You really want to kiss me even though I have pass out breath?"

He laughs back, "I would kiss you with any kind of breath."

She closes her eyes with the contentment of his love as the wisps of his five o'clock shadow and his masculine breath hover over her lips.

"I love you, Thian," she says softly.

"I love you too, Corrinne."

Avery opens her eyes, "Wait, What? What did you say? What did you call me?! Who did you call me?!" Avery repeats this as she flails her arms and throws her fists.

Eleanor throws a small cup of water on her face and shocks Avery out of her night fighting. She shakes out of it and looks around with wild wide eyes and blurred vision. She is burning up. Her sheets are soaked with a combination of sweat, urine and vomit stains. Her stomach is churning, rumbling, and bloated. She feels hungry and nauseous at the same time as her head thumps to the rhythm of her rapid heartbeat. Eleanor watches Avery closely as she struggles to collect herself.

"I have to go to the bathroom," Avery says weakly.

Eleanor helps her out of the bed and into the bathroom. Avery stumbles over to the sink to get a glimpse of herself in the mirror. After a few minutes of blur, she is able to focus and sees an unrecognizable image staring back at her. Her once perfect skin is now porous and covered in red and crusty splotches, her hair is matted, there are three sties clustered on each eye, her lips are blistered, her cheeks are bloated, her hands are shaking uncontrollably and her pajamas are covered in vomit and an unknown green mucus.

"Eleanor, please bring me my pills."

Eleanor looks at Avery with the concern of not wanting to aid her in killing herself.

"Please, bring them to me," she requests again in her

newly hoarse voice.

Eleanor leaves to get them. Avery examines the rest of her body and notices welts and scabs as well as an ugly discharge from her belly button. She stands and looks at herself.

"But at least you'll have the body you want," she says to the image mocking her in the mirror.

Eleanor somberly returns with the Upsyzeum pills and a fresh pair of pajamas. She is not supposed to show any emotion or opinion towards her clients. She could already be fired for sleeping on the floor at the foot of Avery's bed without permission, but she knew those pills would not set well with her after reading the side effects when she cleaned up her room. Eleanor had a feeling Avery would not be able to ask for help when needed. And she was right.

Avery takes the bottle from Eleanor and tries to open it, but her hands are shaking too much. Eleanor offers no assistance. She should have left the room by now, but she stays and watches instead. Avery doesn't seem to mind. After several minutes of trying and pounding the bottle in anger on the side of the counter, the lid flips off. Avery gives a small victorious laugh then looks at the bottle. She walks unsteadily across the bathroom and flushes them down the toilet. Eleanor almost tears in relief. Avery looks over at her.

Eleanor straightens up, "Bath?"

"Please," Avery manages to croak out.

"Consider it done."

After a long, cool bath, Avery, with the help of Eleanor, washed her caked-up brittle hair where several clumps of tresses managed to escape into her hands from the toxins that were attacking them. It only took two Upsyzeum pills and six hours for Avery's body to overreact. She thought possibly she would suffer only one of the side effects, not a whole carnival of them. Eleanor blow dries her hair on cool so as not to further irritate the soars on her scalp that are starting to scab.

Having been a nurse in her previous career, Eleanor knew just how to handle all the beasts as they appeared. Avery is exhausted, defeated, but mostly angry. Eleanor helps her to bed with the new linens and duvet she changed while Avery was soaking in the tub. Avery asks Eleanor for her phone in almost a whisper as her throat feels like she has been gargling with razors.

"I'll be right outside if you need me."

"Thanks."

This is the most Avery has said please and thank you in

the past fourteen years.

Eleanor leaves the room.

Avery speed dials Dalton.

"Hey Doll. Did you see Dr. Fillups?"

Avery answers in an inaudible whisper's whisper.

"You're gonna have to speak up and speak fast because I've got clients who are actually working right now," he tells her in his usual obnoxious way.

But this time his tone sparks a rage in Avery that she has never felt before. She always took his attitude with a grain of fame and a stack of cash, but this is different. She's sick and has no idea if she'll ever get back to her original health. Because of his gain-weight-fast ideas, she is left humiliated and possibly ill and scarred for the rest of her life. Her heart starts banging at her chest as if it's going to kick it open. An inner swelling in her belly lends way to a deep and fresh inhale that allows a guttural roar from her suffering throat to her mouth.

"Go to hell, Dalton! Go deep, long, and heavy to hell! You selfish, hateful, troll of a non-human-piece-of-shit-crap-loser-ass-in-a-suit-bottom-feeding-barnacle-eating-bastard!" she venomously spits out loud and rapidly.

"Wha…what the hell's gotten into you?!" he asks, taken completely off guard.

"I've gotten into me! That's what! And your irrelevant ass is gaslit fired!"

She hangs up first. That being the most satisfying part of it.

Avery falls back onto her pillow and exhales heavily then laughs. She is tickled with the joy of feeling in control. Her joyous laugh is silent as her throat can no longer summon sound and tears roll down her face. She starts to feel energized and kicks her legs in the air as if pedaling a bike. She does this for the next two minutes then slows down and finally stops out of pure exhaustion. Avery looks terrible but feels fantastic.

Dalton looks shocked and saddened after Avery hangs up. Araya puts her hands on his cheeks.

"Honey, what's wrong?"

"She fired me. She really fired me after all these years." his voice quivers barely above a whisper.

"Who fired you?" Araya whispers back

"Avery," he barely gets it out.

"Oh Dalty," she says softly as she gently caresses his face.

They are silent as she reflects his heartbroken eyes back

at him. Suddenly, they burst into maniacal laughter.

"It's about damn time! I'm so glad I won't have to tell her that I signed Rella and that she got the Zavier contract today!"

"You always come out on top, Baby!" Araya tells him.

"Just the way you like it!"

"You know it!"

They kiss passionately as they grab inappropriately at each other; completely ignoring the confused and slightly terrified luxury car salesman sitting behind the desk waiting for their signature.

Eleanor softly knocks on the door. She has no idea of Avery's victory.

"I have some broth and tea you need to eat to replenish your nutrients and flush out your system. May I come in?"

Avery props herself up and rings the bell twice for yes. Eleanor had set up an easy system for Avery to communicate with her without talking. She enters and places the food tray on Avery's lap.

"I loaded your t.v. with nothing but comedies. Laughter will be the best medicine for you right now," she says as she places the remote control next to Avery and heads towards the door.

Avery picks up the bell and rings it three times, meaning she wants Eleanor's attention. Eleanor stops and looks at Avery as she writes on a pad of paper.

Avery holds it up for Eleanor to read, "Stay and watch with me."

Eleanor smiles.

"Sure."

Eleanor sits in one of the plush round chairs next to the bed as Avery scrolls through her choices of comedies to watch.

Knowing that she is way overstepping her bounds, Eleanor states, "You should also flush whoever suggested those pills."

Avery puts down the remote control and writes on the pad and shows it to her, "Consider it done."

Chapter Twenty-One
Meat and Greet

Avery decided to drive herself to the new and exclusive retreat in Malibu. She just needs to get away and figure out what to do next. She has more than enough money to continue her lavish lifestyle for three eternities without ever having to work again. She has no dependents, no pets (because she hates animals), not even a plant, and her parents are set for life. For the first time, Avery has no one telling her how to look, what to wear, what to eat, what not to eat, who to date, what to say, how to say it, when to say it, where to live, where to go, how to get there, when to be there, how to stand, how to walk, how to pose, how to smile, when to laugh, where to be seen, who to be seen with, what time to go to bed, what time to wake up, what products to use, or who to impress. Nothing and no one is stopping her from doing what she wants. And right now, all Avery wants to do is drive her new red sports car up Pacific Coast Highway, better known as PCH, but Avery fondly calls it "The Peach."

It took three and a half weeks for Avery to truly recover from the two doses of the Upsyzeum pills. After Avery went into cardiac arrest following her second dose, she was rushed to the hotel's fully functional and staffed hospital located in the basement. Eleanor was specifically assigned to Avery as she was viewed as a high-risk, high-profile guest to ensure her safety while undercover as her "assistant." Had Eleanor not been in place, Avery would have died alone in that hotel suite trying to keep up with phantom standards. She had stuffed herself with so much sodium, sugar, carbs, and fat along with those pills, that it completely changed her body's chemistry and functions to the point her heart did not know what else to do. It was confused and exhausted from the fight of the enemies she had let in. Fortunately, Eleanor was there to give her CPR and revive her in time before being taken down to the hospital. Following treatment for various infections inside and outside of her body, Avery was released back up to her room. She had no idea Eleanor had saved her life nor exactly where the hospital had been located. The whole situation was very discreet. No family members, friends or press were called to the scene. The week and a half of her hospital stay was a haze of in and out of consciousness, hallucinations, and nightmares.

Eleanor was key in her recuperation and full recovery and they became good friends, something that was quite foreign to Avery.

The cynical part of her is still waiting to see a picture of herself at her worst and for Eleanor to turn up on television talking about their experience. Even though she signed a non-disclosure and privacy agreement with the hotel, the payment and notoriety for such an encounter would well cover any costs of legal fees and loss of integrity.

At this point, Avery doesn't even care. Let them see her war wounds from a much unneeded and self-inflicted battle. She had reached the pit of degradation and beyond, so nothing more could touch her. She is free. Free to be Avery. Whoever the hell that is.

After the twenty-five-minute drive up The Peach, Avery arrives at her hidden destination. No signs. No greeters. Just a call box.

"Hello, how may I help you?" a kind songbird southern voice asks.

"Um…I'm not sure but I think I'm in the right place but maybe not…," Avery stammers as she is not accustomed to having to explain her presence. She was always allowed in. No questions asked no I.D. required.

Eleanor had recommended she go to this particular resort to sort herself, figure out next steps, and explore life away from it all. Avery liked the idea so much that she bought out the place for the next eight weeks. She didn't want to share her self-exploration with others because she didn't want to feel self-conscious and worried about what others thought of her. As a special favor to Eleanor, the owners permitted it and cancelled the other guests that were scheduled in order to accommodate Avery.

"Is this Avery?" the voice sings.

"Yes…yes I am," she stammers again, taken aback at how happy the voice sounded that it might be her.

"Well come on up, Sugar, we've been waiting for you. So glad you're here!"

The tall golden gates open inward in grand style, smoothly and noise-free. Avery is comforted by the welcoming sight in front of her as she drives through the gates onto a perfectly paved driveway lined with clusters of red rose bushes that fragrant the air. Butterflies and hummingbirds go about their business fluttering and chatting as she cruises by. She can hear the ocean waves as she approaches the sprawling one-story building that looks more like a home than a resort. A feeling of warmth comes over Avery as she parks her car and steps out. The giant front door opens and out gallops a tall man in his mid-forties, with a surprisingly well-styled mullet, and a short, roundish, pretty, big-haired blonde, about the same age, in an art-deco dress and high heels. They stand on the porch and wave to Avery.

Ah...the staff greeting committee. I wonder if they'll be taking my bags.

Avery pauses and sniffs the air.

"Is that barbeque I smell?" Avery asks as she walks towards them.

"You know it is, Young Lady! Now get on in here and let's get you some!" the man says in a booming southern voice.

"Okay, but what about my bags?"

"Oh Sugar, don't you worry 'bout them. That'll all be taken care of. Just you come on in and leave the rest to us," says the woman with that same song-bird voice from the gate.

Avery had never been greeted like this. Everything had always been so formal, so regal, so intimidated. *These people act like I am an everyday person, a civilian, a local, someone they know.* She is conflicted in her feelings of this type of familiarity from the servants. When Avery reaches the porch, the woman gives her a big unexpected hug. She smells of expensive intoxicating flowery perfume. The man reaches out his massive hand and shake's Avery's as if they had just made a bet.

"Welcome to Wexx and Bril's!" he says proudly.

"What's Wexon Brills?" asks Avery having never heard of such a place and feeling a bit annoyed with their lack of hierarchical social boundaries.

"Why Darlin' that's us. I'm Wexx."

"And I'm Bril and this is our home."

Avery tries hard not to look as surprised as she is and smiles a gigantic smile to cover her dropped jaw.

"Now you come on in so we can show you where you'll be restin' your bones for the next eight weeks," says Wexx as he escorts her through the front door into the breathtaking foyer with its high ceilings and enormous sparkling chandelier.

Straight forward is a large luxurious yet comfy living room. Avery can see the ocean as if the house was floating on top of it.

"Now, this is the not-so-common area where everyone just hangs out, watches t.v., eats, plays games, chit-chats, whatever they wanna do. But since it's just you, do whatever **you** wanna do," explains Bril.

"To your right, here, are where all the beds and baths are. There are eight private rooms and baths and you are free to use all eight of 'em if you like," Wexx chuckles.

Avery follows them and explores each master bedroom which seems better than the next with their decadent master bath that is fully stocked with plush robes, thick and soft sets of towels, silk pajamas, slippers, candles, soaps, etc…

Avery can't help but notice that Wexx and Bril have been holding hands this whole time. After they finish showing her the theater loaded with the latest movies (and those that will be released soon in theaters), the game room, gym, indoor pool, sauna, bowling alley, and meditation room, Avery is the ready for a nap. But there is still outside to see and getting to bottom of that barbeque smell.

"Now, our living quarters are on the other side of that door," says Bril as she points to the gold double doors in the living room. "Those quarters are usually off limits to guests during their stay, but since you're here alone, if you need anything from us just ring the doorbell."

Bril's statement of 'Since you're here alone' suddenly gives Avery a sense of loneliness even though there is a full staff just for her.

"There's more house than this house?" Avery blurts out as if she just found out there's more ice cream flavors than chocolate and vanilla.

"Oh, Honey, our personal living quarters has another seven bedrooms and baths and is just a little bigger than this side."

"You didn't think we'd give all this room away to strangers and we live like raccoons, did you?" asks Wexx jokingly.

Avery is taken aback at being called out while still trying to soak in the vastness of the situation.

"Uh, no, not raccoons, I thought the house out there was yours." She refers to a house the size of an average three-bedroom home she saw out of one of the windows of the gym.

"No, that's just used for supplies."

Avery catches her breath, "Oh."

"Actually, this house could fit inside our house in Texas. You Californians sure like to live in tight spaces."

"Our home, now yours too, for the next two months, runs on two things. Kindness and respect. We ask that you treat our staff respectfully. All services end at 6:00 p.m., because they have a life too."

"Do they live on the premises?"

"Yes, we have a house for them on the other side of the property," says Wexx.

"And we also ask that you do two kind deeds while you're here. The first one is be kind to yourself and the second is do something kind for someone else outside of this house," Bril tells her.

"Come on, let's get over to what we're famous for!" roars Wexx enthusiastically

"What's that?"

"Barbeque!"

"Yes!" Avery exclaims before she can catch herself.

The smell has been calling her hunger pangs. Something she is very happy to experience since she was unable to take in solids for three weeks as her body recovered and recalibrated itself from the Upsyzeum adventure. Every time she feels hungry, she feels grateful.

Wexx and Bril laugh in delight.

"Now that's the kind of enthusiasm we like to hear!" says Bril.

They take Avery outside and along a rose lined trail towards the heavenly aroma.

"If you don't mind me asking, what is it that you all do?" Avery asks having her curiosity get the better of her.

Wexx stops in his tracks and turns to look at Avery. She shrinks back.

"If you're gonna ask a question, ask it right. It's not you all, it's y'all."

Avery laughs in relief, "Oh, sorry. What is it that **y'all** do?"

"That's so much better. Well…"

They reach the pool and luxury outdoor kitchen with an explosive spread of potato salads, cole slaw, macaroni and cheese, greens, breads, and barbequed ribs, chicken, tri-tip brisket, links, and steak.

"We are the cooks and owners of 'Wexx 'n' Bril's Texan Grill."

Avery puts her hands over her mouth then exclaims, Oh…my…goodness! I am so stupid! I didn't even put you and two together! I absolutely love, love, love, love your food! Me and my grandma used to eat at your place in Indiana all the time when I was a kid!" Avery can't believe she's fanning out like this.

Wexx and Bril have been a staple in the food industry for twenty years with the barbeque sauce recipe the two of them came up with in college. They cooked and sold it on campus and soon were catering college events. Not long after, they married and opened their first restaurant in Dallas, Texas and from then on never worried about money again. They soon franchised to all fifty states and seven countries and have been an unbelievable success.

Their brand of big food at small prices gratifies all wallets and palates (says their logo tagline). Although they are big personalities, they prefer to stay out of the limelight and surround themselves with good friends, family, and sound business decisions. They decided to open their Los Angeles home as a retreat to help those who have gotten tangled up in situations that have compromised their well-being. It's not therapy, it's not rehab, and it's not soul searching because they believe the soul was never lost. It's just plain ol' gettin' back to basics (in luxury).

Wexx and Bril smile broadly at Avery's delight. This kind of reaction is what they live for.

"Wanna know what our secret ingredient is?" Bril asks Avery.

"I sure do!"

Avery leans in as Bril moves in close, secret telling style.

"It's joy."

Avery leans back and smiles, knowing she's been had and gotten at the same time.

"Ya see, Miss Avery, anything you put joy in will bring you many great returns," Wexx tells her.

"And with that said, please partake and enjoy your

meal!" says Bril with a big smile and a warm hug. "I hope you find what you're looking for," she whispers sweetly in Avery's ear then releases her.

Avery can't help but tear up.

"Thank you, Everybody, and take good care of our girl!" Bril says to the awaiting staff.

The staff all wave and say in unison, "Sure thing, Miss Bril."

"Wait! Aren't you going to stay and eat with me?" Avery asks in disbelief. She had grown accustomed to company at mealtimes.

"Oh, Sweet Sugar no. This is your time without distractions. Normally there would be seven other people with you to share and bond with, but we can't be those people. In fact, we have a plane to catch. But we will be back in a few days."

Avery looks like a seven-year-old who has just been told there is no Santa.

"They're gonna take real good care of you. You'll see. Bye now," says Wexx as he takes Bril's hand. They turn and walk away.

Avery watches them as they disappear around the path. Her heart deflates. She turns back around and sees the smiling staff waving her over to come and explore.

For the next week and a half, Avery fills her long days with sleeping in until 10:30 a.m., swimming, working out, walking along the beach, having three hearty and healthy meals (that were not all barbeque), napping, playing tennis with an instructor, taking saunas, watching movies, bowling, taking dance classes, playing solitaire, reading, getting massages, her hair done, manicures, pedicures, waxing, and watching a lot of cooking shows. She had forgotten how much of a passion for cooking she had as a kid before fame came and spoiled that appetite.

At 6:00 p.m. sharp, all the staff pack up and head for their living quarters. This is the time designed for guests to hang out together. There are tons of board games from childhood to adulthood to play, interactive video games and quiet corners carved out in the living room for personal conversations, but Avery had none of those. This was the toughest time for her. She would walk around the room picturing what it looked and felt like to have people there playing, chatting, laughing, eating, including her in conversations, interested in what she had to say and vice versa. The house feels so empty and quiet. What made it worse was seeing all the empty rooms that should have been filled with other people. People she may have gotten to know and like and who may have liked her. People she probably bumped off their experience because she was being selfish. During this time is when Avery chose to watch movies in the theater to pass the night away and feel drowsy enough to sleep until she knew the house was packed again with staff.

Wexx and Bril were nowhere to be found. She had no idea if they had returned from their trip. For the first time, Avery missed having people around. She was too ashamed and afraid to ask some of the staff to stay and hang out with her for fear of looking desperate and mostly not wanting them to lose their job. They all seem so nice and she could hear them making plans to hang out after work. She wished she could ask to come along with them but knew she couldn't.

By the end of the third week, unable to stand herself by herself, Avery decided it was time to explore the property. First, she wanted to know where the kitchen was. Where and how the magic happens. She steps out of the front door and around to the other side of the house. She is greeted by several landscapers as the rest of the huge dwelling reveals itself around the back. She looks to her left and sees another large one-story building and several barbeque smokers on the side of it. She walks into the building and sees what looks like Santa's workshop for chefs. It is an enormous kitchen with multiple stoves, ovens, endless counter space, cabinets, and refrigerators. People in lavender coats and jeans with either paper caps or chef's hats work busily and happily preparing food. The aroma is that of heaven's idea of heaven. Someone quickly approaches

Avery and puts a paper cap on her head.

"If you're going to be in here, Miss, you have to wear this," a young woman in her early thirties wearing a deep purple jacket and eyes to match says as she tucks Avery's long thinned out locks under the cap, "And this...," she hands her a baby blue coat, "this one's for visitors."

Avery does not protest as she puts on the jacket and buttons it up because this is where she wants to be. If she only knew how ridiculous she looks with this white elastic paper cap that is skewed comically to one side of her head.

"Hi, I'm Cinder, Head Chef for the estate." She removes her plastic glove to shake Avery's hand. "Now wash your hands and put these on," she orders as she pulls out two plastic gloves from her pocket.

Avery obeys Cinder's orders and is off to an incredible tour of the kitchen and how things work for the food at the estate and the restaurants. She is fascinated and feels a sense of home and happiness in this kitchen. It started bringing back memories of time with her grandmother.

As a kid, Avery would watch as many cooking shows as she could and recreate the dishes that were made after getting their recipes online. They came out extremely well, especially after she set about putting her own twist on them.

Avery feels honored for the opportunity to be here and from this day forward, the kitchen is where she chooses to spend her days. After receiving permission from the estate manager, Carusso, who spoke with Wexx and Bril, Avery donated the services she would have taken advantage of to the staff so they could enjoy the food and amenities with each other.

Unbeknownst to Avery, throughout her recovery, she would talk in her fevered sleep and babble on about cooking. This is where Eleanor got the idea to call in that special favor to Wexx and Bril. They made sure their kitchen had a creative space for Avery to do whatever she wanted to. Had she not discovered the kitchen on her own by the end of the fourth week, Wexx and Bril were going to take her there themselves.

For the next two weeks, Avery gets up at the crack of dawn to be at morning line up and is even given her own table to try out her own recipes from an amazingly stocked pantry just for her. One early morning, a very handsome young man with boy band hair and a cowboy swagger walks in with boxes of breads and pastries.

"Hey Rookie," he says to her.

Avery is completely taken off guard. First by his striking looks, second by his familiarity, and mostly by the revision to her title recognition.

"Are you talking to me?"

"You're the only one in the baby blue coat," he says as he sorts the deliciousness beside her.

Before she can say anything else, he has moved on and out of the building. No delivery boy had ever spoken to her like that. In fact, no delivery boy has ever spoken to her. *He must not have recognized me in this outfit.* She was starting to know what it felt like to be an "Ordinary." The title she gave people outside the realm of fabulation. This same routine went on for the next couple of weeks. He would come in and call her "Baby Blue" and she would act annoyed and ignore him. It got to the point where Avery looked forward to his arrival. She would casually look towards the door at 7:00 a.m., see him enter, then look away and busy herself with her newest recipe.

On this day, Avery has a couple of blueberry cinnamon muffins she made earlier that morning sitting next to her in a napkin lined basket. The delivery boy enters as usual and places his items next to Avery.

"Mornin' Baby Blue. What's cookin'?"

"There's a couple of extra muffins I had left over if you want them," Avery tells him, trying to sound nonchalant while tending to the business of rolling dough that will soon disappear if she doesn't slow down.

"You made these for me?" he asks with a grin.

"They were just extras. I was going to throw them out anyway."

"Oh, well, I feel so honored! Thank you for thinking of me that way," he retorts sarcastically.

"No, I didn't mean it like that," Avery tries to say apologetically without pleading for his forgiveness. She truly didn't mean to insult him and hopes this won't stop him from talking to her.

"I know you didn't because most people don't put their trash in cute picnic baskets with napkins and a fork," he chuckles. He knows she likes him and enjoys their cat and cat game.

"Whatever," Avery says as she rolls her eyes. *He's on to you. Play it cool.* "Are you going to take them or not?" she asks him with slight irritation.

"You bet your basket I will!" he says as he takes them out of the basket.

"Aren't you going to take the basket?" Avery asks.

"No, I'll leave it here for tomorrow's treat."

He winks at her and leaves.

Avery tries hard not to smile, already planning tomorrow's goody.

After working in the kitchen and observing all day, Avery is dog tired and in bed by 8:00 p.m., then up and refreshed by 5:00 a.m., ready for another day.

Today she makes Delivery Boy her self-proclaimed famous double chocolate espresso brownies. Avery feels anxious with anticipation for his praise because she knows she can bake him dishwater cookies and he'll love it. This time she has four treats stacked neatly and appetizing in the basket.

He walks through the door as usual, is greeted by everyone and makes his way towards her. She continues to busy herself with adding ingredients and hand mixing them in a bowl. In the past week she has made sure that the paper cap lays on her head as fashionably as possible and makeup has been subtly introduced, especially mascara to accentuate her eyes in order to burn them into his memory when she chooses to give him a peek.

"Hey Rookie, great muffin yesterday," he says with a big smile.

Avery tries not to smile too big and turns slightly to acknowledge him, "You're welcome."

"But it was missing just a hair of salt," he tells her.

Avery is involuntarily disappointed then defensive.

"Well I know what it should be missing," she says.

"And what is that?"

"Your opinion!" she says a little too loud and a little too proud.

"My, my, my, you're mighty touchy for a rookie," he says slightly amused.

"And you're mighty opinionated for a delivery boy," she retorts.

"Oh, I get it. Since I'm just the delivery boy I should be grateful for anything you give me?" he says slightly hurt.

Avery can sense it. The upper hand handed back.

Yes! Dammit yes! That's how it works in my world! she wants to say.

"Just so we're clear here," he states matter-of-factly, "I'm also the baker."

Upper hand taken away.

Avery takes a deep breath as she takes in this breaking news, "A mighty sensitive baker, I see."

"You can't think you're going to go from superior model to superior chef in just a few weeks. Take notes from everyone because it's everyone whose opinion counts." He picks up the basket and takes it. "I look forward to trying these," he says as he struts towards the door, then without looking back, "And don't think I'm angry because you're way out of my league."

Avery smiles and calls after him, "Ahhh…A baker and a mind reader!" Upper hand back and in her pocket.

Chapter Twenty-Two
It's Just Desserts

This evening, Avery is feeling more alone than ever. She has become accustomed to being around people in the kitchen during the day, sharing meals, stories, laughs, and recipes but when 3:00 p.m. rolls around, most of them pack up and leave to get ready for dinner service at the restaurant. She is never asked to go along and is too prideful to ask. She sticks around with the estate staff and works on her recipes until 5:00 p.m. when the kitchen closes for the day. There's no other place she'd rather be.

Just like she's done every evening since she's arrived, Avery goes to the large gold door that divides the resort from Wexx and Bril's living quarters to see if she can hear any sign of their presence. The heavy door reveals nothing, and she won't dare ring the doorbell. The only thing she really needs is company and the lack of that is her fault. As she turns to walk away, the door clicks and opens slightly. Avery whips around, eager for the invitation but finds no one there. She opens the door herself, steps in on the other side and closes it quietly. What should feel like a spooky moment feels more like excitement. The long well-lit gold hallway boasts pictures of Wexx and Bril and their restaurants.

As she walks down the hall, Avery can hear the cheerful voices of chatter and laughter. She freezes. *Oh no, they're having a party. I'm not dressed for a party*! Avery thinks to herself as she looks down at her pink sweatpants and matching top she put on after her shower. Her hair is pulled back into ponytail and she has on no makeup. But at this point, curiosity is stronger than vanity.

The laughter gets louder as she comes to a doorway to her left and peeks in. It is a beautifully decorated large kitchen with every amenity anyone could wish for. Just on the other side is the spacious family room where Wexx and Bril and two teens are playing charades. Wexx is up and acting something out and the other three are trying to guess. They laugh at his animated movements and each other for getting it wrong.

He sees Avery admiring the situation and calls out, "Come on in, Darlin'!"

The other three turn around.

"Hey Sugar! Come and join us!" Bril says as she waves Avery over.

Avery wants to run in and jump on the comfy couch but plays it cool.

"Oh no, I don't want to disturb your family time," she says, hoping they would insist on her staying. Praying they would.

The two teens, a boy thirteen and a girl fifteen, look at Avery with two different expressions. The boy, in awe as his fantasy girl is now standing in his kitchen. The girl, slightly annoyed.

"Oh, you're not disturbing us," booms Wexx.

"Well she kinda is," says the girl under her breath. Bril gives her a now-now-be-nice look.

"Well maybe for just a few minutes," Avery says as she walks briskly to the couch telling herself that she's doing **them** the favor by hanging out.

Wexx and Bril could see Avery at their door every evening because the sensor bell would go off in their house every time someone got two feet to the door. They would look at the door monitors that are placed throughout the house for who is at their door. This evening they decided to invite her in by pushing the button located on Bril's phone. They just knew curiosity and loneliness would get the best of her one day.

The boy gets up and tries to make himself more handsome and taller by running his hands through his hair and holding in his slightly pudgy stomach. He is grinning from kitchen to bedroom.

"This is our son, Falcon. As you can see, he's a big fan,"

says Bril.

Avery reaches out her hand and shakes his.

"Very nice to meet you, Falcon. What a cool name!"

She means it. It's been a long time since anyone has said they were a fan of hers. She is overwhelmed with a feeling of gratitude and almost tears up. Falcon can hardly speak.

"And this is our daughter, Swan," says Wexx. Swan, a tall, slightly overweight girl with luxurious long brown hair and perfectly shaped grey cat eyes set in a beautiful heart shaped face, reluctantly walks over to Avery, and gives her a wet noodle handshake. Now this was the reception Avery had grown accustomed to over the past few months.

"Hey," she says dryly without looking at Avery. "I wanna call Clover. May I be excused?" Swan asks her mother.

"Oh, don't let me stop your family time. I just wanted to say hi and to let you know that I'm having a great time."

Avery hurries out of the room which seems to take forever. She doesn't want them to see how hurt her feelings are. *Why are you so sensitive? She's just some stupid kid!* she thinks to herself to stop from crying.

Avery walks briskly down the long hallway that at first was so inviting but now feels suffocating. The door to freedom is a hazy vision that seems unreachable.

Bril stops her.

"Hey, Honey, you don't have to go," she says in her sweet tone.

"Guess she's no fan of mine," says Avery with an awkward smile.

"Actually, she is. I hope you get a chance to talk to her before your stay is over," Bril tells her.

"I'd like that." Avery means it.

"Good! How 'bout you join us for dinner at six tomorrow?"

Avery nods and smiles through her pooled tears begging them not to drop.

Bril gives her a hug. The tears drop. Damn, this woman and her hugs!

The next morning Avery is at her station with a basket of six blueberry cinnamon muffins. Delivery/Baker Boy arrives as scheduled with the deliveries and makes his way over to an already flushed Avery. He puts the empty basket down from the day before and looks at the newly filled one and smiles.

"I have to give it to you, Rookie, those brownies yesterday were perfect and delicious. Great job," he tells her as he leans his back against the counter to face Avery as she pretends to be deep in the concentration of mixing.

"Thanks, Baker, that means a lot coming from you," she says without looking at him.

"Are you serious or sarcastic?" he asks.

Avery doesn't know how to play this humble herself game. She's always been the one sought after, humbled to, with no questions or justifications. It was always up to her to say yes or no. Not today and possibly never again. Avery puts down the bowl and takes a deep breath to fortify herself then looks at him. He is already looking at her.

Oh, he's so cute! Keep it cool *but not cold.* "What do you think? You're the mind reader, remember?"

He chuckles. Avery is relieved and smiles back.

"I think you're sincere and a seriously good baker. These for me?" he asks as he points to the basket of muffins, picks one up and takes a bite before she can answer.

"I uh…took your advice…and added some salt," she states humbly.

He looks at her as he chews and grins the grin of someone in flavor ecstasy.

"This, this right here, oh yes! You added some extra butter too, didn't you?"

Avery is overjoyed by his reaction. She is unaware and doesn't care how childlike goofy her smile is by this compliment. He finds it endearing.

"Yes, I did. I thought it would make it even more moist and rich."

"Well, you were right. This is absolutely delicious!" He picks up the basket to leave, "I'm going to do my best not to eat all of these on my drive back to L.A. Great job, Rookie."

"You can just call me Avery," she tells him, letting him know she's interested.

"Okay, Avery it is."

"And…what can I call you?"

He looks at Avery for a long second. *Is he going to kiss me?*

He finally says, "You really have no idea who I am, do you?"

Chapter Twenty-Three
Special Affects

Avery blinks and leans back, confused.

"Should I?"

"Well maybe not since we only worked together for six years on 'Only Avery!' I played Cody, the nerdy classmate who was in love with you."

Avery gasps deeply in disbelief, "Cruddy?!"

"Yup. That's what you used to call me on and off camera."

Avery is speechless as she looks at him and searches for the little nerd boy with the crooked glasses and stuffy nose both on and off screen.

"Oh my gosh! I always wondered what happened to you!"

He looks skeptical.

"Did you?"

"Well of course! I wondered what happened to all of you. We were supposed to have an 'Only Avery' reunion to help launch my dress campaign with Zavier last year but my agent said he couldn't find anyone and just assumed you were all dead."

"Did you at least send flowers?"

Again, Avery looks confused.

"Actually, we were all contacted...but none of us wanted to go."

Avery looks bewildered, "What? But why? Was it because of my agent? He could be quite rude…"

"No, it was because of you. You were the rude one."

"Me?! What did I do?"

"You were the star, the princess, the one who had to have things her way all the time. We had to only have the foods you liked to eat on set, play with the toys you only liked and only after you were done with them, played games you wanted to play with the rules you made up that were always in your favor. Man, I had no idea four-square had so many rules," he breaks it down to her half kidding half venting.

"But you guys always came to my birthday parties away from the show," she says hoping that there is a redeeming point about to be made.

"We were paid to come. It was in our contract because no one else would show up. If you remember, we were the only so-called friends you had. We couldn't wait for the show to be over so we wouldn't have to hang out with you anymore. The whole crew and cast had a party on their own to celebrate our freedom," he recalls. There is such a pleasantness about him that even when he's delivering harsh statements, it's done without any animosity.

Avery is not sure how to receive this other than as fact. She is forced to react minus resentment or pretense. Her red face is canvassed with the perfect palette of surprise, confusion, and humility. She had no idea she was so hated back then. *But they all acted like they liked me.* Then it dawns on her. *"Acted," they were all actors. Everyone, except for me. I was just being myself. An entitled brat, all the way up until eleven and a quarter weeks ago.* She could feel a tight squeeze of regret in her heart as her mind races through various situations where she had disparaged others.

"So, is that why no one could ever make it to the television reunion specials the studio kept trying to set up?" she asks, trying to sound brave.

"Bingo! Oh, but we have our own reunions. More like a support group. We still get together and have dinner and hang out and discuss how we survived those six years with you," he says trying to sound more humorous than cutting. He can see that he's struck a nerve and realizes he may have gone too far. "But that was a long time ago. No worries. All is forgiven...at least for me." He chuckles casually, trying to pull her out of the bed of despair he made and tucked her into.

Avery tears up and looks sincerely into his spell-casting eyes, "Wow, I had no idea. Wow, I'm really sorry…" *What the hell is his name?*

"Jason, my name is Jason," he responds, smiling.

She never took the time to get to know any of her co-stars, let alone their names. And he knows it.

Avery is completely embarrassed as she hangs her head. Then recovers and quips, "I was going to say that."

Jason smirks at her.

"Really? Before or after I said it?"

"After. Waaaaay after."

They both laugh. Avery is surprised by her own humor and relieved that he's not angry with her.

"Is there anything I can do to make up for it?" she asks, hoping that a schoolboy crush has turned into a grown man's desire.

"Definitely!"

She's still got it.

"Keep baking like this," he says as he pops a piece of muffin in his mouth and turns to leave with the basket.

Though slightly deflated that he didn't pick up on her flirting, a surge of excitement races through Avery's body like lightning. A sense of accomplishment, a job well done that has nothing to do with how she looks or what she's wearing.

Avery spends the rest of the day replaying and analyzing her encounter with Jason as she bakes two dozen vanilla and chocolate micro-mini three-layer cake muffins for dinner with Wexx and Bril that evening.

At 6:00 p.m. sharp, Avery rings the doorbell to Wexx and Bril's part of the house. Once again, the door opens and Avery steps through to make her way towards the kitchen.

"Hey Sweetness! So glad you're here!" sing songs Bril. She notices the basket in Avery's hand. "What do we have here?"

"Oh, I've been testing out my baking skills and made **y'all** some goodies as a thank you."

Bril laughs warmly, takes the basket and hugs her. She breaks away and says, "Now, dinner's runnin' a little late but I think this would be a good time for you and Swan to get to know each other."

Oh no! Not another confrontation! "Sure!" she says in

the most positive tone she can gather as a boulder drops in her stomach.

Bril directs Avery to Swan's bedroom which is down the rest of the long hall to the right past the formal living room, dining room, two bathrooms, six bedrooms, a theater, and game room. Swan's room is nestled in a cul-de-sac at the end of the house where Avery would have done well to drive there. She rounds the corner and sees a flood of neon green light from beneath the door. She can hear the faint sounds of girly giggles and teenage rhetoric. Avery hesitates to knock as she knows the worst way to start a conversation with a teen is to interrupt a fun phone conversation.

Swan is the reason Avery came to be at this home in the first place. Wexx and Bril would never grant a request such as Avery's had it not been for Eleanor. They do not believe in anyone being better than the next. But when they received the urgent call on their private line from Eleanor about Avery's dire situation, they cancelled the guests they had reservations for, reimbursed them, and gave them a free two-week stay in the future.

Wexx and Bril met Eleanor fifteen and a half years ago when Bril went into labor in a department store in Texas. Eleanor was there for her sister's wedding and was shopping for accessories. Bril went down in a blaze of hollerin' (as Wexx likes to tell it). She was only six and a half months pregnant and had no previous complications when her water broke, right there between the scarves and purses. Eleanor calmly stepped in and promised the painfully contracting Bril that her preemie baby girl was going to be just fine because obviously she has a will to shop. That statement tickled Bril so, that it gave her the last push she needed to deliver her tiny girl. As an exhausted Bril was being loaded onto the stretcher by paramedics, she was so grateful, she wanted to name her baby after Eleanor; even though she wasn't crazy about the name. Eleanor begged her not to because she wasn't crazy about it either.

"Then what's your last name?" Bril asked her.

"Swan."

"That's it! I love it!"

Bril was going to name her Magnolia Fern, after her mother's mother, but Swan sang to her like a choir on Easter Sunday.

Wexx and Bril gave Eleanor a lifetime certificate to any of their restaurants and they have kept in touch all these years through holiday and birthday cards. They told Eleanor if she ever needed or wanted anything to just call. She never did, until that day to help Avery.

"Knock knock," Avery calls out trying to sound cool and casual when she's really scared and scattered. *What are you so nervous about? She's just an immature teenager. An immature teenager who obviously hates your guts.*

"Come on in!" says the young southern voice that echoes Bril's.

Avery wishes she had been told to go away as she slowly opens the door and steps into magic. Avery is immediately transported to the rain forest that is Swan's room with its floor to ceiling real-life replica trees and exotic birds and animals. The walls are wallpapered with forest imagery and the green granite floor has a wide strip of glass with a blue running river of water from the entrance to the end of the room. It's like stepping into another world until you see the California King bed draped in sparkly pink netting and the silhouette of a teen girl sprawled across it on the phone.

Wexx and Bril believe in giving their kids anything they want, as long as they do four things: Always respect and obey them, respect each other and themselves, be kind to everyone, and volunteer their time to make life better for others. And with that philosophy they are raising two terrific kids who love and look out for each other, enjoy spending time with their parents and volunteer at various non-profit organizations two Saturdays a month.

"Hang on for a second," Swan says into the phone. She

pulls the netting aside to see who has entered her domain. She is disappointed to see Avery. "Oh, hi."

"Hey!" Avery responds, bypassing Swan's dry greeting.

Swan speaks into her phone, "Cedar, let me call you back." She hangs up and looks at Avery. "What's up?" she asks in a what-do-you-want tone.

"Uh…this room! That's what's up!" Avery says trying to sound hip and complimentary, hoping to thaw Swan's glacier.

"Thanks. I decorated it myself," Swan responds, trying to hold back the glee of her idol being in her room thinking she's cool.

There is an awkward silence that Avery can no longer take.

"So, why do you hate me?" she asks bluntly.

"Why do you hate me?" Swan bites back.

Avery looks stunned and says, "Hate you? Why would I hate you? I don't even know you!"

"Exactly," says Swan.

Avery is completely confused. Swan can see this and pulls her netting to the side, inviting Avery to sit. Avery takes the cue and sits next to Swan.

"What do you mean? I don't understand."

"I used to worship you. I wanted to be like you. Not body-wise because as you can see with my genes that is never going to happen, and that's okay. But I could fix my hair like yours, do my makeup like yours and maybe one day have a life like yours."

"Well I think the one you have right now is pretty great," says Avery looking around.

"I don't mean money and material things but having people interested in what you have to say and caring about what you think and being able to make a difference with just one sentence. That's what you have…had."

"Yeah, I definitely don't have that anymore. But what does that have to do with hating you?"

"That comment you made about Corrinne on Oscar Night about how you couldn't blame Thian for wanting to keep her a secret because she was fat," Swan tells her matter-of-factly.

Avery double-takes as the harsh statement verbally assaults her ears. It sounded so ugly so terrible.

"I didn't say it like that," she responds defensively.

"But that's what you meant."

Avery looks at Swan as she searches for a clever or even

consoling answer. But there's no lying to this girl. Avery had never been confronted like this before.

Avery surrenders and says, "You're right, you're right. I was just sooooo angry that night. Thian had broken up our Hollywood romance at the last minute. I was expecting to be the date of an Oscar winning actor, instead I ended up with a dressmaker. Although, a very famous one, but still, it wasn't the same as a so-called boyfriend. I was embarrassed that the world knew that he didn't want me and that the whole relationship was fake."

"But I thought you were in on it and being a good friend. Everybody did. We all thought you were so cool for doing that for them."

"That was the story Thian and Corrinne told to help make me look better and to save me from embarrassment. But I was so mad and jealous that I couldn't let it be. For some reason I thought the world would be on my side…"

"Because you're skinny and she's not," Swan interjects.

"Exactly," Avery answers honestly. It was true. "I felt that since everyone told me I deserved better because I looked better, I was entitled to **be** better."

"Wow!" exclaims Swan with wide eyes.

Avery can't believe she really said that out loud.

"I guess you really hate me now."

"No, no. That is the most honest thing I think I've ever heard."

"I think that's probably the most honest thing I've ever said."

"I mean, you gave off this impression of being so perfect, almost super-human, like nothing bothered you and you were living the best life anyone could ever live, but in reality you have feelings and problems and a lot of insecurities."

"Well, I wouldn't say a lot of insecurities," says Avery trying not to sound defensive which is what she's now starting to feel.

"But enough though," Swan tells her.

Avery gives her a curious look and asks, "Does that make you happy? That I may be unhappy with myself?"

"No, not happy. Relieved. And not relieved that you're unhappy but relieved that you're not just mean."

Avery smiles. *Whoa, this kid is deep*!

"Happy or not, that was still wrong of me to say."

"Yes it was because it made girls who look like me feel like girls who look like you hate us because we don't look like you."

"That's so not true, though," Avery says tearing up.

Swan takes Avery's hand and tells her, "Mama and Daddy taught me and Falcon ever since we were little that we were special and that special affects others more than ordinary. And to most people we are going to be considered special because we are, so what we say and do means more. Just like you."

"I never thought of it that way. I thought people only cared about how I looked and not what I had to say." She squeezes Swan's hand. "I'm sorry. I really didn't mean it that way. I really wasn't trying to hurt people."

"Corrinne and Thian are people," Swan reminds her. "Have you apologized to them?"

"No, I haven't. Think I should?"

"Do you think you should?"

Avery pauses for a moment, having never thought to do so.

"Yeah, I guess I should."

"But don't go all public and cryin' on t.v. or anything like that 'cause that seems phony. Just call them up and say I'm sorry."

"Think they'll forgive me?"

"I think so. And if they don't, you still did the right thing."

Avery looks surprised then tells her, "You are so smart."

"Yeah, it's what I do," Swan responds playfully.

They both laugh. The tension officially severed.

Avery sobers.

"Listen to me, that stupid statement isn't who I am and it's not who I think you or anybody else is. You know that don't you?"

"Now I do. It was more about jealousy than judgment," Swan says with sympathy.

She's right. I was jealous. So, so, so jealous. Avery throws her hands up and shakes her head.

"And what do I do? I turn around and try to gain weight to try and fit in. So, what kind of a person does that make me?" Avery asks, afraid of the answer.

"A real one."

Swan hugs her tightly. Happy to have her idol again.

Avery exhales heavily. Happy to have herself again.

Chapter Twenty-Four
Perceiving Is Deceiving

The next week goes by briskly as a happy Avery continues to bake and flirt with Jason.

"So where are you getting these recipes from?" he asks her on Friday as he bites into a lemon pistachio macaron.

"Some I remember from my grandmother and others I make up as I go along."

"You're really talented."

"Thank you. It means a lot coming from you."

Jason looks surprised.

"Really?"

"Really," she says with a smile.

"Well, you have something else coming from me,"

Avery perks up as he reaches into his pocket. *Finally! It must be tickets to a concert or a ballgame. Either way, I'll say yes of course.*

Jason pulls out thirty-five dollars and hands it to Avery.

"Oh…Umm, what's this for?" she asks, trying not to sound disappointed.

"We've been selling your desserts. They're a hit and this is your cut."

"You sold them? But I made them for you."

"I know, and believe me, I've had my share."

"Why didn't you tell me?"

"Because I wanted you to keep baking from your heart."

"Oh, so that's what you think I'm doing?" she responds defensively, feeling exposed.

"Yup," he answers playfully.

"And how do you know that?"

He points to the macarons and answers, "Because nothing this good comes from just putting ingredients together."

They look at each other for a moment. Avery can't fight the truth and has nothing in her cranial lexicon to dispute it.

"So why are you telling me now?" she asks, happy to formulate words into a sensible sentence.

"Because the owner wants to meet with you," Jason says as he grabs the basket of macarons and makes his way to the door.

Avery is dumbfounded.

"Huh? Who? About what?"

Jason waves the basket in the air.

"Til tomorrow, Rookie!"

That evening, Avery reflects on the dinner she had with Wexx and Bril with the lively banter at the table, s'mores making and funny story telling in the backyard, but mostly on her conversation with Swan and realizes Corrinne and Thian aren't the only people she needs to apologize to. She decides to give her last two weeks at the retreat to someone and their friends and family she had treated very poorly.

Avery calls Shadoh, the stylist on her last Zavier Zero Zipper shoot.

"Hello?" says the lilting voice on the other end.

"Hi, is this Shadoh?"

"Yes, it is. Avery? My goodness. How are you? Where are you?"

"I'm fine and I'm in a good place."

"This is such a relief. Word on the runway is that you overdosed and either died or were in rehab," says Shadoh as she types a press release to the media titled, "I Found Avery!"

Avery had unplugged from public life right after her stint on "Losers At Gaining." She shut off from any updates on how and what the public was feeling or thinking about her. And it looks like Eleanor kept her promise not to reveal Avery's life-threatening experience. Meanwhile, there had been a frenzy of supposed sightings and stories of her in France, in homeless shelters, working as a high-priced escort, losing all her money, living in motels, strung out on drugs and worst of all, having lost weight. Shadoh fills her in on all the speculations. Avery can't help but laugh.

"No, none of that is true, and please put that in your story to the press."

Shadoh stops typing. Busted.

"Anyway, I just called to get the name of the girl who was your assistant on our last shoot together."

Suddenly, Shadoh bursts into multiple waves of loud high-pitched laughter that would cause a pack of hyenas to flee for their lives. Avery puts the phone down as the shrieks pierce her ear like frozen needles.

"I'm sorry. I thought you knew," she finally says after all the king's horses and all the king's men were able to put her back together again.

"Knew what?" Avery asks with a spritz of irritation.

"That my assistant, Cori, is Corrinne. The Corrinne! Your Thian's Corrinne!" Her tone is filled with the mirth and merriment of a lottery jackpot winner.

The shock of this news ambush holds Avery's breath hostage as she slowly sits down and remembers their last encounter. She tries to make out Corrinne's face and body behind those unforgiveable clothes. She can't really see her as Avery barely looked at anyone who wasn't famous. What she does remember was Thian talking to her and she not liking it at all. Avery now feels like the villain in a romantic comedy who gets her comeuppance as she is the last to know. This is where the movie ends, on Avery's contorted face.

After what seems to be an eternity of rabid jubilance at her expense, Avery is finally able to summon enough air to put vowels and consonants together to break through Shadoh's sirens of hilarity and says, "Make sure to include that in your story too. This should guarantee you won't have to work for at least two years. And you can quote me on that." Avery hangs up, not sure if that was the right thing to do, but it's done, and it feels good. Tonight's entertainment news headline ready for presentation. Avery lays back on her bed and stares at the ceiling, conjuring up the promos, "Avery Strikes Again!" "Again, Avery's Foot In Her Mouth, Most Calories She's Had All Week," "Avery, Lost And Found; Stay Lost!" She can't help but laugh at the irony of the whole situation.

After the phone conversation with Shadoh, Avery knew exactly who she should extend the invitation to.

Twenty-four hours later, Avery picks her grandmother up from the airport.

One week later…

Avery arrives at the address given to her by Jason to meet the owner of the restaurant where he works to discuss her baked goods. Having never been on a job interview, Avery asked Wexx and Bril and Swan for advice on what to wear, how to introduce herself and present her delectable desserts. Falcon was no help as he stared in fascination, still unable to break free of his crush. Dressed in cream colored dress pants, a pear green blouse and modest three-inch heels with her hair pulled back in a tight neat bun (just in case she's asked to bake something on the spot), her face is clean with just a dash of foundation and one swipe of mascara. Avery never looked or felt better than she does right now.

The place is nothing like what she expected. It's very casual, there are people on laptops, listening to music, talking on their phones, drinking coffee and sipping smoothies. She starts to step out to see if she has the right address until she witnesses someone happily eating the bite-sized strawberry cream cheese cupcake she made for Jason this morning. Avery thought she would be meeting with a famous chef at a five-star restaurant who wanted to take her under his wing. A flash of dismay comes over her as she looks around the place. Had she taken a moment to look the address up online, she never would have come, thinking this was a joke being played on her. Revenge, in fact.

A smile crosses her face as she focuses in on the counter where an oval tray with a handmade sign on a coffee stirrer reads: "Baby Blue Bakes." It is written inside the drawing of a cupcake with a bite taken out of it. Avery has a warm feeling of flattery that only one of her desserts is left since she made two dozen just three hours ago.

A young man rushes in, "Dude! Thank gravy there's one left! My boss would have fired me if I came back to the office without today's bite."

Avery can't help but beam and blush. She wants so badly to tell him that she's the creator with a basket full of bites to prove it. But she plays it cool. Savoring this delicious moment of pride for something positive she's done without anyone knowing it's her.

Avery comes to terms that Jason never led her to believe that she'd be interviewing at a five-star restaurant. It was her own perception of the situation and what she thought she was entitled to. Like most of her life. She starts to giggle. Half at herself and half out of relief. Relief that she doesn't have to prove herself to an elite audience who may just want her on notoriety alone. She now feels even more motivated to remain as professional towards this owner as she would have if this were "Maison de Red."

Avery looks around the place with fresh eyes and rather likes its cool and relaxed vibe.

An employee approaches her and says, "Welcome to Coffee Being. What can I get for you?"

"Oh, uh, I have an appointment with the owner."

The employee turns around and calls, "Jason, your eleven o'clock is here!"

Three Years Later…

Well Red

With her strawberry red hair blowing lazily in the spring air, she lounges comfortably overlooking the city from a plush patio chaise lounge. Zavier happily brings her morning coffee that he makes every morning. "Here you go, Baby," he says lovingly as he hands her the oversized mug that reads: "ZANGEL."

She takes the mug as she leans up to meet his awaiting lips.

"Thank you, Honey," she replies sweetly then kisses him. She is still as beautiful as the first day he met her forty-three years ago. Ambereene, Zavier's wife of forty-three years.

They met when they modeled for the same fashion show in New York. Zavier was inexplicably and overwhelmingly smitten by Ambereene, the only red head in the bunch, giving a splash of color in an otherwise beige room. He knew in that moment she would never be out of his life. He wanted to marry her that day, down the runway, but he had to get her name first. So, he waited. Six days later, they were married.

Although part of Zavier's image was to be surrounded by models as his dates and suggested love interests, it was all for show. He never once cheated or ever thought of cheating on Ambereene. She was and still is the only love of his life. After a life-altering fall from a six-foot high runway, which was the designer's fault, Ambereene never modeled again. She was at the height of her modeling career when the accident occurred and was ridiculed by the media, fans, designers, and models for being clumsy and unprofessional. Following two surgeries and a three-week stay in the hospital, Ambereene signed a non-disclosure agreement with the world-renowned designer, promising to never tell what really happened that day. She received an enormous amount of "Don't Ruin My Reputation" money and became a recluse on the massive compound she and Zavier bought and live on today.

Zavier quit modeling and took his talent for clothes design and his burning desire for revenge on all who hurt Ambereene and started his own clothing line with his signature brand of contempt.

He and Ambereene enjoyed decades of coming up with new and ridiculous fads and trends just to see how far people would follow. There was the tangerine trend where that was the color to wear head to toe for a summer. The fringe pocket jeans and the ever-so-popular inside-out dresses were what put Zavier in front of the fashion line. Then they decided to see just how far they could go with manipulating body image. Zavier started making clothes that were impossible to fit because they were well below the size he purported them to be in order to create the illusion of size exclusivity. It started off with size four (actually, size three and a half) then little by little Zavier started making clothes smaller to make women feel like they were getting bigger. Thus, catapulting the diet industry's weight loss gain off the stock market charts where he and Ambereene have huge investments. They are also the secret owners of "Seams Like It" and "Also Sewn As." The stores that make and sell Zavier's knock-off designs at discount prices. This is where most of their fortune is sewn up.

Then the body image switch blew up without Zavier's knowledge or creative needle and thread on the pulse. He was taken off guard. His brand and command over what people should look like and wear had been taken away by one person. Though he hustled and made it look like it was his idea and genius, it rattled him. For the first time he realized that he may not be able to manipulate people forever and that there were others out there who can make changes just by being themselves. His name, his reputation and all that he had built was almost taken away from him that Oscar Night. Zavier never had to work to prove himself. **He** set a trend and people obeyed. Boom. That's it. It was against his nature to resort to stunts to appease others. Luckily, he was able to turn it around but next time he may not be so lucky. Knowing that he was no longer the king over being, designing just wasn't fun anymore. After a year of the Zavier Zaftig Design line, he decided to retire. He closed the store which left twenty people out of a job with a big fat severance check and a healthy retirement plan that would take care of them all.

Zavier and Ambereene opened an exclusive fashion institute and design school called "From Z to A," in that same Beverly Hills building. It is wildly successful and teaches aspiring designers how to make clothes for women of all shapes and sizes. Parents of unborn children have put their embryos on the list for eighteen years from now just in case the fashion talent is there.

Zavier enjoys dropping in to wow the students and staff and attending some of the end of semester fashion shows to collect his accolades. Ambereene works as the runway consultant for the students and models. To this day, no one knows they are married or who Ambereene really is.

Zavier and Ambereene recline comfortably on their fourth floor balcony drinking their coffee as they anticipate the arrival of a class of third graders for a field trip of their grounds.

"What time will she be here with the kids?" Zavier asks.

"They'll be here around eleven, take a tour of the rescued animals petting zoo then have lunch."

"I love seeing her with the kids. She looks so happy and really enjoys teaching."

"I know, it's so cute how they all call her Miss Tassidy. By this time next year, she'll have her degree, teaching credential, and her own class."

"I am so proud of her!" Zavier beams.

Tassidy was the only other person, besides Ambereene, who could see through Zavier and did not fear him. Being one to even tolerate someone comes very few and very far between, but Zavier fell in love with Tassidy that first day of the photo shoot. Not as a lover but as a father. Her brash fearlessness and quick wit resembled his own personality and she looked so much like Ambereene. Had they had a daughter she would have been Tassidy.

After a year of being the spokesmodel for Zavier's Zaftig Zipper, Tassidy decided to decline the renewed contract offer and instead go to school to fulfill her true dream of becoming a third-grade teacher. The money she made more than paid for tuition and a nice apartment. She refused any monetary help Zavier and Ambereene presented her with because she wanted to do it all on her own. Over the past two and a half years they have become a family complete with weekly dinners either for elegant meals at the compound or at Tassidy's two-bedroom apartment for burgers, home-made popped popcorn and a movie. They vacationed, celebrated, and gave much needed business and life advice on both ends. Tassidy loves being considered the only child to Zavier and Ambereene and they love it even more.

Terrible Twos

Dalton and Araya live together in wicked bliss in a beautiful six-bedroom home in the Hollywood Hills with their kids, two-year-old daughter, Reign, and ten-month-old son, Edge, who are an exact and frightening fusion of their mom and dad.

Dalton left the managing business to solely advise, not manage, Araya because Araya is not someone who can be managed. Araya sold "Weight Wanters" over a year ago when she became bored. Together, they started their own production company, "Reigning Edge," that produces Araya's new show called, what else? "Araya!" It is a cross between self-help life enhancement and gotcha-all-your-secrets-are-out where not a guest leaves without her kind words of wisdom and their self-respect intact. It is the number one afternoon talk show in the nation with four seasons of sacrificial hams waiting to be guests.

Araya literally has Dalton wrapped around her finger as he proposes to her on the eighth of every month. She now has twenty-eight dynamic diamond derangedment rings. He keeps asking her because he loves the sadistic game of her turning him down then making passionate love. He knows one day she will say yes. And one day she knows she will.

Go Figure

Corrinne has fulfilled her dream of becoming a full-time designer and opened her own beautiful store in Los Angeles for sizes zero to thirty-two called, "Inclusive." They are the same high-quality, trendy, and practical designs from jeans to evening gowns from infants to adults. If there is a customer who cannot fit one of her sizes, she personally alters it for their body type.

As a lifetime wedding gift to Corrinne, Thian put back on his construction worker's hat with his father and brother and built her store from scratch.

The store's clientele ranges from lower to middle to high income to celebrities to kids to teens to seniors. The store also sells Morganna's custom jewelry that has become so popular, a separate section had to be built and staffed to help keep up with inventory and sales. All clothes and jewelry are made on site in a beautiful and air-conditioned warehouse behind the store.

Right next door is "Malinda's Complete Beauty" (MCB) salon where Malinda has taught all her stylists her special skills and techniques for every type of hair. Malinda married Thian's brother, Dominic, two years ago.

Thian went on to win another Oscar for his dramatic role

as an assassin and reluctant caregiver to two precocious orphaned kids and their pet goose.

Corrinne's still thin twin Lorrinne is currently working the beauty pageant circuit. After not even being accepted for an audition for the Miss Los Angeles pageant, Lorrinne decided she would rather judge than be judged. So, she managed to use the clout of first-hand experience and the fame of being a famous person's sister and sister-in-law and found herself a seat on the "celebrity" panel. She is now known as the tough judge who holds nothing back in her opinions and sends contestants running and crying off stage, which has shot ratings through the sky. At one of the pageants she meets Creign Kitchell, and the cataclysmic collision of their sarcastic and shallow personalities mesh into a romance that will make future reality show history.

Corrinne and Thian were able to avoid Priscilla's winter wonderland wedding extravaganza complete with an ice-skating rink where professional ice skaters were to perform amazing and elegant love stories on ice (including theirs) and the Swarovski Crystal adorned room with hidden snow machines that would have covered enormous pine trees. Each guest was going to be gifted a snow sculpture of Thian and Corrinne's initials in a large glowing aqua-colored bottle. Corrinne also avoided having to get married in the ridiculously expensive and excessively bejeweled princess gown with a twenty-pound, forty-foot train that Priscilla had co-designed with beyond-the-top wedding gown creator, Wicker.

Even though Priscilla had happily settled into her natural size ten, (still a bit disappointed at not reaching fourteen) she still likes to reminisce about her glory days as a size two. And you can bet your life savings if that trend comes back, she'll be down for it.

Priscilla changed her mind about the big wedding after Corrinne told her it was a Hollywood faux pas for Oscar winners to have big weddings. She believed it and decided to let Corrinne handle her own wedding plans. This outcome worked perfectly for Priscilla because she had been secretly dating the architect/contractor, who was going to construct this monstrous event. Priscilla couldn't help but be attracted to his rugged good looks and chivalrous attitude. She knew he wasn't the millionaire she was accustomed to dating, but there was something adventurous and maybe a little dangerous about him that she found appealing. He didn't treat her like a beautiful fragile piece of china or try to go out of his way to impress her. He was just himself, Greene Winters.

For their first date he told her to dress in casual duds. So, she put on her white Chanel jumpsuit with only three-inch pumps. He was dressed in jeans, a long sleeve t-shirt and work boots.

When he saw her, he just shook his head and said, "Okay."

When they arrived at their destination, a lot, with a partially built house, Priscilla thought he had to consult with someone about the job before getting on their way. It wasn't until he opened her car door and handed her a pair of work boots, did she realize that this was no extraordinary date.

"You won't be needing those," he said pointing at her well-heeled feet.

Priscilla spent the day awkwardly hammering, carrying beams, breaking nails, drinking out of plastic bottles, wiping sweat and very expensive melting make-up from her face and laughing with average people; things she had never done a day in her adult life. By the end of the date, she was exhausted and slept, mouth open and snoring all the way back home. She woke up the next morning with no fingernails, every muscle sore, aching feet, a little sunburned, and a feeling of purpose. She couldn't wait for their next date. Thian knew of Greene as he studied all his books and followed his career. He was more excited to meet him than Greene was him.

After Corrinne and Thian's simple cliffside wedding in Hawaii, Priscilla traveled everywhere with Greene on new adventures as he tries to save the world. She had no idea he was a man of incredible means until five months in when he flew her on his private plane to help install pipelines after a storm in Indonesia. They eloped eighteen months later in Las Vegas with their favorite celebrity look-alikes in attendance as well as family and friends. Corrinne receives postcards and pictures of them from around the world building, feeding, counseling, and providing emergency aid. Priscilla is now a different and adventurous person who has given up the manicured nails, makeup, designer clothes, and perfect hair (for most occasions). She is now jumping out of planes, riding motorcycles, horses and skateboards, surfing, white water rafting, and she even knows how to install plumbing.

Priscilla had even evolved to the point of refraining from sending her ex-husband and Morganna a wedding gift of her own stunning wedding picture with Greene.

When they are in town, Greene and Priscilla spend time with their families together. Priscilla often jokes that maybe Gregge would have been a great catch after all as she winks at Thian.

Remodeled

Avery signed on as a baker at “Coffee Being” where her Baby Blue Bites continue to be one of their biggest sellers. They became so popular, they are now packaged and sold in stores all over the country but sold exclusively fresh at “Coffee Being.” Avery also signed on as Jason’s wife a year later.

After sending the ladies of “Chews ‘n’ Views” a huge variety basket of her bites, Avery was invited on the show. She told the truth about her relationship with Thian, how she felt when Corrinne came on the scene, her failures at trying to make a comeback, her near-death experience, and all the ugly that came with it. The cast from “Only Avery” joined her. This was the first time they had been re-united in public since they were kids. There were painful revelations, tears, apologies, and forgiveness; something that had already taken place while she and Jason were dat-ing during a dinner party at his place six months prior. The fans ate it up and this particular show won “Chews ‘n’ Views” their first daytime Emmy.

Avery lathered up enough courage to invite Corrinne and Thian to her home to cook for them and apologize. She was terrified they would say no or hang up on her. They accepted her invitation and it wasn’t as hard as she thought. They were just nice and easygoing people who harbored no resentment. They talked, laughed and reminisced the night away. Since then they double and triple-date with Malinda and Dominic. Corrinne even designed Avery's wedding gown.

Today, Avery and Jason are still in matrimonial merriment in their Holmby Hills home with their two dogs, Baker and Rookie. The adult cast of "Only Avery" are back on television in a spin-off where they all work as the owners and chefs of a restaurant/bakery where comedic calamity ensues. They even got most of the old crew back. The set now feels like a family filled with laughter, pranks, good food, and respect. Swan interns on her summer vacations as a set designer, and it is often catered by "Wexx 'n' Bril's Texan Grill." It is the number one rated comedy show and has been picked up for three more seasons. Avery insisted the show be called, "Taste Buds."

And they all live happily ever as themselves.

THE BEGINNING

Dictate How You Participate

Book Club Questions

1. **Who do you identify with more, Corrinne or Avery?**
2. **Whose issue would you rather have, Avery's or Corrinne's?**
3. **How much do you think fashion and the media dictates how people feel about themselves?**
4. **How far have you gone to fit in?**
5. **Is the opinion of others about your body more important than yours?**
6. **What is the craziest thing you have ever done to gain/lose weight?**
7. **How important is your body image?**
8. **Is body image more mental than physical?**
9. **In your life today, how would you handle being in Corrinne's position?**
10. **Have you met people like Dalton and Araya?**
11. **What perceptions did you have just by seeing the cover of the book?**
12. **By the end of the story, which character(s) did you grow to like more and least?**
13. **Do you think this story could really happen? Why/Why not?**

Made in the USA
San Bernardino, CA
09 June 2020

72896315R00219